THE TREACHEROUS NET

T0275422

Books by Helene Tursten

THE IRENE HUSS INVESTIGATIONS
Detective Inspector Huss
Night Rounds
The Torso
The Glass Devil
The Golden Calf
The Fire Dance
The Beige Man
The Treacherous Net
Who Watcheth
Protected by the Shadows

THE EMBLA NYSTRÖM INVESTIGATIONS
Hunting Game
Winter Grave
Snowdrift

An Elderly Lady Is Up to No Good: Stories

THE TREACHEROUS NET

HELENE TURSTEN

Translation by Marlaine Delargy

First published in Swedish under the title *Det lömska nätet*
Copyright © 2008 by Helene Tursten
Published in agreement with H. Samuelsson-Tursten AB, Sunne, and
Leonhardt & Høier Literary Agency, Copenhagen
English translation copyright © 2015 by Marlaine Delargy

First English translation published in 2015 by
Soho Press
227 W 17th Street
New York, NY 10011

Library of Congress Cataloging-in-Publication Data

Tursten, Helene.
[Lömska nätet. English]
The treacherous net / Helene Tursten ; translated by Marlaine Delargy.
(An Irene Huss investigation)

ISBN 978-1-61695-767-4
eISBN 978-1-61695-403-1

1. Policewomen—Fiction. 2. Murder—Investigation—Fiction. I. Delargy,
Marlaine, translator. II. Title.
PT9876.3.U55L6513 2015
839.73'8—dc23   2015014950

Printed in the United States of America

10 9 8 7 6 5 4 3 2

To Anita and Stina:
It's time for Superintendent Sven Andersson
to retire!

THE TREACHEROUS NET

As usual I have taken considerable liberties with geographical facts. My philosophy is that I do not adapt my narrative to reality; instead, reality is adapted to fit the story where necessary. The characters featured in my books are always fictional, but the descriptions of real-world historical events and individuals are accurate. Even if I take liberties when I write, it is not in my power to change things that have already happened and are documented.

Helene Tursten

ELOF PERSSON HAD to die. The only possible course of action was to get rid of him. In spite of the fact that he was a member of the General Security Service, a secret intelligence organization, the idiot didn't understand what a dangerous game he was playing. He was arrogant and overconfident. His aggression had been frightening the first time he got in touch just over two months ago, and his physical strength, terrifying. He had taken pleasure in showing off his prowess, grabbing the other man so viciously by the throat that the tender red mark had taken twenty-four hours to fade.

With undisguised contempt, Persson had let loose with a stream of scornful invective and threats. His victim was so shocked that all he could do was stand there and take it, paralyzed by the realization that the man in front of him could destroy his entire future. Elof Persson had stumbled upon his crime, and now Persson must be paid to keep quiet.

But the worst thing was the threat of public exposure, which would inevitably lead to a trial and a jail sentence. The mass media would revel in his shame, and the situation would be unbearable. His entire social life and career would be wrecked. It would amount to total ruin, and in that case he might as well kill himself.

Right now everything hung in the balance: life against life. His own against Elof Persson's.

THE MAN LURKING in the dark doorway clutched the butt of the Tokarev pistol in his coat pocket. It was made of Bakelite and was damp with the sweat from his palm. His fingertips traced the round logo with its five-pointed star. The Russian semiautomatic wasn't the most reliable or the best quality model, but this particular gun had other advantages. No one was aware he had it. He knew how to handle it; his friends had taught him how it worked. Furthermore, the Russians had produced the Tokarev in huge quantities both before and during the war, so there were plenty around on the black market. It was the perfect murder weapon.

He pulled his hat down farther and peered out of the doorway, tentatively wriggling his toes in his wet shoes to try to keep the circulation going. The newspaper he was using instead of insoles seemed to be drawing in the dampness rather than providing any kind of protection. Shoes and clothes were only available using a ration card these days; he wouldn't be able to buy new shoes until December. Not that he could afford anything, thanks to the man he was waiting for.

The street was in complete darkness. People had closed their blackout curtains or covered the windows with black paper. Most were probably asleep by now. He had to make sure that a patrol didn't spot him; it would be difficult to explain why he was hanging about in a doorway after night had fallen. A damp, chilly wind whirled a flurry of rustling autumn leaves along Hornsgatan. The doorway from which Elof Persson would emerge at any moment was just a short distance away.

They had arranged to meet in Tantolunden, but he had no intention of waiting there. Better to surprise the man as he stepped out into the street.

It had probably never even occurred to the cocky security cop that his home address could be tracked down. Or that his pathetic little victim could suddenly become a threat to his own life. Persson no doubt saw him as a fussy busybody, someone he could exploit as it pleased him. He was an arrogant bastard, and that would be the death of him.

This time the man's victim wasn't carrying an envelope stuffed with money.

Just a loaded gun.

IT SEEMED SAD, somehow. When this demolition project was done, only one wooden building would remain standing on Korsvägen. It had been renovated and now housed several small companies and a part of the university's administration. It was protected as a cultural landmark, of course. The wooden palace was situated a little way up the hill, with its extensive glass veranda facing the traffic down below. Everyone passed it on the way to the university library or Näckrosdammen. It was good that at least one building remained, but it was a pity that this one had been so badly damaged by fire that it was going to have to be demolished.

Göran Jansson sighed. He was born and raised on Mölndals-vägen, just a stone's throw from the spot where he was now standing. He was very familiar with the area around Kors-vägen. Most of the wooden buildings had been in poor condition already by the end of the sixties, but they had still lent a certain charm to the busy intersection. Two of his friends had lived in the houses on the spot where the Museum of World Culture and the Universeum science center now stood.

Jansson worked as a foreman with the building company that was responsible for pulling down the remains of the fire-damaged property. His men would then fill in the hole in the ground and obliterate the final traces. He felt a pang of nostalgia as he raised his hand and gave the signal to get things under way.

The chimney was a sturdy red-brick structure. Apart from the thick granite cellar walls, it was the only part of the building that had emerged more or less unscathed. All the timber had been consumed by the fire. According to witnesses, the whole place had been ablaze in less than ten minutes. The firefighters had concentrated on stopping the conflagration from spreading to the neighboring property, but an elderly man who lived in one of the apartments had lost his life. It had proved impossible to determine the cause of the fire.

The chimney might still be standing, but it was leaning to one side, which was why the decision had been made to clear the site as quickly as possible. There was a risk that it could collapse in a strong wind.

The heavy wrecking ball suspended from the crane swung toward the brickwork. Over the next half hour it gradually demolished the chimney, and the excavator filled the truck with debris. Eventually only the section in the cellar remained. Göran Jansson clambered down and checked the foundation. It looked unusually thick on one side and was an odd shape. Kind of skewed. *We'd better take down that side before we remove the boiler,* he thought.

It was the first warm day after two weeks of wind and rain. It felt good, but he was wearing too many layers. He took off his orange hard hat and used his sleeve to wipe the sweat from his hairline before climbing back up the ladder. He positioned himself a short distance away from the edge in order to assess the best way of proceeding. He wondered why someone had made one side of the chimney so thick. By his estimates, it was at least eighteen inches wider than the other side. Perhaps they had bricked up an old hot water tank? Or a wood store? Not impossible, back in the old days . . .

His thoughts were interrupted as the wrecking ball smashed into the chimney at full force. However, the sound it made was not a dull thud, as expected; instead the brick wall came crashing down.

Göran Jansson saw it at once. He started waving frantically to stop the crane driver from deploying the ball again.

A sleeve was sticking out of the hole in the wall, a claw-like hand protruding from the end of the sleeve.

THE WITNESS WHO called the police at 9:14 A.M. had been right. There was a dead body at the water's edge. The technicians had quickly gone out to Nötsund to secure the scene. After two hours' intensive work they were done, and the corpse could be removed and placed in a body bag.

Detective Inspectors Irene Huss and Jonny Blom waited patiently. Then Irene carefully examined the puffy grey face before zipping up the bag.

"Alexandra Hallwiin," she said in a resigned tone of voice.

They had suspected as much, but it still felt ineffably sad to be able to confirm that the girl was dead. They hadn't been involved in the case while the girl had simply been listed as a missing person, but as soon as the call had come in about the discovery at Nötsund, along with the information that the body was that of a young girl, they had printed out the available case notes. Jonny Blom drove while Irene read aloud.

Fourteen-year-old Alexandra had been missing for five days. According to her parents she had never shown any signs of wanting to run away, nor had she had any reason to do so now. They described her as a typical horse-crazy teenager—a little shy, perhaps. Hardworking at school, but no indication of bullying. Alexandra's teachers and school friends had backed up her parents' view of their daughter.

Alexandra's face had been all over the front pages over the

weekend. She came from a well-off family, and kidnapping had been a possibility right from the start. If she hadn't been abducted, the police still suspected that a crime lay behind her disappearance. A girl who just wants to get away for a while usually tries to take some clothes and money with her, but according to her mother the only thing Alexandra had taken before she went missing on Walpurgis Night, April 30, was a wallet containing her bus pass and three hundred kronor at the most, the clothes she was wearing, a telescopic umbrella and her cell phone. Nothing else.

Alexandra had told her parents she was meeting some of her classmates in Brunnsparken. In spite of the pouring rain, they were going to see the Chalmers University of Technology's traditional annual parade, known as the Cortège. Then they were heading back to Torslanda to hang out at the home of one of the girls. She would be home by midnight at the latest. Her parents were going to a party with friends and didn't have time to give her a lift, so Alexandra said she would catch the bus into town. When she waved goodbye and walked out through the door, that was the last time anyone was known to have seen her alive.

The 6:05 P.M. bus had been full, and the driver didn't remember her. The driver on the next bus hadn't noticed her either. There were lots of young people heading into the city center to watch the parade and celebrate.

None of her friends had arranged to meet her in the park. Even the two girls who were regarded as Alexandra's closest friends had no idea what she was planning to do on Walpurgis Night. When they had asked Alexandra about her plans the previous day, she had said she would be training Prince in preparation for the show on Sunday. Since they knew how important the horse and competitions were to Alexandra, neither of them had pursued the matter.

No one could say for certain whether the girl had traveled into town on the bus. When her worried mother had started calling her cell phone after midnight, it had been switched off.

From the moment Alexandra closed the garden gate, it was as if the ground had opened up and swallowed her.

Now they had found her.

IT WAS A Labrador that discovered her. He was young and playful, and at first he was delighted to find a friend who had hidden herself so cleverly. A second later his sensitive nose registered a strange smell. Exciting, acrid, and a little bit frightening. He began to bark agitatedly, sticking his rump in the air as he circled the interesting odor, gradually getting closer. When his master called him—"Elroy! Elroy! Here, boy!"—he grabbed a scrap of fabric that was lying on the ground and proudly scampered back with it in his mouth. There was a brief struggle, but eventually Elroy let go of his trophy. The man shuddered when he looked down at the torn, bloodied black lace thong in his hands. The word SUNDAY was embroidered on the small triangle at the front, surrounded by a border of red rosebuds.

The body had been pushed into a crevice in the rocks; the murderer had piled a few branches and stones on top in an attempt to hide it.

"SO IT'S ONLY the beginning of May, and we've already had our murdered teenage girl of the summer. Along with another one, just to be on the safe side. On the same day," Detective Inspector Jonny Blom said with a sigh.

His colleagues nodded with an air of resignation. Two murders at the same time meant a heavy workload for the team, particularly in view of the fact that the gang war in the city had begun to escalate once more. It had been relatively calm on that front during February and most of March, but over the Easter weekend they had launched two murder investigations within three days. The victims were a thirty-four-year-old father of three, and a twenty-three-year-old rookie. Both had belonged to the warring factions: the criminal network known as Asir, and the notorious biker gang Bandidos.

The investigation also covered a car bomb, although only minor injuries were reported. The car had belonged to a would-be gangster who carried out his activities using the restaurant he owned as a front. Presumably he hadn't been willing to pay the price for the protection of one of the gangs, although it wasn't clear which one. Those who are willingly or unwillingly drawn into dealings with the biker gangs never talk to the police. Most people have a certain instinct for self-preservation. At the moment Asir and Bandidos were equal, with one loss each. The question wasn't *if* reprisals would follow, but *when*. And which of them would strike first.

Irene Huss was only half-listening. She couldn't get the image of Alexandra's dead body out of her mind. When she had looked at the girl's face she had noticed something that was later confirmed by the preliminary autopsy report: some kind of plastic twine had been pulled tightly around her neck. A thin washing line, perhaps. There was no doubt that they were dealing with a homicide.

The meeting with Alexandra's parents the previous day had been just as difficult as these meetings always are. During the afternoon Irene and Jonny were intending to go out to Torslanda to speak to them again, and to take a look at the girl's room. Hopefully CSI would be finished by the end of the morning.

The door leading to the corridor was open; they were waiting for their boss, Efva Thylqvist, to arrive. Her deputy would probably turn up at the same time: DCI Tommy Persson, Irene's classmate back at the police academy.

After they qualified, Irene and Tommy had both ended up in central Göteborg, and they had been colleagues for over twenty years. They had grown very close—unusually close for colleagues of different sexes. This had given rise to a number of rumors, but thanks to the fact that these rumors had been completely groundless, their friendship had survived. Before Tommy and his wife, Agneta, divorced four years ago, the two families had often hung out; they had even gone on vacation together. They had been godparents to each other's children. For eighteen years Irene and Tommy had shared an office in the Violent Crimes Unit—right up until a year ago, when their former chief, Superintendent Sven Andersson, had moved over to the Cold Cases Unit, and a new chief had taken over.

Irene and Tommy's office was right at the end of the corridor, well away from the main door. Superintendent Efva Thylqvist had decided she wanted her deputy closer to her, and after a rapid reorganization, Tommy found himself in the room next door to the superintendent. Which meant he was at the opposite end of the corridor from his old office.

"It will be nice for you to have your own space after all these years," Efva Thylqvist had said, gently placing a well-manicured hand on Irene's arm.

Irene hadn't thought it was nice at all, just lonely. She would no longer have anyone to chat with or bounce her ideas off. It had taken a great deal of self-control on Irene's part to refrain from shaking off the superintendent's hand.

That was the tricky thing about Efva Thylqvist. To begin with, everyone had a good feeling about the new chief. She had seemed friendly and genuinely interested in her new colleagues, but after a while Irene realized that her interest was mainly directed at the men. She always smiled at them, took time to have a proper conversation with them. All the guys on the team really liked her. Efva Thylqvist was an attractive brunette in her forties, with thick, shoulder-length hair. Her figure was slim but curvaceous. She certainly knew how to wear even the most severe skirt suit or pant suit; the blouses or tops she wore under her jackets were usually very low-cut, and she always wore high heels. Irene assumed this was to compensate for her lack of height. As Irene herself was six feet tall in her stocking feet, she felt like an elephant standing next to her dainty boss. They were about the same age, but Irene was slightly older. Rumor had it that Efva Thylqvist had been married at the beginning of her career as a police officer, but that the husband had disappeared at an early stage. They didn't have children, anyway. There was talk of affairs with high-ranking colleagues, some of whom had been married. Of course there was no way of assessing the accuracy of this gossip; in her more charitable moments Irene thought this was the kind of thing that was always said about women when they overtook men on the career ladder. At other times she thought it was possible that there was a certain amount of truth in the rumors. However, there was no denying the fact that Superintendent Thylqvist had led an outstanding career so far. Irene consoled herself with the thought that she was unlikely to be content to remain with the Violent Crimes Unit until her retirement.

After only a month Irene had noticed that her new boss was less and less interested in hearing her views. She hardly ever dealt with Irene personally, not even if something major was going on. She usually sent an email. On one occasion Irene had tentatively asked why she did this. Efva Thylqvist had smiled sweetly and said, "It saves me coming all the way to your office."

Any assignment that appeared to be remotely routine ended up on Irene's desk, and she had started to feel marginalized. She realized that her self-confidence had taken a knock, but sometimes there was light at the end of the tunnel, and she had the opportunity to get involved in the operational side of things. Like yesterday, when the call about the dead girl in Nötsund had come in. Then again, that was probably because only she and Jonny had been available to go out there.

Another reason why Irene was feeling lonely was no doubt because Birgitta Moberg-Rauhala was on leave. She had started reading law at the university back in the fall, and she had at least another year to go. After that she would be able to start applying for higher level posts within the police service. When they had met up for a quick lunch a month ago, Birgitta had hinted that she might carry on with her studies; she was considering training to be a lawyer or a prosecutor. Things were going well for her, and she was really enjoying the course. Her husband, Hannu Rauhala, was still on the team, and according to Birgitta he was happy to support whatever decision she made. Their son, Timo, was almost five years old, and they had decided not to have any more children. The grief had been too great after the late miscarriage Birgitta had suffered a few years earlier. As usual, Hannu hadn't said a word to his colleagues. The ice-blond man from Tornedalen had been as inscrutable as ever.

At the moment Irene was the only female inspector in the department, and she suspected that this suited Efva Thylqvist perfectly.

Just as the thought flitted through Irene's mind, the superintendent walked in, closely followed by Tommy Persson.

"Good morning! Has everyone got a cup of coffee?"

Efva Thylqvist smiled as her gaze swept around the table. Irene noticed that she barely registered on Thylqvist's radar; it definitely looked as if she was avoiding eye contact with Irene. On the other hand, the superintendent lingered on Fredrik Stridh's handsome face. He had recently gotten married, and was due to become a father at the end of August. To everyone's surprise, the department's eternal bachelor and ladies' man had fallen head over heels for a nurse during a vacation to Barcelona the previous spring. Everything had happened very quickly after that: a wedding on New Year's Eve, the move to a larger apartment, and now a baby on the way.

Irene suddenly became aware of a strange feeling. She vaguely recognized it, and realized it had been bubbling inside her for quite some time. It took a while before she was able to identify it, but she got there in the end: rage. Pure, unadulterated rage. A second later she made a decision. Whatever happened, she was no longer prepared to be treated like an inferior being by Efva Thylqvist. She was no longer prepared to put up with that woman's disparaging attitude. It wasn't going to be easy; Superintendent Thylqvist was her boss, and she wouldn't hesitate to pull rank if she felt threatened.

Jonny Blom had placed the preliminary autopsy report on Alexandra Hallwiin on the table in front of him. Irene reached across and grabbed the pile of papers; she moved so fast he didn't have a chance to react. He glared at her and opened his mouth as if he was about to protest, but Irene merely gave him a placatory smile. The irritation in his eyes was gradually replaced by a certain level of confusion, and before he had time to speak, Efva Thylqvist took charge.

"Okay, let's make a start." She smiled and looked at Fredrik Stridh.

"Anything new on the car bomb?"

He seemed pleased to be the focus of her attention, and answered quickly. "No, but I'll be speaking to a fresh witness later today. A man walking his dog saw an older model Merc parked next to Roger 'the Hulk' Hansson's brand-new Jag. The timing is interesting; it was about eleven fifteen. Hansson left the restaurant at his usual time, just after one thirty. And as we know the bomb went off when he opened the car door."

"How serious was the injury to his foot?" Thylqvist asked.

"Only superficial. The force of the bomb was directed

toward the passenger side of the car; it had probably been set up incorrectly."

"Useless bastards—they never get anything right," Jonny Blom said, just loud enough to be heard.

Efva Thylqvist managed a half-smile and turned her attention to him.

"Has anything come in on the Alexandra Hallwiin case?"

Before Jonny could answer, Irene took the initiative.

"It has. We received a preliminary autopsy report this morning; the forensic pathologist will get back to us later this afternoon with more details, but definitive information will take a few days," she said.

She glanced down at the papers in front of her.

"Dental records have enabled us to officially identify the body as that of Alexandra Hallwiin. She went missing on Walpurgis Night, and according to the report it seems likely that she ended up in the water during the first twenty-four hours following her disappearance. This means she had been submerged for approximately four days. There was a thin electrical cable wrapped tightly around her neck when she was found. The cause of death is probably strangulation. She was wearing only a black lace bra. There are knife marks on her inner thighs, around her breasts and up toward her neck. However, these are not stab wounds; it looks as if the perpetrator used a knife to inflict a series of deep scratches. Damage to the area around the anus and vagina suggests penetration with a blunt object. Even though the autopsy has not been completed, it is obvious that the body has been subjected to serious sexual violence. There are also knife wounds around the pudenda; the ME thinks the killer tried to make a pattern using the knife."

Irene stopped reading and looked up.

Efva Thylqvist was gazing at her expressionlessly. After a few seconds she turned to Jonny. "Are there still no witnesses who saw Alexandra after she left home?"

"No," Irene replied quickly, before Jonny had the chance to speak.

Without looking at Irene, the superintendent said in a neutral tone of voice, "Jonny, you carry on with the investigation into Alexandra's death."

Then she turned to Hannu Rauhala. "What do we know about the other girl?"

"She's also been identified with the help of dental records," Hannu replied. "Moa Olsson, born September second, 1992. Fifteen years old."

Alexandra Hallwiin was exactly a year younger than Moa, Irene thought.

"She lived in Salviagatan, not far from the place where she was discovered; two and a half kilometers as the crow flies. The body was found in the forest at Gårdstensbergen; it's a recreational area with designated running tracks. But it was cold and wet the week leading up to Walpurgis Night. There weren't many people around. According to Moa's mother, she went missing the previous weekend, probably Sunday, April twenty-eighth. The mother's name is Kicki Olsson. She's been given early retirement. Mental problems, alcohol abuse. She got home at around nine on Sunday morning and doesn't remember whether Moa was there or not. But she thinks so."

"When was she reported missing?"

"On the following Tuesday."

"So she'd been gone for . . . seven or eight days," the superintendent said, looking pensive. "Who reported her?" she went on.

"The mother. I assume she'd started to sober up by then," Hannu said dryly.

"So she has a serious problem with alcohol."

"Yes. There was an older brother who died in a car accident three years ago. He was seventeen; no driver's license, drunk at the wheel. The car was stolen from Angered Square fifteen minutes before the crash. Kicki Olsson hasn't been able to work since."

"What did she do?"

"She was a cleaner at IKEA in Bäckebol."

"What about the father?"

"Out of the picture; the two kids had different fathers," Hannu explained.

"Okay, we need to check out both fathers. And find out whether the mother has a new man on the go; if so, check him out too. What does the ME say about the cause of death?"

"Nothing definite. Decomposition had set in, and animals had been at the body. Entomological samples have been taken for testing. They estimate that she'd probably been lying there for at least a week. She seems to have been subjected to extreme sexual violence, based on the appearance of some of her injuries. She was completely naked. The dog that found the body had picked up her panties. They'd fallen off as the killer dragged her up the hill to hide her in a crevice in the rock."

"The hill? He climbed a hill with a dead body?" Jonny exclaimed skeptically.

"A small hill, with a path leading to the top," Hannu said.

"Can you drive there?" Tommy wondered.

"Yes. There's a parking lot no more than a hundred meters from the spot where she was found, and a gravel path leading from there to the hill; it's perfectly possible to drive all the way. CSI has secured several different tire tracks. The problem is all the rain we've had since she disappeared."

The superintendent nodded; she realized this could cause problems. She gave a start as Irene suddenly spoke up again.

"It feels as if everything is a bit much right now. We've already got several ongoing investigations piled up, and now these new cases . . . I'm just wondering when we'll be getting a replacement for Birgitta," she said calmly.

"We don't have time to discuss that at the moment," the superintendent replied brusquely.

"But I think we'd all like to know where we stand in terms of reinforcements," Irene persisted.

"Robert Backman was only available for three months," Efva Thylqvist snapped.

"Yes, but that was before Christmas. We haven't had anyone in place of Birgitta since then."

You're saving money, Irene thought, making every effort not to show what was going through her mind. Thylqvist was starting to look uncomfortable.

"It's not that easy; people start taking their vacations in June," she defended herself.

"I agree with Irene. We've been under far too much pressure since New Year's, and all through the spring. We need a replacement as soon as possible."

Irene was both surprised and grateful as Tommy spoke up. By now it was clear that the superintendent was far from happy, and she couldn't hide her annoyance.

"Every department has the same problems! There's nobody available. Birgitta's leave of absence ends in August; she might be back then."

"She won't," Hannu pointed out.

And he ought to know. Even Efva Thylqvist wasn't about to contradict him. Instead her face suddenly lit up. "Oh, so she's decided to carry on with her studies?" she said in a pleasant tone of voice. "In that case we need to act in accordance with this new information."

As if you don't know that already, Irene thought. Both she and Hannu knew perfectly well that Birgitta had applied for an extension of her leave of absence several weeks ago.

The internal telephone suddenly crackled to life.

"Hello? Are you there? Superintendent Thylqvist?" said a female voice.

"I'm here," the superintendent said, leaning toward the speaker on the table.

"We've just had a call. A body has been found on Kors-vägen, walled up in a cellar. Can you send someone over to take a look?"

No one in the room moved or even blinked. They were all dumbstruck, staring at the soulless grey plastic box as if it had suddenly turned into a hissing viper.

"You didn't give Efva much room to maneuver," Tommy Persson remarked.

Irene was sitting beside him in the passenger seat. She turned and looked at his profile; was there a hint of reproach in his voice?

"Somebody had to say it. Thanks for your support," she said, keeping her tone light.

"I agree with you—the workload is starting to become untenable. But maybe that wasn't the right time to bring it up."

He kept his eyes fixed on the road ahead. Was there something he wanted to say but couldn't quite bring himself to spit out?

"Maybe not. But right now it feels as if it's never the right time to bring up any problems in the department. These two fresh homicides just make it all too much. That's how I felt, and somebody had to say something."

"Efva is extremely conscientious, and of course she wants the department's work to flow as smoothly as possible. But she's got a lot on her plate. I see how hard she works . . ."

Tommy left the last sentence hanging in the air. He was obviously keen to defend the superintendent, which made Irene feel a little sad, if not exactly surprised. It wasn't unexpected. Efva Thylqvist was good at her job, and she could be immensely charming when it suited her. Irene had noticed that she was always charming toward Tommy. He had spent a year in close proximity to her by now.

"Jonny didn't look too pleased when you said you were coming with me to Korsvägen," he went on.

"Well, Efva told him he was working on the investigation into Alexandra's death, so I thought it was self-evident that he ought to write the report. It's his responsibility after all," Irene replied, her tone completely neutral.

To tell the truth she was very pleased with the way she had handled the situation. If Thylqvist wanted Jonny to head up the case, then it was only fair that he took on the boring paperwork. She wasn't his private secretary. He hadn't even managed to come up with a good excuse. He had reluctantly snatched the preliminary autopsy report from Irene before she followed him out of the room, smiling to herself.

"Don't forget where we're going. Another body. Walled up, apparently. If we're lucky it happened a hundred years ago, otherwise we have another homicide on our hands," she said, trying to remain positive. It hadn't been a long journey; it is just over a kilometer from police HQ to Korsvägen.

THEY CLIMBED DOWN a steel ladder to reach the bottom of the cellar, and stepped over piles of debris. Göran Jansson, the foreman, led them over to the chimney. The hole in the brickwork was approximately one and a half meters in diameter, and about half a meter above the ground. The sleeve of a dark jacket was sticking out of the hole, with a shriveled hand protruding from the sleeve.

Irene and Tommy moved over to the hole and peered inside. The body was in a half-sitting position. The beam of their flashlight showed a grinning cranium with parchment-brown skin stretched over the bones. The yellowing teeth gleamed as the light caught them.

"A mummy," Irene said.

"Male, judging by the clothes," Tommy said.

Irene tried to see how the body was dressed. It was covered in a thick layer of dust from the demolition. The only things she could see clearly were the sleeve and dark pants.

"It's a waterproof jacket, maybe a windbreaker. He hasn't been here for a hundred years, unfortunately." She sighed.

"I guess you're right."

"I don't think Efva can keep on saying no. We have to have a replacement for Birgitta. Right now."

Irene was trying not to sound too aggressive, but a sideways glance from Tommy told her that he had picked up something in her voice.

Instead of answering, he turned to Göran Jansson. "What happened when you discovered the body?"

"It was pretty gruesome. When the wrecking ball hit the chimney, it almost looked as if the guy had stuck his arm out through the hole! Like, deliberately! I saw the arm come out and and I started waving and shouting at Janne to stop him swinging the ball again. Although I expect the . . . body . . . was damaged anyway, with all the stuff that came crashing down . . ."

"Probably, but thanks to your vigilance it looks in pretty good shape," Tommy said, smiling reassuringly at the foreman.

Göran Jansson managed a wan smile in return. Finding a body had been both surprising and stressful. Seeing that kind of thing on cop shows on TV is one thing, but experiencing it in real life is something completely different.

"Can I get you guys a coffee?" he said, pointing to a temporary office parked a short distance from the site.

"Please. We'll need to cordon off this area until forensics has finished. They're working on two other cases at the moment, so they won't be here for at least an hour. Unfortunately you won't be able to carry on working until they're done," Tommy explained.

Jansson's face clouded over for a moment, but he realized

there was nothing he could do. A walled-up, mummified corpse couldn't be ignored.

THEY STOOD OUTSIDE drinking freshly made coffee. The sun was shining, and it was very pleasant in the shelter of the office. Irene leaned back against the wooden wall and turned her face up to the sun. It had been notable by its absence, as her mother, Gerd, used to say.

"I grew up in one of those blocks over there," Göran Jansson said, pointing in the direction of Mölndalsvägen.

He turned and pointed to Universeum and the Museum of World Culture on the other side of the roundabout. "Some of my friends lived in the timber buildings that were pulled down when the city decided we needed to start showing off."

"Did you know anyone who lived here?" Tommy asked, nodding toward the gaping hole in front of them.

"Not really. There was some kind of office on the ground floor, though people lived here too. There were two or three apartments, I think. I remember one of the teachers from my school lived here with her sister, but they were already old back then. They've probably been dead for years."

"When was this?"

Jansson thought for a moment.

"Mid-60s. I started school in '62."

"As I understand it, only the old man who died in the fire was living here at the time," Tommy went on.

"Yes. There was an architect's office downstairs; we've found the remains of computers, that kind of thing. But all we can do is scoop it all up and take it to the dump."

"Everything was destroyed?"

"Yes. The fire spread in no time, and they didn't manage to get the old guy out. The whole place was ablaze by the time the firefighters got here."

"Do you know what caused the fire?"

Göran Jansson made a 180-degree turn and nodded in the direction of a small tobacconist and candy store at the bottom of the steps on Korsvägen.

"No idea; everything I've heard came from Anna, who owns the tobacconist's over there on the corner. We were at school together."

"So she's stayed in the area," Tommy said.

"Her parents bought the store. Talk about a goldmine! And she's still in the apartment where she lived when we were kids, just over there."

"You didn't find anything else of interest in the remains of the fire?" Irene asked.

"No . . . Well, maybe. A room full of empty bottles. We've already taken them away, but the place was packed—bottles from floor to ceiling!"

"Wine and spirits bottles, I assume?"

"Exactly. Someone really went for it, there's no doubt about it."

"And where was this room?"

"At the opposite end of the cellar from the chimney."

They finished their coffee and thanked the foreman.

"We'll go and have a chat with your old school friend," Tommy said. "What's her surname, by the way?"

"Svensson. Anna Svensson. At least that was her maiden name. I can't remember what her husband is called, but her daughter's married to a nigger—I met them when I was in the store last week. I came down to check things out before we started pulling this place down."

Irene could feel the tension in her face. She clamped her lips together to prevent the words in her mind from coming out. A nigger. She loathed the word. Irene's daughter Katarina had been with Felipe Median for two and a half years now; his father was Brazilian, his mother Swedish. Felipe was dark-skinned, and he had been called all kinds of names. But "nigger" was the worst. It was so insulting, and had such strong negative connotations even in Sweden, where the biggest exposure to the word came from American rap music.

"Do you think this Anna Svensson, or whatever her surname is, might know something about our mummy?" Irene asked as she and Tommy made their way down the steps to Korsvägen.

"You never can tell. She ought to know if any of the tenants have disappeared over the years, since she's lived and worked here all her life. That would save us a lot of time. And I'd like to find out more about the old guy who died in the fire."

Tommy chivalrously held the door open for her as they entered the little store. The sweet aroma of loose candy and freshly baked buns from the oven in the corner rushed toward them, overlaid with the smell of fresh coffee. Someone had managed to cram candy, tobacco, magazines, games and a café into just a few square meters. There was even a little round table just inside the window where people could drink their coffee. The real miracle was that the place didn't seem in the least bit crowded or untidy.

They were the only people in the store, apart from a heavily pregnant young woman. She was filling up a stand by the cash register with packs of cigarettes. Her long red hair was caught up in a high ponytail.

"Hi there," she said with a smile.

Tommy introduced himself and Irene. He asked if Anna Svensson was available, and added that they had some questions about the fire in the old wooden building.

"Mom's been Anna Jonsén for almost thirty years," the young woman said as she added a few more packs of Marlboros to the stand. "I'm Petra."

Before Tommy had the chance to repeat his question, she went on.

"Mom's at home. Or she might be out with Felix—he's her dog. She doesn't start work until three o'clock."

"Do you live nearby too?" Irene asked.

"Not far away—in Kålltorp."

"So you didn't see anything of the fire three weeks ago?"

"No, it happened late at night. But Mom and Dad saw it."

"Could we have your mother's address and telephone number? We'd really like to get these questions out of the way as quickly as possible," Tommy said with a smile.

Petra nodded and gave him the information.

THE APARTMENT BLOCK was made of gloomy dark red brick. It looked solid, resting on its sturdy granite foundations. Above the main entrance was the year 1906. Creaking and protesting, an elevator that had seen better days carried them up to the fourth floor.

When the apartment door opened, Irene and Tommy were not welcomed by the same pleasant aroma that had met them in the store. This place was impregnated with cigarette smoke. A black miniature poodle jumped around their legs, its shrill yapping echoing in the stairwell.

Anna Jonsén's coloring was a little paler than her daughter's, but she had the same build. Which wasn't a compliment, given Petra's advanced pregnancy. But Anna had a pretty face, and she was smartly dressed in a denim skirt and light blue blouse that matched her eyes. Her smile seemed warm and genuine.

"Come on in. Unfortunately, I don't think I can be of much help. I didn't see . . ."

The end of the sentence disappeared in a murmur as she led the way through a long hallway and into a large living room.

"Please sit down. I've just made some coffee—I'm sure you'd like a cup?"

They both said yes. Irene thought that it had been a good

start to the day in spite of everything; she was about to have her sixth cup of coffee before lunch.

They sat down on rococo armchairs upholstered in silk. Like the matching sofa, the faded fabric was a dismal vintage rose color. The chairs were hard and uncomfortable. A small chest of drawers with a marble top seemed to be part of the suite; it was cluttered with framed photographs and small souvenir dolls. Through an open sliding door Irene could see a soft leather sofa and a reclining armchair with a footstool. Something told her that was the TV room, where the Jonséns sat when they were alone. She could understand that, because the elegant silk-covered seats were anything but comfortable.

Anna came in carrying a tray, and placed it carefully on the little table in front of the police officers. The aroma of cinnamon rose from a pile of warm buns on a china plate. They looked very similar to the ones they had seen in the store.

"According to your old friend Göran Jansson, you've lived here all your life, and you know what goes on in the area," Tommy began.

"I'm not so sure about that. It's impossible to keep an eye on things on Korsvägen these days; there's so much traffic, so many people . . ."

"Of course. But I was thinking more about the people who live around here. You must know them pretty well."

"Well . . . some of them, maybe."

"We're interested in everything you can tell us about the building that burned down, and above all we'd like to find out as much as possible about the old man who died. But please tell us a bit about yourself first."

"Goodness me . . ."

She broke off and thought for a moment, then took a deep breath.

"We moved here from Annedal when I was five. My father

bought the tobacconist's store, and at the same time my parents got a hold of this apartment. I thought I'd died and gone to heaven—I had my very own room! We'd gone from one room and a kitchen to all this space. Can you imagine?"

She took a big bite of her bun, munching away with obvious pleasure before she went on. "My father developed heart failure, and died of a heart attack in 1973. I'd already started working in the store a year or so earlier. Mom and I ran it together until she died eleven years ago."

She fell silent, biting her lip.

"Were you living in this apartment at the time?" Tommy asked.

A gentle smile flitted across Anna Jonsén's face.

"I was the only child. My mom was so lovely . . . Lasse and I were living in a two-room apartment in Johanneberg. When our second child was on the way, Mom suggested we swap spots. She thought this place was too big for her, and we needed more space. So that's what we did, back in '82 when Jessica was born."

"And now you're about to become a grandmother yourself," Irene said with a smile.

"I already am; this is Petra's second child."

She got up, went over to the chest of drawers and picked up a photograph.

"Axel," she said proudly, handing the framed picture to Irene.

The boy looked about two years old. He was laughing at the photographer, his pearly white front teeth gleaming against his dark skin. He had dark brown, curly hair. His eyes sparkled with the joy of being alive. In one hand he was holding a little red car, clutching it firmly to his chest.

"Grandma's little prince," Anna said as she replaced the photograph. The proud smile still lingered on her lips as she sat down again.

"Do you know whether anyone in the area has gone missing?" Tommy asked.

"Missing? But when?" Anna was understandably confused.

"We're not quite sure, but probably during the past fifty years."

Irene was taken aback at first, then realized that he had made the time frame as generous as possible just to be on the safe side. Thanks to the windbreaker, they knew the mummy was less than fifty years old.

Anna shook her head.

"Not that I know of, and I think I would have heard something . . . but no. Unless it was before we moved here."

Tommy nodded, but didn't pursue the matter. Instead he changed the subject. "Tell me about the fire three weeks ago."

"I didn't see it start. I heard sirens just as we were about to go to bed, and I noticed that the fire engines stopped nearby. When I looked out I could see that the wooden block was in flames; the fire swept through the whole place in no time. It was terrible. And then I saw the firefighters wearing that special breathing apparatus. They tried to save Calle Adelskiöld, but it was no good."

"Calle Adelskiöld?" Tommy made a note of the name, even though it wouldn't be difficult to remember.

"Yes, Carl-Johan Adelskiöld. He always told us to call him Calle, with a C. He used to have a special order of cigars from me. They stopped importing the ones he smoked, so he changed to Davidoff Long Panatellas. He always used to pick them up on a Friday, and he'd hand in the week's harness racing coupons at the same time—a whole heap of them! He started doing that as soon as he moved here."

"And when was that?"

"1980. The year Petra was born."

"Twenty-eight years ago," Irene said after a quick calculation.

"Yes. He'd retired and moved back to Göteborg. He used to say it was good to be back in dear old Lorensberg."

"Do you know anything else about him? Did he have family?"

"Not that I'm aware of. He was always alone when I saw him. Although he did have a cousin. I remember Calle telling me that both he and his cousin used to work for the Foreign Office. He used to talk about it when he came in smelling of booze, which he sometimes did. Pretty often, to be honest."

Her tone was indulgent. It was understandable that an elderly gentleman might need to cheer himself up with a good cigar and a glass or two of Cognac now and again.

"Although in recent years his cousin used to come in quite often to pick up his cigars and hand in his coupons. After all, Calle was ninety. His cousin is no spring chicken either."

"So he smoked cigars and drank brandy . . . and got to ninety. I wonder what the health fanatics would have to say about that?" Tommy said.

Anna Jonsén fished out a pack of cigarettes and offered them around. Both Tommy and Irene declined. Anna lit a cigarette and inhaled deeply, with obvious pleasure.

"Do you happen to know the name of this cousin?"

"No. He's not as talkative as Calle."

Anna broke off for a minor coughing fit, then continued. "He's not unpleasant, not at all, but he's more . . . reserved. Kind of . . . distinguished."

They asked a few more questions, but although Anna Jonsén did her best to be helpful, it was obvious that she didn't know much more about the old man.

Felix started yapping again as he and his mistress showed them to the door.

As they were on their way down in the elevator, Irene said, "That dog isn't going to live to a ripe old age. What with the air quality around Korsvägen and the smoke in that apartment, it hasn't got a chance!"

"Jonny and I are heading out to Torslanda," Irene said, tugging on her jacket.

"And I'll write up the report on our visit to Korsvägen," Tommy said, without even trying to hide the acidity in his tone. Irene chose to ignore it.

"Well, the chief did say you were to take the lead on the mummy case. Bye bye!"

With a teasing smile she slipped out of his new office. The one that was closer to the seat of power than his old office, which was now hers.

The impressive cream-brick mansion was on a hill, with a view over the roofs of the houses below in one direction, and Torslandavägen in the other. It had huge windows, and extensive patios on three sides. Irene thought it was a real seaside villa that ought to be in solitary splendor on a peninsula somewhere, but then of course it would have cost several million kronor more.

The garden was surrounded by a hedge in full bloom. There was a garage by the wrought-iron gate that separated the paved driveway from the street. Jonny pressed down the gold-painted handle and they made their way toward the blue front door, which had a round porthole window at eye level. The owners were obviously keen to stick to the maritime theme, even though they were several kilometers away from the sea.

Jonny had to keep his finger on the bell for a long time before someone answered. The man who yanked open the door was Alexandra's father, Jan Hallwiin; they had met him the previous day. He had sat in an armchair, his face rigid as Irene told him that the police had found his daughter. His wife, Marina, had sunk down on a stool in front of the open fire and wept. Irene had found it strange that the parents remained at opposite ends of the room; when people are given that kind of news, they usually gravitate toward each other, hugging and trying to offer consolation. Jan Hallwiin had made no attempt to approach his wife. But shock can make people behave irrationally; Irene had seen many examples over the years.

"What the hell is the matter with you!" Jan Hallwiin roared at Jonny. He stood in the doorway swaying slightly. Even from several meters away, Irene could smell the alcohol fumes.

"We'd arranged to meet at three o'clock," Jonny said calmly.

Jan Hallwiin didn't reply but merely glared at them with bloodshot eyes.

"May we come in?" Irene asked.

Before he had time to say anything, she and Jonny pushed past him into the hallway. They kept their jackets on, in spite of the fact that it was a warm day. Jonny turned to the man who was still holding on to the open door; he probably needed some help to stay upright.

"Is your wife home?"

Hallwiin merely pointed upward without speaking. Irene exchanged a glance with Jonny and set off up the stairs. She could hear muffled sobbing; she followed the sound and pushed open a door that was slightly ajar.

It was obviously Alexandra's room. Her mother was sitting on the bed, her head buried in the pillow. Perhaps she was trying to suppress the sound of her weeping, or perhaps she just wanted to cling to the lingering smell of her daughter.

Irene went over and placed a hand on her shoulder. Marina Hallwiin gave a start.

"I'm sorry, I didn't mean to scare you," Irene said gently.

"No, it's . . . I . . ." Marina mumbled.

Her eyes were red-rimmed, and she looked bewildered. Irene bent down a fraction and discreetly took a deep breath. Nothing but perspiration and something unidentifiable. Did grief have an odor of its own? Marina Hallwiin hadn't been drinking, at any rate.

The room was large and airy, with a double bed by one wall. Sheer white fabric hung from the ceiling; Irene thought it looked like a malaria net, but she knew that drapes of this kind were popular with young girls. Otherwise the colors in the room were quite bold: a cerise throw; lime green cushions; a cerise, lime green and white striped rug; and white walls. Not that there was very much white to be seen; the walls were covered with pictures of horses. All kinds of horses. One of the pictures had attracted Irene's attention as soon as she walked into the room: a huge poster of a shimmering coal-black horse that hung above the head of the bed. It was rearing up, its mane flying against the blue of a summer sky. A young man was sitting on its back, his muscles rippling beneath his tanned skin, gleaming in the sunlight. It was clear that he was completely naked.

On the desk some loose cables and a lonely printer bore witness to the fact that forensics had taken the girl's computer.

"Will we . . . will we get her things back?" Marina snuffled.

Irene could see that she was trying to pull herself together. Once again she placed her hand on Marina's shoulder.

"Yes. Everything will be returned once we've gone through it. We're most interested in her computer since we haven't found her cell phone. Did Alexandra have her own computer?"

Irene asked the question even though she already knew the answer. Marina Hallwiin nodded and swallowed hard, pointing to her daughter's desk with a trembling hand.

"There. That's where . . . the computer was."

Irene looked around as if she had just noticed all the pictures.

"Alexandra seems to have been pretty keen on horses," she said.

"Yes . . . She has her own horse—Prince. The two of them . . ."

Marina's voice broke and she let out another sob. She pointed to the wall above the white bookcase, where rosettes of every color were displayed behind a bank of cups of varying sizes.

"Talented . . . so talented," Marina murmured, her voice thick with tears.

"Absolutely. How long had she been riding?"

"Since she was seven."

"But she hasn't had Prince for that long?"

"No, he . . . she's had him for three years."

All Irene knew about horses was that one end could bite you and the other end could kick you. Keeping a conversation about horses going felt like tiptoeing across very thin ice. As far as she was concerned, she had already exhausted the topic, so instead she decided to broach a question she had been pondering ever since the morning briefing.

"Where does Alexandra keep her underwear?" she asked.

Marina gave a start; she looked directly at Irene for the first time. Slowly she got to her feet and nodded, as if she understood why Irene had asked. She pushed a mirrored sliding door to one side, revealing a stack of wire baskets.

"That's something I'd . . . wondered about . . ." she whispered.

Irene pulled out the baskets one by one until she found one

containing bras and thin socks. There were five bras, all size 70A: one red, one black, one pale blue and two white. They were all very similar: the material was smooth and shiny, the cups padded and firm.

"Did Alexandra have any other type of bra?" Irene asked.

"No . . . she always thought her bust was too small. She bought these at Lindex . . . I've been thinking about it since yesterday . . . that bra she was wearing when she . . . It wasn't hers!"

The last few words were almost a scream, and they confirmed what Irene had been thinking. The bra Alexandra had been wearing when she was found was unusually sexy for a fourteen-year-old girl obsessed with horses. It was made of see-through black lace with tiny embroidered roses between the cups; it was very low cut, leaving the nipples partly exposed.

"So you've never seen Alexandra with a bra like that?"

"Never!"

The response was unequivocal, and Marina Hallwiin unconsciously stood up a little straighter.

"Do you know which bra she was wearing when she disappeared?"

"It must have been a black one. I bought her two of those, and there's only one here."

When Irene had shown the parents a photograph of the lace bra the previous day, neither of them had reacted. The shock of being told their daughter was dead was too great. Both of them had simply shaken their heads and said they didn't recognize it, but now Marina had had time to digest the information, and she had reached the same conclusion as Irene: when Alexandra was found, she was wearing a bra that didn't belong to her. The killer must have forced the girl to put on the sexy scrap of lace, or else he had done it himself after the murder. Or she could have put it on of her own free will. That seemed unlikely, but it couldn't be ruled out at this stage of the investigation.

According to her details, Marina Hallwiin was forty-three, but right now she looked significantly older. Her husband was fifty-six.

"Do you have any other children?" Irene asked.

"Janne has two, but they're grown up. Thirty-one and twenty-nine."

"Do they live here in Göteborg?"

"No, they stayed with their mother in Gävle, and now both boys live in Stockholm. Janne moved here . . . when we got together."

The tears spilled over once more.

"Perhaps we should go downstairs?" Irene suggested, turning toward the door.

"Perhaps . . ." Marina said. She slipped into the bathroom opposite Alexandra's room. Irene heard her blowing her nose, followed by the sound of running water.

As always in cases involving young homicide victims, Irene felt powerless. There were no words to lessen the grief, no words to bring solace.

"MISERABLE BASTARD," JONNY said, sounding his horn crossly as a cab pulled out in front of their car.

Irene knew he was referring to Jan Hallwiin rather than the cab driver.

"Because he was drunk?"

"Because he was so aggressive and stupid. Although that was probably because he was drunk. It's still no excuse."

Irene noted his point of view with a certain amount of satisfaction. A few years earlier Jonny himself had had major problems with alcohol. Rumor had it his wife had given him an ultimatum: stop drinking, or I'm leaving and taking the four kids with me. Irene had to give him credit for the fact that he seemed to have managed it so far. Over the past three years she had never seen him under the influence or hungover.

"He didn't have anything interesting to say?" she asked.

"No. He just kept sounding off about how incompetent the cops are, about this pathetic society of ours that lets killers out of jail after twelve months. They don't face any real punishment nowadays. You know how it goes—same old same old."

Irene nodded. She had heard it all before, many times.

Was it possible that Alexandra's murderer had a record? He might not have killed before, but could he be a rapist who had been released? She decided that her priority for the rest of the day would be to check Alexandra's homicide against previous cases where the victim had sustained similar injuries, but not necessarily been killed.

IRENE COULDN'T GET used to the silence that met her when she opened the front door.

She had to accept that her twin daughters had flown the nest once and for all. Jenny was on a cookery course in Malmö; she would be there for at least another year, then she was intending to apply to a cookery school in Amsterdam, which provided specialist training. Her goal was to become a high-class vegan chef.

Katarina and Felipe would be home in a few weeks after spending five months in Brazil. They were in Natal, working on the same capoeira project they had been involved with twice before. If the street children attended school, they were allowed to participate in a program of capoeira training, and they also received a meal at the center each day. For many of the children it was their only hot meal. If any of them missed school, they were immediately kicked off the project. It was tough, but it was the approach that worked. The basic philosophy was that education is the only way out of poverty. There are no shortcuts.

Capoeira is a Brazilian martial art that was originally brought to the country by African slaves. They used dance moves to disguise their training, so that the slave owners wouldn't suspect they were practicing a form of self-defense. In recent years the popularity of the sport has grown all over the world. Both Katarina and Felipe were skilled practitioners. They were working as trainers and leaders at the center in Natal, but it would be good to have them home again before too long.

And Sammie was gone. One cloudy day in March he had fallen asleep forever, with one front paw resting in Irene's hand. At the ripe old age of fourteen years, nine months and four days, his heart had stopped beating. Now he was running around the Elysian Fields in doggy heaven, with grilled chicken for dinner and liver paste sandwiches every single day.

Irene's throat closed up as she thought of Sammie. She missed him terribly, but she and Krister had agreed that they wouldn't get another dog. They worked such long, unsociable hours.

Almost two years ago, Irene's mother, Gerd, had slipped on a patch of ice and broken her hip. She had also hit the back of her head and sustained a severe injury to her skull, which was the reason for the constant dizziness that plagued her these days. The hip hadn't healed properly, and the operation had to be done all over again. The result was better, but far from perfect. At about the same time, her partner, Sture, had died of a heart attack. It had all been too much for Gerd; she had lost her spark. She still lived in her apartment in Guldheden, but she no longer went out on her own. She was afraid of falling again because she was dizzy and unsteady on her feet. Irene and Krister did the shopping for her, and every other week someone from the home care service came to clean the apartment. In between times she was terribly lonely. "I've been around for too long. I'm nearly eighty. All my friends are dead or gaga or too feeble to come and see me," she would say. Irene tried to jolly her out of it, but she realized there was a lot of truth to what Gerd said. Admittedly the various clubs and societies her mother had been a member of sometimes got in touch, but that was usually around Christmastime. The person who called in most often was a lively lady of about the same age who lived in a neighboring apartment. They had known each other for forty-five years, ever since Irene's parents had moved to Doktor Bex Gata. Irene had grown up there; she hadn't left home until she moved to Stockholm to study at the police academy in Ulriksdal.

Irene walked into her silent house. Krister was working the evening shift, and was unlikely to be home before midnight.

The only positive thing about the fact that her daughters had moved out was that Irene no longer had to eat Jenny's vegan food. She hadn't escaped completely, however; Krister had started to take an interest in vegetarian cuisine. As a professional master chef, he could turn the dullest root vegetables into a delicious delicacy. It was a talent she definitely lacked. Since she was married to a chef, she had never bothered to learn how to cook, and it wasn't something that interested her.

She would make a sandwich and a pot of tea. While the water was heating up she defrosted two rolls in the microwave. A few slices of cheese and two dutiful slices of cucumber on each; that would have to do. She put everything on a tray and carried it upstairs to the TV room.

The local news began with confirmation from the police that Alexandra Hallwiin had been murdered. They were asking for information from anyone who had seen anything on Walpurgis Night, in the vicinity of the bus stop on Torslandavägen, in the area north of Lilleby and around Nötsund. They were particularly interested in hearing about any cars in the area that might have picked up Alexandra.

Surely someone must have seen the girl after she closed the gate of that impressive house on the hill, but not one single witness had come forward, presumably because of the wet and windy weather over the weekend. There had been no gangs of kids gathering on the shore for a barbecue; everyone had stayed indoors.

The police have also confirmed that the young woman whose body was found in the Gårdstensbergen area yesterday was the victim of a homicide. She went missing approximately one week before she was found. The police are not revealing her identity until all the relatives have been informed.

The newsreader moved on to their second case involving a murdered girl.

Irene nodded to herself. They still hadn't managed to track down Moa Olsson's father. Hannu was working on it, so Irene had high hopes of success. Could the missing father be the killer? From a purely statistical point of view, it was certainly possible. But there was something about the MO that made it seem unlikely. The injuries to Moa's body indicated extreme sexual violence with a sadistic twist. There were no reports to suggest that Moa's father had subjected her to any kind of sexual assault. According to the mother, he hadn't even seen Moa since she was one year old. He had major problems with drug and alcohol abuse; he had drifted away to the periphery of society, and had broken off all contact with his daughter.

. . . as the remains of the building were being demolished.

Irene suddenly became aware that the next big story was the discovery of the mummy. The recently purchased flat-screen TV was showing pictures of the cordoned-off area around the exposed cellar, though the police cars were obscuring the view. The cameras had just managed to catch a shot of the corpse being taken away in a body bag.

It appears that the body had been walled up in an aperture next to the base of the chimney. The police are not prepared to comment on the identity of the victim at this stage.

The mummy was still a mystery. Tommy had spent the afternoon compiling a list of men who had disappeared without a trace over the past forty years. It had turned out to be a very long list. They had agreed to wait for the forensic pathologist's preliminary report, which should tell them how long the body had been walled up. It would also be interesting to get an idea of his age; that would enable them to cross a lot of names off the list.

Irene had gone through the database searching for sex offenders with sexual violence as part of their MO. Alexandra's injuries indicated an extremely violent perpetrator, possibly with ritualistic tendencies, according to the pathologist. She had given a copy to Hannu, as there seemed to be certain similarities to the case of Moa Olsson.

She too had ended up with a long list. She had been able to delete several names right away because the violence had been directed at the woman the man in question was living with or had lived with. A further three men had been deported after serving their sentence, which left twenty-three names on the list. Tomorrow she and Jonny would start going through them.

Before she left for the day, Irene had called forensics to find out what had been used to strangle Alexandra. To her surprise it turned out to be a common computer cable; the various components of virtually every computer were linked by such thin cables. The killer had looped it around the girl's neck, pulled it tight, then looped the rest around again. Which was an odd thing to do; it was as if he wanted to make sure it stayed put.

The three recent homicides would stretch the department's resources even more, Irene thought. Fredrik Stridh was supposed to be working with a special team that was concentrating on the biker gangs, but in reality all his time was taken up by the two ongoing murder investigations linked to the gang war. They knew from experience that there was a significant risk of escalating violence over the summer; the gangs wanted to mark their territory before the fall. This was about power and big money. Neither of the gangs would back down.

Efva Thylqvist was in a difficult position, caught between the pressure to save money and the increased workload. It would be interesting to see if she had the skill to sort things out. Irene smiled to herself. She knew it was unkind, but she wanted to see her self-assured chief sweat a little, look slightly less competent in the eyes of her subordinates. Particularly as some of them didn't appear to realize how manipulative she could be. Was Irene really the only one who could see what she was like?

"THE FORENSIC PATHOLOGIST is going to look at the mummy today; we'll have a preliminary report sometime after three o'clock at the earliest. The body was lying on a rug, which forensics is analyzing now. At the moment I don't know if it has anything to do with his death," Efva Thylqvist announced as she opened morning prayer. Everyone nodded as they tried to fortify themselves with the contents of their coffee cups. It was going to be a hard day.

The teams reported back on the events of the previous day and how they were intending to proceed with their respective investigations. Just when they all thought the meeting was over and began to get to their feet, Hannu raised his hand.

"I took another look at the underclothes the girls were wearing. They belong together. The bra and the panties."

As soon as Hannu spoke, Irene knew he was right. That lacy bra had bothered her right from the start; the suspicion that it probably hadn't belonged to Alexandra had seemed important, even though she couldn't quite work out why. It had remained there at the back of her mind, chafing away.

"Are you sure?" the superintendent asked.

"The fabric and the pattern on the lace are exactly the same. And the same brand." He looked down at his notebook: "Sexy Thing."

"Have you tried to trace the manufacturer?"

The look Hannu gave his boss was answer enough, but he replied politely, "Yes. It's a common brand sold through mail order and in sex shops. Europe's largest wholesaler is based in Hamburg. The clothes are made in Southeast Asia."

The room fell silent as everyone thought about this new information.

"So you think we could be looking at the same killer," Efva Thylqvist said eventually.

"Perhaps."

The superintendent pressed the palms of her hands against the surface of the table and gazed down at her bare fingers. She played a brief drum solo with her nails, then looked up.

"This puts things in a completely different light. We could be dealing with a serial killer targeting young teenage girls. In spite of the fact that the killings took place in different parts of the city, we can perhaps assume they were carried out by the same person. The crux of the matter is that we can't be sure we have a serial killer on our hands, which means we must continue to pursue the two investigations separately, without bias. However, from now on we will coordinate the two teams and ensure that there is an ongoing exchange of information. We also need to inform forensics of our suspicions and ask them to look out for details that could link the two murders."

She fell silent, and her gaze swept the room.

"And not a word to the media. We need to find out how he made contact with the girls, and we need to find him fast! Because if our suspicions are correct, he will kill again. If he hasn't done so already."

"The Internet," Fredrik Stridh said.

Several people nodded. The Internet was the most likely route if someone wanted to hook up with teenage girls.

"There was that guy in Malmö last year, remember. He was in his thirties, but online he pretended to be a twenty-five-year-old woman looking for young models. He talked them into everything from posing naked in front of a webcam to meeting up with him. They managed to prove fifty-six cases of rape. There were probably a lot more, but the girls weren't prepared to come forward. They were all in their teens," Fredrik went on.

"There are plenty of similar cases where a man has conned a girl into meeting up and then raped her, but none of them has led to murder," Tommy pointed out.

"Not in Sweden. Overseas. There have been several in the US," Hannu said.

"How can these girls be so naïve? Don't they realize they're arranging to meet a complete stranger? As a parent you don't have a clue what they get up to online!"

Jonny spread his hands wide in a helpless gesture. Irene understood how he felt; his two girls were fourteen and twelve. His boys were slightly older.

"So it seems most likely that contact was established online," Superintendent Thylqvist stated. She turned to Fredrik. "Could you make sure that Alexandra's and Moa's computers are checked?"

"I'll speak to Jens."

Jens was their IT expert, and he was highly skilled. As he sauntered along the corridors in his low-slung jeans and woolen hat he looked like a skateboarder who had left his board somewhere and gotten lost, but in fact he was thirty years old and had just become a father. Little Zelda was named after a princess in a popular video game. But then Jens was a bit different, and Irene always thought of him as their "IT oddball."

"Thank you, Fredrik. Apart from that, I assume you've got your hands full with the gang murders. Jonny, Hannu and Irene—I'd like you to work on the two girls; Tommy, you're on the mummy. Unfortunately, I have a meeting that will take all day."

Efva Thylqvist got to her feet, signaling that the briefing was over.

THEY DIVIDED UP the twenty-three names on Irene's list among the three of them. Only two of the men had convictions for homicide. Others were guilty of violent rape, serious assault and extreme threatening behavior. Jonny and Hannu each took one of the men convicted of homicide.

Irene spent the rest of the day working through her eight names. Three of them were still in jail and hadn't been out on parole, so they could be crossed off right away. She was also able to eliminate another man who was in a state psychiatric institution. If he had done half of what was in his file, he was more than qualified for the role of serial killer on the hunt for young girls, so to be on the safe side Irene checked that he hadn't been let out for any reason toward the end of April, and he hadn't. His case worker made it clear that it would be a long time before he was even considered for parole.

Of the remaining four, one was held in an open jail and was on day release. He was employed in a car repair workshop and was doing well, according to the governor. On April 30 he had worked half a day and had spent the evening in front of the TV with some of the other inmates. His alibi seemed legitimate.

The last three names were trickier. She got a hold of the youngest, an eighteen-year-old, at his mother's house in Tynnered. After a lengthy discussion, first with the mother and then with the boy himself, they arranged to meet the following day. He was adamant that he didn't want to come down to the police station. "I get these traumatic flashbacks," he insisted. *Someone's obviously had therapy*, Irene thought. They agreed that she would come to his mother's apartment at ten o'clock the following morning.

Then she hit a wall. Neither of the remaining two men answered on the number that was given in their contact details. In one case she heard an automated message informing her that this number was no longer in use, and when she dug a little deeper in the database, she discovered that the man had died two weeks earlier. The cause of death was listed as suicide. He had been released the previous month, after serving a sentence for the repeated rape of three little boys. After two years he had gotten out of jail, and a month later he took his own life.

A guilty conscience? Hardly. Irene had interviewed enough pedophiles over the years to realize that they rarely felt guilty about what they had put the children through. They usually defended themselves by insisting that the child had been a willing participant or had even taken the initiative in the sexual transaction. They claimed that pedophilia is a sexual orientation and that it is forbidden to persecute a minority.

It is almost always the social stigma and rejection that breaks a pedophile. They have the lowest status in jail, and are frequently subjected to harassment. It is rarely possible for pedophiles to return to their former workplaces, since most of their colleagues know what they had been up to. They often have to move because the neighbors know why they have been away. Pedophiles are abhorred everywhere, and by everyone.

And yet there are more and more of them.

Why? The Internet. It has brought about a revolution for pedophiles all over the world. The opportunity to access images has increased, as has the volume produced. No one needs to smuggle pictures and magazines across the border from one country to another these days. All you have to do is take pictures on a cell phone and post them on the net, where they spread at the speed of light. They will be there forever, and the victim has no way of getting them removed.

A note further down the page caught Irene's attention; it was a link to a site called Pedophilewatch. She clicked on the link and brought up a site showing pictures and names of men, along with the occasional woman. The rubric explained they were convicted pedophiles, exposed on the Internet. Most were Americans, since the site was based in the US, but other countries were also represented. The names were arranged by nationality, so she quickly found the page showing Swedish names. The man who had committed suicide two weeks earlier was almost at the top of the list, with his photograph, description, education and training, former workplaces, convicted crimes and his last known address. Two more of the men Irene had found through the police database were also there.

It was obvious that the victims and their relatives were keeping the site updated. It would be virtually impossible for anyone on this particular register to find a place in the world where he or she wouldn't have to worry about being recognized.

The sharks that hunt in the dark depths of the cyber ocean can get caught in the net themselves, Irene thought, *with no chance of escape.*

The idea didn't give her any sense that justice was being served. Instead she was becoming increasingly aware that anyone at all can become a hunter online, and anyone can become a victim. All you have to do is click on a link, read a blog or enter a chat room. An innocent person who is hung out to dry on the net has just as little chance of escaping reprisals as a guilty person.

The Internet is a monster with a life of its own, and it's growing at a mind-blowing speed, beyond all human and legal rules and restrictions, she thought pessimistically.

JONNY HAD THREE names of interest left on his list, while Hannu had two. Together with Irene's two, that made a total of seven men they wanted to talk to about the murders of Alexandra and Moa.

"We'll do this together," Jonny decided.

"I'm meeting Tobias Hansson at his mother's apartment on

Smaragdgatan in Tynnered at ten tomorrow morning," Irene said. "He didn't want to come here. Said he was completely traumatized by the place."

"Poor bastard. What does he have on his delicate little conscience?"

"The rape of a thirteen-year-old girl and the attempted rape of a twelve-year-old. The twelve-year-old's father heard her screaming and came to the rescue; he happened to be out in the garage with the door open. He was able to give a good description of Tobias, who was picked up later that same evening. At first he insisted he was innocent, but he was linked to the attempted rape through DNA. The girl had managed to scratch him and had traces of skin under her nails. There were also scratch marks on Tobias's forearms, and his DNA was found in the sperm taken from the thirteen-year-old rape victim. When he was confronted with the DNA evidence he changed tack and claimed he had lost his memory, due to the influence of both alcohol and GHB."

"So his MO is a surprise attack on his victim?"

"Yes."

"Where and when did these attacks take place?"

"Almost exactly a year ago, both within a kilometer of the apartment where Tobias lives with his mother. He's just been released; he was given a reduced sentence because he was under eighteen."

"He doesn't really sound like our man. That kind of rape is governed by impulse, whereas Alexandra and Moa's killer seems to have planned everything. He was very careful not to leave any traces. He was bent on homicide right from the start," Hannu said thoughtfully.

"I agree. Plus the fact that little Tobbe operated in his own neighborhood in both cases. Our girls were murdered in completely different parts of the city, a long way from Tynnered," Jonny pointed out.

"I think you're right, but we'd better speak to him anyway so that we can eliminate him from the investigation if nothing else," Irene said.

Hannu nodded. "I'll come with you."

"Good. In that case we might manage another name from the list for the morning," said Jonny.

Irene turned to him and smiled.

"And maybe you could help me find out a bit more about this guy? I haven't managed to track him down."

Jonny looked far from pleased as he stared at the piece of paper she put in front of him.

"There's so much to do when you're leading a case," Irene said, pretending to sympathize.

Jonny snorted, but couldn't come up with a cutting reply. For once, Hannu smiled.

"I promise I'll come out with you in the afternoon, just to make things fair," Irene went out.

"No thanks—I'll take Hannu. You can stay here and write up your report on what you find out in the morning," Jonny said with a triumphant grin.

THE ENTIRE APARTMENT reeked of cat piss and cigarette smoke. After only a few minutes Irene was starting to feel slightly nauseated. A ginger cat hissed at her and slid under the tattered sofa in the living room. Perhaps it just didn't like mornings. We grow similar to those we live with; neither Bettan Hansson nor her son seemed to be morning people.

The mother had opened the door and sullenly introduced herself. She was a faded blonde who weighed at least 260 pounds. She had squeezed her abundant curves into a dirty pink tracksuit. The jacket was zipped only halfway up, generously exposing her heavy breasts. As far as Irene could tell, she wasn't wearing anything underneath. Just above one breast was a tattoo that had presumably been a small lizard once upon a time, but Bettan's increasing weight combined with the forces of gravity meant that it now looked more like an alligator.

"Tobbe's in the bathroom. He won't be long," she said curtly.

She shuffled past the coffee table and sank down in a battered armchair. As the seat began to sink toward the floor with a squeak of protest, Irene realized why the cat had wisely chosen to hide under the sofa.

"What's this about?" Bettan Hansson asked.

She was trying to take an aggressive tone, but the anxiety in her voice was unmistakable.

"We just want to ask Tobias a few questions," Irene said.

"About what?" Bettan asked again.

Neither Hannu nor Irene answered her. They could hear the sound of the shower from the bathroom; after a while it stopped, and they heard someone moving around, followed by a hacking cough. It was almost ten minutes before Tobias Hansson emerged. He stood in the doorway of the living room, glaring in silence at the two police officers. He was big—enormous, in fact. He was of normal height, but the width of his body meant that he could barely get through the door without turning sideways. Pumped biceps strained the sleeves of his black T-shirt, which had the logo OLYMPIC GYM across the chest. He couldn't put his arms down by his sides, but held them slightly bent outward. His black jeans hugged the muscles in his calves and thighs. Tobias was a shining example of how several hours of strenuous strength training each day could build muscle. But he was only eighteen years old; something told Irene that anabolic steroids might have a role to play here.

His round, shaven skull looked shrunken, perched on top of his huge body, and his cherubic cheeks gave him the appearance of a giant baby. Perhaps that was why he had acquired several substantial tattoos on his arms and around his neck. White crystals sparkled in both ears, and his lower lip was pierced by a silver ring. None of which made a great deal of difference; he still looked like a grotesque baby. Perhaps the expressionless pale-blue eyes contributed to the overall impression.

Irene and Hannu introduced themselves. As expected, they got nothing more than an inarticulate grunt in response. Tobias slowly began to shuffle toward the other armchair. Irene caught herself holding her breath as he thudded down. The chair creaked alarmingly, but it didn't break.

"We really just want to check where you were on Walpurgis Night," Irene said, looking Tobias straight in the eye.

"He was here," Bettan Hansson said immediately, before her son even had the chance to open his mouth.

Her hands were trembling as she shook a cigarette out of an open pack on the scratched coffee table. A fleeting expression of surprise passed across Tobias's face, but the next moment those pale-blue eyes were blank once more.

"Were you at home, Tobias?" Irene persisted.

He managed a nod.

"Were you here all evening?"

"Yes," Bettan snapped.

Another nod from the giant baby in the other armchair seemed to indicate confirmation.

"That's unusual, a guy of your age sitting at home with his mom on Walpurgis Night," Hannu said calmly.

Tobias glanced at him, then quickly looked away.

"But that's what happened," Bettan insisted.

"Is there anyone else who can confirm that you were here all evening?" Hannu went on, still addressing Tobias.

"It was just the two of us," Bettan said firmly.

Hannu kept his eyes fixed on Tobias, paying no attention whatsoever to his mother. She looked furious as she greedily sucked on her cigarette, spilling ash all around her. *Nervous*, Irene thought. *Probably with good reason.*

"And what did you do the previous weekend?" Hannu asked.

Tobias looked confused, but Bettan came to his rescue once more.

"We were together all weekend. He went to the gym with some friends during the day, but in the evenings he was here with me."

"So you and Tobias are best friends?" Hannu said, turning his attention to the big woman for the first time.

Her face immediately flushed the same color as an overripe strawberry.

"He'd only just gotten out of jail, goddammit!" she said.

It was true that Tobias had been released from the youth offenders' institution on April tenth; but the two girls had been killed after that. From that point of view he remained of considerable interest.

But we're not going to get anything out of him with his mother hovering over him, Irene thought. She caught Hannu's eye and they exchanged an almost imperceptible nod. They got to their feet simultaneously.

"We'll be in touch. You'll probably have to come down to the station," Hannu said, his eyes fixed on Tobias, who was doing his utmost to avoid that searching gaze. Beads of sweat had appeared on the boy's shaven head. Irene could see that he was extremely nervous too, which was interesting in itself.

"He makes one mistake, and you keep on hassling him!" Bettan hissed.

The smoke from her cigarette went down the wrong way, and she started coughing violently.

Neither Irene nor Hannu bothered to reply.

"We can't dismiss him," Irene said when they were back in the car. She pulled out into the stream of traffic heading for the city center.

"No." Hannu looked pensive. "But it's not him. The two homicides were planned."

"And he's too dumb and impulsive," Irene agreed.

"Exactly."

Even though Irene shared his view, she wanted to hear his thoughts.

"What makes you believe the murders were planned?"

"No witnesses have seen either of the girls with a stranger. Neither of them mentioned that they'd arranged to meet someone. No clues, no evidence. The killer has been in touch with them, arranged to meet. And persuaded them to keep quiet."

"What about the girls' computers? Anything there?"

"Jens is going through Alexandra's computer; Moa's is missing."

"Missing?"

"Yes. She had a laptop through the school. She was dyslexic, and was taking part in an experiment. She was having extra lessons with specialist teachers. According to her mother, she carried the laptop around all the time, in her rucksack. The students don't get a new one if they lose it."

"So they won't be tempted to sell it," Irene said with a grimace.

"Presumably."

They both sat in silence, thinking things over as they approached the police station.

"I don't suppose her boozed-up mother could have sold it?" Irene wondered.

"No. Her mother said that Moa spent most of her time skipping class over the past two years, but apparently since she joined this dyslexia group, she'd pulled herself together. And it's all down to the laptop; the girl used to spend several hours a day on it."

"Hmm. Why does that give me a bad feeling?" Irene said, glancing over at Hannu.

He nodded in agreement. "We have to find Moa's computer. Her cell phone is missing too. I'd like to try to get over to Gårdsten this morning; two colleagues are talking to Moa's teachers and school friends, but I'd like to speak to her mother again."

"Poor woman. She's lost both her kids. Her son died in a car crash, and now her daughter has been murdered."

"Yes, some people really do suffer. But I'm not sure it's always a coincidence," Hannu said.

"You mean it's a question of environment, that kind of thing?"

"Yes. My impression of Moa's mother is that she's . . . absent. In every sense of the word."

"What do you mean?"

"She's an alcoholic. She goes out boozing with her pals. Sometimes she's away for several days, according to social services."

Irene thought about what he'd said.

"That could be a link between Moa and Alexandra. When Jonny and I went over to Torslanda yesterday, Alexandra's father was completely wasted. We couldn't get a sensible word out of him. At first I thought he just couldn't handle the grief, but . . . Her mother was a mess, but he wasn't giving her any support. When we got there, he was downstairs and she was upstairs. It was as if they couldn't get far enough away from each other. I got the feeling that . . ."

She broke off, trying to find the right words before she went on.

"The house is incredibly extravagant. Alexandra has her own horse. Jan Hallwiin was married before and has two grown-up children who were raised by their mother in Gävle. They're about thirty now and live in Stockholm. It doesn't sound as if they've had much contact with their father over the years. Alexandra's mother is twenty-three years younger than Jan, and Alexandra is her only child. Both parents work long hours. I have a feeling that Alexandra was a lonely girl. Yes, she had a horse and loved riding, but . . . she seemed lonely."

Hannu nodded to show that he understood. A cop has to rely on gut feelings.

THE NEXT PERSON on their list was in his hair salon. He finished off a client, then showed the two officers into a small staff room, hidden away behind a rattling bamboo curtain. His name was Bengt Robertsson, and he was forty-three years old. His thin bleached-blond hair was cut very short, but he sported an impressive mustache with the ends waxed and optimistically turned upward. He had a watertight alibi for the time of Moa's death; he had been in Thailand when she went missing and had gotten home three days before Walpurgis Night. He had spent April 30 and the May Day holiday in the company of good friends on the Stena line ferry to Kiel. Without a moment's hesitation he gave them the names of a dozen people who could confirm he was on board the ship at the relevant time.

The visit to the hairdresser had taken only fifteen minutes. The next person on Hannu's list had been horrified at the suggestion that the police come and speak to him at his new workplace, so he had promised to come to the station after five o'clock. Until then Hannu would go with Jonny to see another man on their list. Once all seven had been tracked down and questioned, any possible alibis would be checked. They would then attempt to decide which of the men were still of interest and which could be eliminated from the investigation. Meanwhile they would continue to follow up any new leads or information that came in. It was tedious routine work, but it was absolutely necessary; it was the only way to solve a crime.

"We've got time to go and see Moa's mother. It's only quarter of an hour from here. What's her name again?" Irene asked.

"Kristina. Known as Kicki. Thirty-nine years old. Regularly picked up for alcohol abuse ever since she was a teenager. Her parents were alcoholics. However, she has managed to look after her own children; they've never been taken into care."

"What about Moa? Has she had any dealings with the police?"

"Nothing at all. However, the brother who died in the car crash was picked up for drunken behavior twice, and he was given a warning for aiding and abetting in the theft of a car. That was two months before he stole the car he crashed."

"So you don't think it was pure chance that the son died in a car crash and the daughter was murdered. I agree with you to a certain extent, but not entirely. Not all children who grow up with parents who abuse alcohol or narcotics end up going down that road themselves."

Hannu glanced sideways at her.

"The survivors. But Moa Olsson and her brother were not among them."

Nor was their mother, it seemed. They parked outside a two-story grey concrete block. The stairwell had recently been freshened up with pastel colors, but someone had already sprayed MDNMDNMDN all over one wall in bright purple. The letters were surrounded by small red phalluses.

They rang the doorbell of Kicki Olsson's apartment. When no one had answered by the fourth ring, Hannu tried the handle and the door swung open. There was a pile of shoes and outerwear in the hallway, and an unidentifiable smell with hints of garbage and sour wine.

They stepped over the mess on the floor, and Irene called out, "Hello! Anyone home? Kicki Olsson?"

She was in the bathroom. There was a high stool right next to the bathtub, with a drying rack propped against one wall. Kicki Olsson had tied a nylon washing line to the ceiling hook for the rack, then she had made a noose and slipped it around her neck. She had stood on the stool, then jumped into the tub. Given the way she looked, it must have happened at least twenty-four hours ago.

"We've got some information about the mummy," Tommy said.

He took a big bite of his cinnamon bun and washed it down

with a good swig of coffee. "We're looking at a man in his forties. He's probably been dead for between twenty and thirty years. The cause of death was three bullet wounds: one in the head and two close to the heart. We won't know the bullet type and caliber until tomorrow at the earliest. The gun that was found with the body is interesting. It was underneath the rug the body was lying on. It seems that the rug was used to carry the body to the opening. The gun is an old model, a Tokarev. Russian. Stopped being manufactured in the mid-50s. Forensics sent a picture."

The image of an old-fashioned gun appeared on the white wall behind him; at first glance it resembled an FN Browning. When Irene looked more closely, she could see a five-pointed star on the butt, with the letters CCCP between the points of the star.

Tommy moved on to the next picture. "This is the rug—a valuable item, according to forensics. Ninety by two hundred and twenty centimeters. The blood on the rug presumably comes from the body, but they're in the process of testing it. They'll get back to us when they've checked the whole rug in detail."

Tommy leafed through the papers in front of him. "Getting back to the mummy itself: he was one hundred and eighty centimeters tall. Slim build, thinning ash-blond hair. Good teeth, but with a number of amalgam fillings. He has a small gold bridge on the upper-left-hand side, so forensics is hoping to identify him with the help of dental records. He was wearing blue Jockey underpants, white tube socks, dark blue corduroy pants, heavy black shoes, a pale blue shirt, a wine-red knit jacket with a crocodile logo on the left breast, and a dark blue Helly Hansen windbreaker with a detachable red nylon lining. On his left wrist he had a watch advertising the *Reader's Digest*. We're in the process of going through the missing persons database."

As usual, Irene was drinking coffee with a dash of milk and steering clear of the cakes. Out of sheer defiance, she took another bun. When she had finished, she licked every scrap of cinnamon and sugar off her fingers. Childish, admittedly, but it made her feel much better, even though she would have to run a few extra kilometers to stop the calories from settling on her hips. On the other hand, she hadn't had time for lunch. The unexpected discovery of Kicki Olsson's body had meant that Hannu and Irene had gotten back to HQ only fifteen minutes ago. They would return to Gårdsten once CSI had finished with the apartment, probably the following day. There was no doubt that it was suicide, but they still needed to check the place over. They were still looking for Moa's computer and cell phone, among other things.

Irene felt depressed as she thought about the dysfunctional family: the son dies behind the wheel in a car crash, the daughter is murdered, and the mother takes her own life. To a certain extent she could understand Kicki's decision. Perhaps her children had kept her more or less stable, and once they were gone, her life lost its meaning.

"Any names that look interesting so far?" Efva Thylqvist asked.

"I've only just got the names; I haven't had time to go through them yet. But I'm optimistic; it hasn't been that long since this guy disappeared. He must be on the list."

Tommy looked determined as he waved his papers.

Nice to know that someone is feeling optimistic, Irene thought.

As usual, Krister's spaghetti Bolognese was a triumph. Jar sauce was banned from his cooking, of course. He made the sauce using ripe beef tomatoes, garlic, basil, a decent slug of red wine and freshly ground beef, which he bought in the market hall on Kungstorget. "I want to see the piece of meat before they grind it," he often said. He had always felt the same, even before it came to light that the stores were relabeling old ground beef. Food wasn't only his profession, it was also his main interest in his leisure time. He was a master chef in one of Göteborg's most famous gourmet restaurants, with one star in the *Guide Rouge*.

"Tough day, sweetheart?" he said, topping up Irene's glass of wine.

"Just half, thanks . . . I've got to get up early . . . Yes, it's been a hell of a day. It's kind of got me down, actually."

Irene sounded off about Efva Thylqvist, who refused to lighten the department's workload by bringing in a replacement for Birgitta. Then she quickly ran through the cases they were working on. As she was telling him about Kicki Olsson's tragic life and death, she could feel her throat closing up. In her mind's eye she could still see the image of the dead woman, her toes almost touching the bottom of the bathtub.

"It's strange; I don't usually let things get to me, but these cases are just so tragic," she said.

Krister nodded sympathetically. "The two girls were so young, and then you find the mother of one of them dead. It's just too much at once. Perhaps this case is getting to you because you're a mother yourself. Our girls might be twenty-two, but you never stop worrying," he said.

"This killer worries me. I don't want another teenage girl to go the same way, but we're not sure how he gets in touch with them. We suspect it might be through the Internet, some youth site maybe."

"Like LunarStorm? I remember what the twins were like when it first appeared!"

Krister laughed at the memory.

"Do you remember how we used to have to nag them to come away from the computer?" he said.

"Yes, but it didn't last long. Just a few months, then they lost interest. And they've always had so much going on in their free time: Katarina had her jiujitsu, Jenny had her music. These days she devotes most of her attention to cooking, but she's started singing with a band down in Malmö," Irene said.

"Has she? I didn't know that."

"She mentioned it when she called last week; I must have forgotten to tell you. And she's found a new apartment."

"I knew about the apartment, but not the singing."

"And in three weeks Katarina and Felipe will be back from Natal. It'll be so good to see them again!"

Krister raised his glass.

"A toast to our wonderful daughters!"

"They got the Hulk," Fredrik informed the team before anyone else had time to speak at morning prayer.

"Who? When? Is he dead?" Efva Thylqvist demanded.

"He's dead. I think we know who's behind it, but we don't have any proof; it's probably the same guys who were responsible for the car bomb. As for when it happened: two thirty this morning. Apparently Hulk Hansson had a girlfriend nobody knew about. Including his wife, presumably. He slipped away last night without telling his bodyguards; he'd actually requested police protection himself. But I guess when you're horny . . . He was shot as he left the apartment block after visiting his mistress. So now we have three murders," Fredrik concluded with a gusty sigh.

Efva Thylqvist pursed her lips, but chose to ignore the sigh. *She's starting to feel stressed*, Irene thought with some satisfaction. Although it wasn't really anything to celebrate, since she and her colleagues would end up under even more pressure.

"They were standing outside waiting for him. Pumped several bullets into his chest. He died instantaneously," Fredrik added.

"You say 'they.' Were there any witnesses who saw more than one perp?" the superintendent asked.

"Not saw, but heard. Several witnesses whose bedrooms overlook the street heard the shots, and at the same time they heard an engine start up, then a car door opening and closing before the vehicle took off with a screech of tires. My interpretation is that the perp who shot Hansson was standing by the door, while his accomplice was sitting in a car nearby. After the shots had been fired, the car drove up and the killer jumped in. They took off so fast it virtually melted the tarmac."

Efva Thylqvist stared at Fredrik, and she wasn't studying his handsome face. Irene knew exactly what she was thinking: Fredrik was going to be completely taken up with the gang war from now on. It had escalated to such an extent that he was going to be out of action for quite some time as far as the ongoing work of the department was concerned.

THERE WAS NO sign that CSI had been in Kicki Olsson's apartment. There were still piles of clothes on the floor. Irene and Hannu stepped over them and tried to get an overview. It was a small, three-room apartment with a kitchen and bathroom. It was light; the living room had a large south-facing window and a balcony. Not that much daylight penetrated through the filthy glass, but Irene could see the sun shining outside, and soon it would attempt to brighten the shabby room. The only piece of furniture that looked new was a big flat-screen TV on a small cabinet. In front of the TV was a worn sofa, an armchair that didn't match and a cracked glass table. The rug had probably once been an attractive pale grey with a pattern in dark beige, but all the ingrained marks and stains had turned it to brownish red and dirty grey. The only picture in the room was a framed print of a weeping little boy.

The kitchen faced east; the morning sun was still shining through the window, highlighting the dirt that was everywhere. On the draining board lay the flattened aluminum bag from inside a wine box; the torn box itself was on the floor, revealing that it had contained the cheapest white wine available from the state-owned liquor store.

Irene went into Kicki Olsson's bedroom. It contained only a king-size bed, a rickety bedside table, and a Billy bookcase from IKEA. There wasn't a single book to be seen; the shelves were crammed with ornaments: mostly dolls and china animals. There were more clothes all over the floor, and the room smelled musty and was in dire need of some fresh air.

Moa's room was small and incredibly messy. Schoolbooks, empty candy and chips bags, clothes, magazines and CDs were strewn everywhere. Irene knew that CSI had gone through the room and found nothing of interest. They had focused on trying to find Moa's computer and cell phone, but Irene wanted to know who Moa was and what she had done during the final days of her life.

A kitchen chair next to the unmade bed served as a bedside table, with a reading lamp and an open pack of tissues. A mirror hung on the wall at the foot of the bed.

On either side of the mirror Moa had pinned up two school photos of herself. Irene recognized one as the picture they had issued to the media. It was taken in the fall, only about six months ago. Moa was gazing straight into the camera, her expression serious. Her eyes and lips were heavily made up, and she had obviously piled on the fake tan. Her thick hair was dyed black, with a center part; it framed her face and fell below her shoulders. She looked good, even though her features were slightly too coarse for her to be regarded as pretty.

In the other photograph Moa was smiling shyly at the camera. Her hair was significantly shorter and lighter, curling above shoulder level. She might have been eleven or twelve years old, and there wasn't a trace of makeup. What struck Irene was the difference in the expression. The younger Moa's smile reached her eyes; the older Moa's gaze showed no emotion whatsoever. Was it her brother's death that had extinguished the smile in the girl's eyes?

Like her mother, Moa had a Billy bookcase. One shelf was

full of cuddly toys in all shapes and sizes. The other shelves contained a few schoolbooks, a pile of magazines, a new stereo, two packs of cigarettes and a small yellow plastic lighter, tons of makeup and several bottles of perfume. These attracted Irene's attention. Six bottles, some half full, others only just started, all different brands. Expensive brands, like Dior's J'adore and Kenzo's beautiful bottle with the flower stopper. Each bottle must have cost at least five hundred kronor. How could Moa afford that? A thought suddenly struck Irene; if she was right, it could provide an explanation for Moa's disappearance. Full of foreboding, she opened one closet door.

A whole row of designer tops were arranged neatly on hangers, several of them unworn. Five pairs of new jeans—three by Armani, the other two by the hip label Acne. A black sweater in the softest angora wool. Several more beautiful sweaters that also looked as if they had never been worn. On the floor of the closet was a stack of CDs, most still in their cellophane wrapping. Two pairs of leather boots, and a pair of high-heeled ankle boots. Irene picked up the leather boots. The price tags were still on the soles; one pair had cost three thousand four hundred kronor, the other three thousand. The ankle boots were more modestly priced at one thousand two hundred kronor. In the corner of the closet was a Versace handbag.

Hannu came into the room. "Anything interesting?"

"Yes. This isn't right. Moa had jeans that cost two thousand kronor, boots at around three thousand a pair, and expensive perfumes. This handbag would have cost several thousand."

"Shoplifting?"

"Maybe some of this stuff, but not all of it. The stereo, the perfumes, the makeup . . . the tops . . . look at this one, it's still got the price tag on it. Eight hundred and ninety-nine kronor!"

Irene shut the closet door and opened the other one, revealing a stack of wire baskets. She started to go through them, and in the top one she found what she was looking for. She pulled it out and put it on the bed. She took out several pairs of old sweats and laid them on the dirty sheet; concealed among the sweats were four sets of underwear. It looked as if Moa had deliberately hidden them.

"Bingo," Irene said grimly.

Hannu reached down and checked the label.

"Sexy Thing," he said, holding up a dark red set in see-through lace.

"It's the same as the girls were wearing, but a different color!" Irene exclaimed.

She couldn't suppress her excitement. They took a closer look at the thong and the skimpy bra. It definitely looked like the same style; the tiny roses were there too. The word SATURDAY was embroidered on the front of the thong.

The other sets were different brands, but certainly not the kind of thing you would expect a fifteen-year-old to own.

"She could have bought them online," Hannu said.

"I think Moa did all kinds of things online," Irene said. "We have to find her computer."

She gazed pensively at the see-through underwear.

"I think Moa was wearing the black Sexy Thing set when she met her killer. He took the bra with him, and forced Alexandra to put it on. Or maybe he put it on her himself afterward. The black bra was the only thing she was wearing when she was found."

"We still haven't found the rest of the girls' clothes," Hannu said.

Their eyes met; each knew what the other was thinking. *This investigation is turning into a nightmare.* And in the worst-case scenario, this was just the beginning.

"WE'VE GOT AN ID on the mummy!" Tommy announced triumphantly.

His colleagues sat up a little straighter, noticeably encouraged by the news. It was Friday morning, and they'd all had a tough week. Irene was already on her fourth mug of coffee, and was gradually starting to feel human.

"His name is Mats Persson—no relation, I should add. Date of birth March fifteenth, 1942. He disappeared without a trace on the evening of Wednesday, November ninth, 1983," Tommy went on.

"Did he go missing in the vicinity of Korsvägen?" Irene wondered.

"The last time he was seen alive was just before six o'clock at the city library on Götaplatsen. He spoke to one of the librarians as they were just about to close, and she saw him leave. And that was the last anyone saw of him. A woman waiting outside the city theater saw a man who might have been Mats Persson, but she couldn't be sure. If it was him, he walked past the steps and around the corner, heading toward the back of the theater."

"Well, he certainly turned a corner," Jonny Blom said, dunking a cookie in his coffee.

"There was an extensive investigation into Persson's disappearance. I spoke to Olle Nordlund, who retired a few years ago. He remembered the case very well; he told me it was given high priority, because Persson's father was murdered during the Second World War. It was in the fall of 1941, six months before Mats was born. His father was shot, and there was some suspicion that Russian spies were involved. The father used to work for the Swedish security service—SÄPO's predecessor, which makes him one of Sweden's first modern security agents. This is all according to Olle Nordlund."

Superintendent Efva Thylqvist had remained silent until now, listening attentively to Tommy's report.

"So that means the case notes from '83 should still be here in the building?" she said.

"Should be," Tommy agreed.

The superintendent didn't say any more, but Irene could see that she was mulling something over. At the end of morning prayer, Thylqvist turned to Tommy.

"Could you come to my office? There's something we need to discuss with regard to the mum . . . Mats Persson."

"JENS WANTS ONE of you to go down. He's found something on Alexandra's computer," Fredrik said as he left the department.

"I think we should all go," Irene said. "It could give us a lead on Moa."

Jonny, Hannu and Irene made their way down to the technical department.

"I've found the contact," Jens said, pointing to a pile of printouts. On the top was an enlarged picture of a smiling young man in a white T-shirt. He was strikingly good-looking, with sparkling brown eyes and perfect white teeth. His medium-length hair was dark, with a few streaks of blond. He was probably between sixteen and eighteen years of age.

"I've checked out the picture; it's on the net, but this one has been cropped. He's actually sitting there jerking off. It's on several gay porn websites."

"How the hell do you know that?" Jonny snapped.

Jens looked at him in surprise, then shrugged.

"It's my job. The first contact with Alexandra was made at the beginning of January on the youth site snuttis.se. He says he's a seventeen-year-old guy named Adam. Claims he broke his leg while he was snowboarding during the Christmas holidays. He's looking for a girlfriend. Alexandra answered. Nothing of note happens during January; he flirts a little and she seems interested. In the middle of February he asks her to send him a picture of her face. She takes one using the webcam on her computer. At the beginning of April she sends pictures of herself stroking her breasts. He'd been flattering her, asking her to do it. And he wants to get together. They arrange to meet up on Walpurgis Night."

"Really?" Irene said.

"Yep. It's him. Typical online grooming."

"Have you traced his computer?" Jonny asked.

Jens gave him a look that made his opinion of that particular question very clear. However, there was nothing in his voice when he spoke. "He uses two. They were reported stolen from a car parked outside the Chalmers University of Technology just before Christmas: a Fujitsu Siemens palmtop and an iBook. He hasn't contacted Alexandra from a fixed broadband connection; he uses free public Wi-Fi zones. They're available in most hotels, at airports and some larger train stations and on some trains and buses. Or you can surf using 3G, but that doesn't work so well on trains, because they're moving, and several people will be using the net. A satellite connection is better."

"Can you trace where he was when he was online?" Irene asked.

"It's difficult if it was a satellite connection, but I'll see what I can do."

They would have to be content with that for the time being. Irene picked up the pile of printouts and left the office with Hannu and Jonny following in her wake.

"WE'LL SPLIT THEM between us. Make a note of anything that looks interesting," Irene said as they were on their way up to the department in the elevator. She divided the pile into three, and they went to their offices to work through the material.

Irene had the last third, covering the period from March 21 to April 29. Tense with anticipation, she began to read:

Alexandra: hi. what are you doing?

Adam: looking at the pic of you and getting . . . ☺ what about you?

Alexandra: soooo bored. good friday! going to skåne tomorrow with mom and dad, gymkhana. don't know why they bother when they're getting divorced anyway. keeping up appearances.

Adam: it'll be better when they split—that's what happened with mine.

Alexandra: when was that?

Adam: 2 yrs ago. i was same age as you. have you got brothers or sisters?

Alexandra: 2 brothers but they're grown up & live in stockholm.

> **Adam:** i've got an older brother. he's 25, has an apartment in gbg. i'm going to take it over when he moves ☺
>
> **Alexandra:** so when's he moving?
>
> **Adam:** don't know. he finishes his business course in a year so he might get a job somewhere else. hope so! ☺
>
> **Alexandra:** what are you doing on easter?
>
> **Adam:** thinking about you! can't you send me a sexy pic? feel i need it!

[Eight minutes elapse.]

> **Alexandra:** no time. got to go to stables. Xx.
>
> **Adam:** Xx.

The next contact is on March 25. Alexandra complains about a miserable Easter weekend in Skåne. The gymkhana went well, but her parents spent most of the time quarreling. She is sick and tired of their constant arguing. Adam is sympathetic, and talks about how things were when his parents were in the process of separating. There is nothing of a sexual nature in their conversation over the next few days, but he becomes more persistent at the beginning of April.

> **Adam:** can't you send me some sexy pics to keep me going til we meet? you look gorgeous in the pics you've already sent, but i want to see more. your breasts for example. please?

[Five minutes elapse.]

> **Alexandra:** ok, but you better not show them to anyone else.

> **Adam:** of course not! you're my girl!

Alexandra poses briefly in front of the webcam. She takes off her top and bra and touches her breasts.

> **Adam:** you're so beautiful! as soon as my leg's better we can get together! nothing wrong with other parts though, if you know what i mean! ☺

> **Alexandra:** i want to see you too.

They chat frequently over the next few days. The sexual references become increasingly overt, and Alexandra starts to become bolder. On Saturday April 26, Adam suggests a meeting.

> **Alexandra:** it's a long way to borås.

> **Adam:** my brother is coming home for walpurgis night, so you could come with him. it's only an hour by car.

[Three minutes elapse.]

> **Alexandra:** can't stay over. competition the following day.

> **Adam:** that's cool, he's going back late in the evening, he's got to study for an exam.

Alexandra: my parents are going out for the evening—when is he coming back to gbg?

Adam: around midnight. he'll drive you home, you don't need to say anything to your parents, they'll never know you've been away. ☺

Alexandra: as long as i'm home by 12 at the latest. i'll tell them i'm going to watch the parade with my friends, then back to someone's house.

Adam: sounds good.

Over the next few days the tone of their conversation is light, and the planned meeting is not mentioned. However, on April 29 Adam spells out the details.

Adam: my brother's name is micke. he'll pick you up in the car from Torslanda Square at 6 tomorrow— you'll be here at 7 and he'll leave here at 11 at the latest to take you home. mom has promised to cook dinner for us, do you like grilled chicken?

Alexandra: sure. i like everything except mashed turnips and broccoli.

Adam: same here, but i don't like peas and beans either. i like you though! ☺

Alexandra: and i like you! ☺

Adam: Xx. can't wait to see you!

Alexandra: same here! Xx.

Irene sat there for a long time, trying to swallow the lump in her throat. Alexandra had walked straight into a trap. She had allowed herself to be drawn into the treacherous net. Easy prey for the skillful Adam, who had so successfully played the unhappy fourteen-year-old longing for love and friendship. He had realized how naïve she was, and had exploited her loneliness. She had been carefully selected. Groomed . . . he had gently nudged her along until she was exactly where he wanted her, preparing her for his ultimate goal: a face-to-face meeting. Adam had intended to kill her all along.

Irene decided she needed to speak to Jens. She gathered up the papers and ran down the stairs to his office. He was still sitting at his computer; he looked up from the screen and nodded to her as she walked in.

"Sorry to disturb you, Jens, but I need to know more," she began.

"No problem. Shoot."

"Who's the guy in the picture? You said he was on gay porn sites . . ."

"He called himself Pablo Eros. An Italian gay porn star, kind of a legend. The picture is at least ten years old. He killed himself two years ago; there's a whole heap of grieving fans out there. This particular picture is all over the Internet."

"So he's still alive on the net," Irene said.

Jens nodded. "Forever and ever, amen."

He waved her over to look at the screen so that she could see the original version.

"So Adam took the picture of this good-looking guy, cropped it and sent it to Alexandra. She must have thought she'd hit it off with every girl's dream," Irene said.

"There's no risk in using this picture. Teenage girls are unlikely to be on sites like this; they're real hard-core stuff."

"Do you think Adam contacted more girls online?"

"Absolutely! They always do. Then they choose their victim. Or victims."

"So he might have had several girls on the go at the same time?"

"More than likely."

"Any chance of finding out whether Moa had been in touch with Adam online?"

Jens shook his head.

"That's tricky. She could have been in contact with him on a different site, and of course he could have used a different name. And so could she."

"But Alexandra didn't."

"She was the perfect victim. Completely clueless."

"Jens, I'm worried that our killer might already be in touch with his next victim. He might have already met up with her and killed her. Is there any way you can look . . . is there any chance . . ."

She left the sentence hanging in the air and made a helpless gesture.

"No way. These sites have hundreds of thousands of users every day. I've already searched for Adam on snuttis.se, but I didn't find anything of interest. He's probably using a different name, which makes it impossible to track him down. You've got to use the mass media to warn kids," Jens said.

"I think you're right. It's time to warn young people and their parents. The disadvantage is that the killer will realize that we know how he got in touch with Alexandra."

"True, but it's the only way," Jens said, his expression grave.

"I HAD THE first third, so I'll start," Jonny said. He looked down at a piece of paper with various scribbled notes on it.

"My section runs from January seventh to February tenth. In his very first message the guy says he's seventeen and at high school, specializing in sciences and technology. He lives outside Borås and had a fall on a ski slope in Sälen over winter break, although he was actually snowboarding. Sustained a complex lower leg fracture. He's bored and wants to get in touch with a girl online. Alexandra replies. After a week or so she sends him a photo of herself taken using her webcam. Adam tells her his camera is broken, but he's sending her a picture that was taken before Christmas. Which is the picture of our gay porn star, of course. He doesn't really give much more information about himself."

Irene jotted down a few notes.

Hannu took over. "February eleventh to March twentieth. There's no contact the first week because it's the mid-semester break; Alexandra is away at a riding camp in Kungsbacka. When she gets back she asks if they can call each other on their cell phones. Adam claims he lost his in the snowboarding accident. That was the third phone he'd lost since last summer; his mom was furious and told him he had to save up for a new one himself. He doesn't want to use the landline because she's always complaining about the phone bills. 'My mom's crazy,' he writes on February fifteenth. Alexandra replies, 'my mom is always worrying about stuff, she nags me all the time. Dad is crazy.' She doesn't give any explanation for that comment, and Adam doesn't ask."

Hannu paused and sipped his coffee before continuing. "On March fourteenth Adam asks Alexandra to send him a nude picture of herself. She doesn't reply for ten minutes, then she writes: 'Not today.' Adam doesn't suggest it again in the section I read."

Irene was writing fast, trying to keep up. When Hannu had finished, she went through her own notes from March 21 to the final contact on April 29. "I've made a list of key words. Here." She showed them a sheet of A4 paper divided into three columns.

Jonny, 1/7–2/10	Hannu, 2/11–3/20	Irene, 3/21–4/29
Adam 17 yrs old	No cell phone	Alex—parents divorcing
High school	Adam—crazy mom	Adam—parents split 2 yrs
Science / tech	3/14 Adam asks for nude pic	ago
Borås	Alex refuses	Adam—brother age 25 has
Leg fracture—Sälen		1 yr left at business
Webcam broken		school
Adam sends pic of Pablo		3/21 Adam asks for sexy pic
		Alex refuses
		4/5 Adam asks for sexy pic
		Alex agrees
		4/26 Adam suggests
		meeting
		Brother will pick Alex up,
		drive her to Borås
		Torslanda Square 6:00,
		4/30 home by midnight
		at the latest

"That's a summary of the information we've managed to extract from four months of chat," she said.

Jonny and Hannu read through the list.

"I'll go and make some copies," Hannu offered.

Jonny and Irene took the opportunity to top off all three coffee mugs. When Hannu returned, they all studied the list in silence for several minutes.

"The question is, how much of it is straight lies? Surely Adam must have unconsciously given away some information about himself that will give us a lead. Can you see anything?" Irene said.

"Borås. That shithole turns up twice," Jonny said right away.

"No," Hannu said.

"Why not?" Irene asked.

"He didn't want to meet Alexandra until she was ripe for

picking, so he chose somewhere that was quite a distance away and said he couldn't come and see her because his leg was in plaster. By the way, did he ever say he'd had the cast taken off?"

Irene and Jonny shook their heads.

Hannu continued. "Surely he can't have had a cast from Christmas to the end of April? Over four months?"

"Hardly. But Borås isn't all that far away, is it?"

"We're talking about a fourteen-year-old girl who lives in Torslanda, is at school and spends a lot of time riding her horse during the week and competing at weekends; she's not going to be able to fit in a trip to Borås. The bus to the central station must take at least half an hour. Then the train to Borås . . . no, it would take too long. I think Adam's suggestion that they meet on Walpurgis Night was quite deliberate. He knew Alexandra wouldn't be competing then," Irene said.

She stared at the list again.

"Hannu, you said he wanted her ripe for picking . . . Adam flirts with her, but he doesn't make sexual demands for the first two and a half months. On March fourteenth he suddenly asks for a nude picture. Alexandra says no. On March twenty-first he tries again, with the same result. On April fifth Alexandra gives in and sends him pictures of her naked breasts. It took him three months to get her to that point."

"He knew what he was doing. I don't think she was his first victim," Hannu said.

"I agree. He could have met up with girls he's been in contact with online. Learned how to lull them into a false sense of security. He might have raped them but not killed them. We don't have any unsolved cases of homicides involving teenage girls in western Sweden over the past few years; I've checked. However, there are a number of rapes where we know the girls were in touch with their attacker online. And there are probably a lot more unreported cases," Irene said.

"Why wouldn't a girl contact the police if she's been raped?" Jonny demanded.

"They're usually too scared of what their parents and the police will say. And they're afraid their teachers and friends will find out what's happened," Irene explained.

"We need to check the descriptions these girls have given of their attacker. And his MO," Hannu said.

"You don't need a degree in criminology to work out that big brother Micke was actually doing the grooming himself," Jonny said grimly.

"And there's our clue. He writes that Micke, who is supposed to pick up Alexandra from Torslanda Square, is twenty-five years old. That has to be reasonably accurate; if he's much older, there's a risk that Alexandra will refuse to go with him. But if a car pulls up and a guy of about twenty-five says, 'Hi, Alexandra—I'm Micke, Adam's brother,' then of course the girl will think everything is okay," Irene said.

"He knew what Alexandra looked like because he had pictures of her," Hannu pointed out.

"Exactly. And there's probably a reason why he arranged to pick her up from the square. Alexandra didn't in fact take the bus into the city center, but everyone assumed she had gone in to meet her friends and watch the parade."

"The weather was terrible. The buses were packed in both directions. None of the drivers remembered her," Jonny chipped in.

That was why Alexandra had apparently disappeared without a trace once she had walked out through the garden gate at her parents' house.

"I spoke to Jens a little while ago. He suspects the killer is in contact with several girls online; that's common practice when it comes to grooming. Jens thinks we should go public and warn teenage girls and their parents," Irene said.

"I'm going to chuck the goddamn computer in the trash can when I get home," Jonny growled.

Irene suspected that one of his daughters was spending a lot of time in front of the computer and that Jonny had no idea what she was up to. Something he no doubt had in common with most parents these days, but that was little consolation.

"We'll speak to Thylqvist when we meet at four," Hannu said.

EVERYONE WAS SURPRISED when they walked in; there was a huge princess cake in the middle of the table, next to a pile of paper plates and an array of coffee mugs. They were even more surprised when Tommy Persson told them that Superintendent Thylqvist had provided the cake. When their former chief Sven Andersson walked in, they were completely thrown.

"I thought there were several reasons to celebrate today," Efva Thylqvist chirped, smiling broadly at everyone as she urged her predecessor to help himself to a slice of cake.

"Only a small piece . . . I have to be careful with sugar," Andersson said. He grabbed the knife and flipped a generous slice onto his plate.

Efva Thylqvist turned to her colleagues. "I happen to know that it was Sven's birthday last weekend, so I thought it was a good opportunity to invite him in. And we're all under a great deal of pressure workwise at the moment, so we definitely deserve a slice of cake with our Friday coffee."

She smiled once again, her gaze sweeping the room. As usual her eyes slid past Irene and on to the next person. Irene suddenly had the feeling that there was something behind this "celebration," although she couldn't for the life of her work out what it could be.

The atmosphere was pleasant and relaxed. Andersson seemed happy to be among his former colleagues, and even

Thylqvist was at her most charming. After a short while the two of them were laughing and chatting easily with each another. Andersson was recounting anecdotes from his time in the department, and Efva Thylqvist's bubbling laughter could be heard throughout the room.

Suddenly Efva Thylqvist poked Andersson in the chest with a perfectly manicured nail and said, "I hear you're brilliant when it comes to solving tricky homicides—you never give up!"

A faint pink flush spread across Andersson's cheeks and ears. "Oh, I don't know about that . . . I'm no better than anyone else."

"That's not true! You're a legend!"

It wasn't long since Irene had heard that term used about a significantly younger man in a completely different context, but Sven Andersson was as far from Pablo Eros as it was possible to get.

"I wouldn't call myself a legend . . ." Andersson said, shuffling slightly. He had a foolish smile on his face, and was generally behaving the way most men did in the presence of Superintendent Thylqvist.

"The fact is that I've spoken to the acting area commissioner, and we're in total agreement. If there's anyone who can solve the case of the mummy, it's you!"

The laughter and the murmur of voices stopped immediately. Before anyone had time to say a word, Efva Thylqvist directed a beaming smile at Andersson.

"The murder of Mats Persson will be out of time under the statute of limitations in exactly six months," she said. "It's the perfect case for the most talented investigator with the Göteborg police service—an investigator who's already working with the Cold Cases Unit!"

Irene couldn't help feeling a certain level of admiration for Thylqvist. Instead of organizing a replacement for Birgitta, she had managed to get rid of one of their most challenging homicide cases in one elegant move. It was also a low priority case. Nor had she needed to groom Sven Andersson for four months to lure him into her trap; a little flattery, a slice of cake and fifteen minutes in her company had done the trick.

Irene remembered what Thylqvist had said to Tommy after the morning briefing when she asked him to step into her office. Of course it must have been Tommy who had told her about Andersson's birthday. How else would she have known? Irene looked over at Tommy, who had been her best friend for so many years. His expression was unreadable.

Superintendent Sven Andersson was not returning his successor's beaming smile. He looked distinctly unimpressed as he pushed away his plate and his half-eaten slice of cake.

IRENE AND KRISTER had promised to visit Irene's mother at around ten o'clock on Saturday morning. It was time to give her apartment a good cleaning, including the windows. The home care service didn't do that kind of thing. They cleaned the living room, bedroom, kitchen and bathroom once a fortnight. According to the Gerd's instructions, they weren't even allowed to touch the little bedroom off the kitchen with the vacuum cleaner, so Irene or Krister would spend a few minutes on it from time to time. It had been Irene's room for the first eighteen years of her life; it was now Gerd's spare room and hadn't been used for several years.

Gerd would be seventy-nine in September. She had always been a strong person in both body and soul, and Irene had somehow assumed that things would stay that way. Gerd had consistently supported Irene and her family, she had looked after her husband when he was diagnosed with cancer, and at the same time she had helped her own parents as they grew old and unwell. Irene's father and her maternal grandparents had died within a twelve-month period, but somehow Gerd had coped. She had carried on working full-time behind the counter in the post office, and when she retired a few years later she had immediately joined several clubs, acquiring a whole range of new interests and plenty of friends. She had met Sture. They had never lived together, but had seen a lot of each other for many years since their apartments were just a few blocks apart. They had done a lot of traveling and shared plenty of retirement activities.

When Sture had died suddenly two years ago, Gerd had lost her lust for life. The day he died she had slipped on that fateful patch of ice as she was on her way to see him. Losing both Sture and her health was too much for her. She rarely left her apartment these days. When Irene tried to persuade her to go out, she made excuses, blaming her dizziness and the pain in her hip. "I can't manage the stairs anymore," she would say with a sigh and a long-suffering expression. There was no point in trying to persuade her to move to a ground-floor apartment. "Never! You know perfectly well that intruders always go for apartments on the ground floor!" Irene had tried to tell her that wasn't the case at all, but to no avail. She simply had to accept that her mother didn't want to move; the very idea was just too much for her. At the same time, Irene realized that the day would come when Gerd couldn't stay where she was, two floors up with no elevator. To tell the truth, that day had already come, since her mother could no longer manage the stairs. She couldn't go shopping alone or out for a walk. When she had a doctor's appointment, she couldn't get down to the patients' cab service. The laundry room in the cellar was completely inaccessible. In fact she needed help with most things if she had to move from one place to another, but she could still cope with personal hygiene, cooking, and light housework.

It took several hours to clean the apartment from top to bottom; Gerd was very pleased with the final result. The smell of detergent and the sight of sparkling windows with freshly ironed curtains cheered her up enormously. Krister had brought lunch: salmon pie with spinach and cheddar cheese, accompanied by a crisp salad and homemade flatbread, to be enjoyed with a little extra-salted butter. Gerd looked very content when they had finished eating and the coffee machine had been switched on.

"It's so kind of you to help me. I hate always having to ask; I'm used to getting by on my own," Gerd said.

Krister put his arm around his mother-in-law's thin shoulders.

"Well, you helped us out for many years when the twins were little. We couldn't have done it without you."

"It was my pleasure. They're my grandchildren after all! To be honest, without them I would never have gotten through the period when Rune and my parents died. I went to four funerals that year: Rune, my parents and my cousin Gunnar. It was a terrible year, but the girls were a glimmer of light in the darkness."

She smiled and met Irene's gaze. Suddenly she became serious again.

"It's such a long time ago now. Seventeen years. Time passes, and so do we," she said wearily.

She looked out of her clean kitchen window at the sparse leaves beginning to unfurl on the tops of the trees.

"All these deaths . . ."

A deep silence fell in the little kitchen. Irene looked at her mother's lined face. How old she looked these days! Really, really old. It had happened so fast. But she didn't say anything; it was Gerd who broke the silence.

"I really need to see a dentist. I've lost a filling, and it's painful. Could one of you go with me?"

Irene sighed to herself. Both she and Krister were really busy with work.

"I'll give your dentist a call and book an appointment for when I'm free," Krister said.

Irene gave him a grateful smile. Her husband was an absolute rock, and she loved him for it.

• • •

"I WANT TO quit."

Irene almost ran into the car in front of them when Krister dropped his bombshell with no warning. She managed to stamp on the brake and avoided ending up in the trunk of the Renault Laguna.

"What do you mean, quit?" she said, taken aback.

"I'm getting sick of the job. That little TV chef spends all his time running around showing off. He's barely turned thirty and he thinks he's the greatest master chef ever, just because he stands in front of a camera on a local TV station once a week throwing a meal together."

He snorted. Krister rarely sounded bitter, but right now it was very clear that was exactly how he felt.

"Has something happened?"

"Not really. It's just something that's been growing, the feeling that I'm stuck in one place, treading water. I need to do something different, something new!"

Irene couldn't help clearing her throat. "Something new . . . Have you got anything specific in mind?"

"Not yet. But I want a fresh start," he said with a sigh.

It wasn't a complete shock. She had known that Krister hadn't been entirely happy in the kitchen at Glady's over the past few years. A new owner had taken over the restaurant, and of course he wanted to keep their star in the *Guide Rouge*. At the same time he had tried to keep down costs by not employing "too many" staff members. As a consequence everyone ended up doing the work of two people. Krister had suffered from burnout a few years earlier, and although he had returned to Glady's, he had never really regained the pleasure he had found in his profession. The TV chef Krister had mentioned hadn't exactly helped matters; he had been given more and more authority over what went on in the kitchen, and Krister felt sidelined.

"Life is not a rehearsal. I want to do something I enjoy

for the last ten years of my career. Or rather eleven," he added.

"If that's how you feel, then think about what you want to do instead. We'll manage, even if you're earning less."

Irene was nine years younger than her husband, and certainly didn't want a change of career. As she told Krister, she already had her dream job.

"Although things aren't great at the moment; I don't like the new superintendent. I'll admit she has her good points; she's competent . . . smart . . . maybe too smart. She's kind of . . . intriguing."

Irene surprised herself when she came up with that word, but it was exactly right.

"In what way?" Krister wondered.

She told him how Efva Thylqvist had managed to lure Sven Andersson into her trap and dump the mummy inquiry on the Cold Cases Unit. To her annoyance, Krister started to laugh.

"She definitely sounds like a smart cookie!" he said.

"That's exactly what I said!" Irene snapped.

Krister glanced at her in surprise. She had to take a few deep breaths before she was able to go on:

"She's so manipulative. She's attractive, and she exploits her appearance, smiling and flirting with all the guys in the department while she doesn't even seem to notice me—she does her best to ignore me completely!"

To her horror she could hear the same bitterness in her own voice as she had heard in Krister's. Suddenly his tone was deadly serious.

"Sweetheart. I think it's time for a change for both of us."

"But I don't want to leave my job! I'm not the one with the problem!"

Irene was almost on the verge of tears. She swallowed several times and tried to calm down.

"You can always look for a new restaurant, but my job is

only available in one place in Göteborg, and I don't want to move away. What I do want is a new boss."

"Couldn't you apply for a transfer to a different department?"

Irene shook her head.

"That's the thing . . . there's no other department I'd want to work in. And why should I move? I'm not the one who's creating a bad atmosphere."

"A bad atmosphere? You mean everyone wants this woman gone?"

Irene remained silent for a few moments before she answered. "No. The guys like her, I think. Tommy seems to get on very well with his new chief. He's her deputy now."

"Do you mean they get on too well?" Krister asked meaningfully.

"I don't know. I haven't seen anything concrete, it's just a feeling."

Krister laughed. "Sweetheart, I trust your feelings one hundred percent. That's why you're such a good cop—you go with your gut instinct. And it's never wrong!"

He leaned over and kissed her on the cheek. She was filled with a warm glow and a sudden surge of confidence. As long as they had each other, they could deal with any setbacks. Together they were strong.

OVER THE WEEKEND the evening papers had gone for thick black banner headlines: "KILLER LURKS ONLINE!" "DO YOU KNOW WHO YOUR CHILD IS CHATTING TO ONLINE?" "THE INTERNET—AN EL DORADO FOR PEDOPHILES!" and so on. They ran interviews with experts from the police, Save the Children and ECPAT. They offered advice to parents on how to talk to their children about the dangers associated with being contacted by someone online. Irene thought it was good that Efva Thylqvist—because it must have been her decision—had spoken to the media. There was no suggestion anywhere that Alexandra and Moa's killer had contacted the girls online, which was also good. It was an advantage if he didn't know they were onto him.

There was an article in *Göteborgs Tidningen* about a man who worked as an Internet analyst, with youth sites as his specialty. He often pretended to be a twelve- to fourteen-year-old boy or girl. On certain sites he was contacted by adult males as frequently as every two minutes! For the past few years he had been traveling around the country giving talks to students in schools, to parents, teachers, social workers, police officers and judges about the methods used by men who exploit the Internet to try to establish sexual contact with children. He also mentioned the fact that in the UK anyone convicted of online grooming can be sent to jail, while in Sweden it is still legal for an adult to build a close relationship with a child online, with the aim of progressing to sexual abuse at a later stage. Only after the abuse has taken place is it regarded as a criminal offense.

At one point in the interview he said:

I know several young people who have been lured into prostitution through these youth sites. They often come from dysfunctional families with a low income. The children received money for supplying sexual services, but some of them were just lonely to begin with, and were slowly drawn into the empathetic web of the man who was grooming them. Eventually he had them exactly where he wanted them. Afterward they felt soiled; they almost had a kind of compulsion to carry on meeting men online. I have encountered several girls in this situation over the years, and even one or two boys. They were all under the age of seventeen.

Irene put down the newspaper and stared into space as she thought about what she had just read. Kicki Olsson had been very short on cash, yet her fifteen-year-old daughter had an entire closet filled with expensive designer labels—clothes, shoes and bags worth several thousand kronor. Irene did a quick mental calculation, and came up with a figure approaching twenty thousand. A mind-blowing amount for any fifteen-year-old, and completely unattainable for a girl in Moa's situation. Had she turned to prostitution via the Internet? Was that what she had used her laptop for? It wasn't out of the question. That would explain how Moa had managed to acquire the money to buy all those exclusive clothes she could never have worn. Her school friends would have started to wonder what was going on if she had turned up in a pair of boots worth three thousand kronor, not to mention designer jeans. Had her mother noticed anything? Maybe not; Kicki Olsson had probably had enough problems of her own.

"Prostitution? That had crossed my mind," Hannu said. He pointed to the notebook by his phone. "Forensics just called. They've found fibers on the underwear. Nylon fibers probably from a bathroom mat or something similar. Red, around three centimeters long. There were three caught in the hook and eye of the bra Alexandra was wearing, and five in the lace of Moa's thong."

"So that proves the connection. Where do we go from here?" Irene wondered.

"We speak to your friend," Hannu said with a smile.

"My . . . Who?"

"Linda Holm."

Of course. Why hadn't she thought of it herself?

They headed down the corridor to the Trafficking Unit. Linda Holm was just leaving her office.

"Hi there! It's been a while," she said, her face lighting up when she saw Irene. She said hi to Hannu as well, then looked slightly indecisive.

"I guess you want to talk to me, but I'm kind of in a rush right now. Can it wait an hour or so?"

"Sure. Come along to my office when you get back and we'll have a coffee," Irene suggested.

"I'll be there—two hours max."

Linda hurried away, her high-heeled boots tapping purposefully on the floor; she was definitely a woman on a mission. As usual she was smartly dressed in a black pencil skirt and a pale grey sweater, matching perfectly with her eyes and her blonde hair. Jonny usually referred to her as "Blondie" with a contemptuous snort whenever her name came up in conversation. He couldn't cope with her appearance—or her competence. It was strange that he didn't react to Efva Thylqvist in the same way, Irene thought. The only thing that could be interpreted as a criticism was a certain amount of whining because Thylqvist still hadn't sorted out a replacement for Birgitta Moberg-Rauhala; otherwise Jonny seemed perfectly happy with a female boss, which Irene found surprising.

• • •

ON THE FLOOR below Irene's office, her former boss was laboring under the weight of two big boxes of case notes from the cellar. With a great deal of grunting and groaning he managed to get them into the room he shared with his two colleagues in the Cold Cases Unit. The two brown boxes took up the entire surface of his desk. He stared gloomily at them. To tell the truth, he was deeply hurt. He had really believed that his former colleagues wanted to invite him in for a slice of cake in honor of his birthday. That Thylqvist woman had taken him by surprise. She had actually said that Per-Eric Wallin, the acting area commissioner, thought the Cold Cases Unit ought to take over the investigation.

Sven Andersson knew that Wallin always had coffee at exactly ten o'clock in the big staff room. They had known each other since the '60s, when they had worked together out in Hisingen. It was a placement for the real tough cops, with all the drunks, whores and criminals who hung out around the docks. The two young officers had had their hands full during every shift. They had relied on each other to get through, and had developed a friendship that was still just as strong today. Which was something that lying witch probably didn't know.

Andersson picked up his coffee cup and sugar-free cookie and sat down at the same table as Per-Eric Wallin. "So was it you who suggested that the Cold Cases Unit should take over the mummy investigation?" Andersson asked, the very picture of innocence.

"Hell, no! It was that pretty little superintendent . . . Thal . . . no, Thylqvist! She came up with the idea of handing it over to you. They're on their knees with this business of the gang war, the two teenage girls who've been murdered, and God knows what else. And since the body has been identified and the statute of limitations on the case runs out in

November . . . I told her to have a chat with you, see what you thought. It was good of you to take it on."

Sven Andersson was so furious he could only nod in response. That bloody woman! Instead of "having a chat" with him and asking if the unit would take on the case, she had presented it as a fait accompli, as if Per-Eric Wallin had already made the decision.

When he got back to his office, Andersson realized that he would have to deal with the case himself. His two colleagues were tied up with a ten-year-old homicide: a thirty-year-old mother with young children. He stared at the boxes without enthusiasm. They contained the usual crap: papers from the preliminary investigation and various jars and tubes containing evidence. There didn't seem to be any kind of order. Andersson always maintained that the biggest obstacle when it came to solving cold cases was the cops who had handled the investigations over the years. Material went missing or was destroyed due to a lack of care. Of course there was one major mitigating factor: as recently as ten years ago, investigators could never in their wildest dreams have imagined how the technology involving DNA would evolve. Today a barely visible drop of bodily fluid was enough to create a DNA profile.

It would take at least eight files to sort all the paperwork in the first box. Which wasn't actually all that many; major investigations could fill more than twenty. In the second box he found several smaller boxes containing old letters and envelopes. There was no evidence, of course—there had been no crime scene, no homicide victim. To Andersson's surprise these smaller boxes were marked E.P. SEPT 16, 1941. What were they doing here? And how come a disappearance twenty-four years earlier had generated so much paperwork? Reluctantly he had to admit that he was beginning to feel a certain amount of curiosity.

At the top of his in-tray lay an internal envelope containing a tape of Tommy Persson's conversation with the mummy's widow. She had agreed to the interview being recorded when she had been informed a few days ago that the mummy had been identified as her missing husband.

I must stop thinking about the victim as the mummy, Andersson decided. Mats Persson. He smiled as he thought back to Jonny's comment on the victim's real name: *"Persson? So you'll be researching your family tree, Tommy!"* Andersson had laughed at the joke; as usual Tommy had smiled politely without in any way revealing what he actually thought.

A sudden noise in the doorway interrupted his train of thought.

"Morning, Sven! What the hell is all this crap?" Superintendent Pelle "The Wrestler" Svensson demanded with a laugh.

He was from Vänersborg, and worked with the Cold Cases Unit three days a week. He had acquired the nickname "The Wrestler" back in the '70s, when the wrestler Pelle Svensson had been a major star within his sport. Pelle Svensson the cop had never in his life tried a headlock on anybody, but he had had to put up with the nickname. He was powerfully built, and he was steadily putting on weight. His jackets strained across his back, his shirts across his gut. Andersson would often note with a certain satisfaction that Pelle was fatter than him. He appreciated Pelle's good humor and booming laugh. He was also a conscientious cop from the old school, which Andersson valued highly.

The man in Pelle Svensson's wake was his direct opposite: tall, thin and almost completely bald. His glasses had unusually thick lenses that served to enlarge his eyes significantly. His dark blue designer sweater and pale grey chinos hung loosely on his skinny body. His shirt collar was far too wide for his scraggy neck, and his Adam's apple looked disproportionately large. Superintendent Leif Fryxender was the team's analyst.

He had lived in Göteborg for thirty-five years and still spoke with a marked Värmland accent. Fryxender was quiet and reflective. He was also the youngest member of the team at fifty-eight.

"New case?" Leif Fryxender ventured, nodding in the direction of the boxes.

"Yes, it's the guy they found walled up on Korsvägen. The cause of death turned out to be three bullet wounds. He's been identified as one Mats Persson, who disappeared without a trace twenty-four and a half years ago. The statute of limitations on the case runs out in six months. Efva Thylqvist, my successor, thought we should take it on," Andersson explained.

"So this will be the first case where we get to conduct the actual homicide inquiry," Leif Fryxender said.

His thin cheeks were flushed. *He thinks this case is going to be interesting,* Andersson thought in surprise. Reluctantly Andersson had to admit he was right; this was an extraordinary case, and an ideal opportunity to show that the old guys still have what it takes. Admittedly they had cracked cases in the past, but as Fryxender pointed out, they had had to rely on data collected by other people. This time they would have to try to gather new information themselves, which was unlikely to be easy after almost twenty-five years. The witnesses might have died or gone senile, while others would be unsure of the facts after such a long time. On the other hand, they were used to working on this type of investigation. Perhaps the Thylqvist woman had a point after all. Although Andersson had no intention of forgetting that she had lied to him.

Decisively he placed the recording of Tommy's interview with Mats Persson's widow in one of the boxes. As with all other cold cases, he would start by organizing the material, then he and one of his colleagues would go through everything with no preconceptions. The next step was to transfer all relevant information to IBASE, a data system that had been developed in Göteborg. It was used in investigations where there were a large number of witnesses and leads. *I hope we can get all this done before the vacation,* Andersson thought. *When we come back feeling rested and refreshed, the hunt for Persson's killer can begin.*

"IT'S JENS. HAVE you got a minute?"

Irene jumped as the internal telephone crackled into life. She leaned closer to the little grey plastic box on the table.

"Sure."

"Can you come down?"

"On my way."

She flicked the switch and left her office. As she was hurrying along the corridor she almost bumped into Jonny Blom.

"Jeez, where's the fire?" he exclaimed.

"Sorry. Jens wants to see me."

"Is it about Alexandra?"

"I don't know; he didn't say."

"Come and tell me if it's about her or the other girl."

Irene nodded.

He really is bone lazy, she thought crossly as she ran down the stairs. On the other hand she was quite pleased that he hadn't insisted on going with her; he could be incredibly annoying when the mood took him.

"Hi," Jens said as Irene walked into his office.

"Hi yourself. Have you found something?"

He nodded and tapped the computer screen. "Do you recognize him?"

Irene moved closer; Pablo Eros was smiling at her. Her heart skipped a beat.

"Pablo."

"Yep, but this time he's calling himself Ivar."

"Is he chatting with someone?"

"Yes. The girl is thirteen. Alarm bells rang when her mother read those newspaper articles. She had noticed that her daughter was spending more and more time on the computer, so she checked her browser history and found this contact. He's asked the girl to pose naked in front of her webcam. Her mother went crazy."

"How did you get a hold of this?"

"Lots of anxious parents have been in touch following the press coverage; anything that looks as if it could be related to online grooming has been passed on to me. Seventeen cases."

"Wow!"

"That's just the tip of the iceberg, believe me."

"How long has this contact been going on?"

"Since Easter."

Which was when Alexandra had been in Skåne with her parents. Adam had used the time to link up with at least one new girl who would be lulled into a false sense of security, ready to be persuaded to meet up when the time was right. Although this time he was calling himself Ivar.

"He's chatting with another one," Jens informed her calmly.

"Another one?"

"Yep." He pressed a key and once again Pablo's smiling face filled the screen. "This girl is fourteen. She called us herself; she was starting to get suspicious. He's asked her for nude pictures several times. This contact has been going on since February. This time he's Gustav."

Adam. Ivar. Gustav. Something was beginning to stir in Irene's memory. Those names . . . Adam. Gustav. Ivar.

"I think I'm onto something!" she explained, gazing eagerly around the sparsely furnished office. "Can you look up the phonetic alphabet? The one they use in the military? Isn't it Adam for A, Bertil for B, something like that?"

Jens quickly typed "Swedish phonetic alphabet" into the search box, and the list appeared on the screen.

Irene found it difficult to hide the excitement in her voice as she read the names aloud:

"Adam, Bertil, Cesar, David, Erik, Filip, Gustav, Helge, Ivar . . . that's what he's using!"

Jens gazed at the list and nodded. "Looks that way. But we've only got three names."

"Can you search for the others? Something tells me you might be able to find Bertil and Cesar; they're not exactly common names for teenage boys."

"I'll do my best, but there's no guarantee you're right."

"No, but it's worth a try."

Irene felt a dash of hope. This could be a lead. Ivar. If he had started off by calling himself Adam, that meant he was grooming at least nine victims online. Two of them were already dead. If he had groomed Moa, of course; he might just have contacted her directly online and arranged a time for a sexual transaction.

"Alexandra's killer got in touch with her on snuttis.se. It's highly likely that he also contacted Moa online. Bearing in mind his MO and the fact that the sexy lingerie set probably belonged to Moa, we know that the murders are connected. Do you think we should go public with what we know?" she asked.

Jens thought for a moment.

"If we do, he'll just keep a low profile until the media interest switches to something else. Then he'll come back. They always do. We have to catch him."

Irene felt a chill that reached to her very marrow. Whatever they did, there was a risk that they were making a mistake, and the wrong decision could mean death for another girl. Trying to hide her fears, she kept her tone neutral. "Hannu and I just caught up with Linda Holm from the Trafficking Unit. She's promised to go through the relevant sites and look for Moa.

We suspect she might have been selling sexual services online."

Jens nodded. "If she's checking sex sites, then I'll check the youth sites. Let's see what else I can find."

WHEN IRENE CALLED into Jonny's office to tell him what she and Jens had worked out, he was on the phone. She stepped back, but he frantically waved her in. His cheeks were flushed, and he was scribbling in his notebook for all he was worth. The sight of this sudden burst of energy was enough to make Irene stay. She sat down opposite him.

"A dark-colored van. Black or dark blue. Shit! Sorry . . . my pencil broke . . ." Angrily he tossed the offending item aside and grabbed a new one from the top drawer of his desk.

". . . black or dark blue. Possibly dark green or dark grey . . . It was nighttime and it was pouring rain . . . of course, I understand. And you say this was almost exactly eleven thirty on Walpurgis Night. Okay."

Jonny grinned and gave Irene a thumbs-up sign.

"In that case I'd appreciate it if you could come in today to take a look at some pictures. Many thanks."

He ended the call and rubbed his hands together.

"A pensioner called Nils Lindberg was out looking for his skiff, which had come adrift some time during the afternoon. He walked along the shore from Björlanda marina down toward Lilla Hästholmen. There was no sign of the skiff, so he went back to his car, which he'd parked at the end of Store Udds Väg. When he'd driven about fifty meters, he met a dark-colored van. He's not sure of the make or the exact color. It carried on past him and stopped by the water, where the road comes to an end. He looked in his mirror and saw the rear lights go out. He remembers thinking: Who the hell drives down to the sea in such bad weather and at this time of night? He looked at the clock, which is why he's sure it was almost eleven thirty."

"Why has he only just gotten in touch?"

"He didn't connect the van with the murder of Alexandra; after all, her body was found almost a kilometer away. But now he's had time to think, and decided it was best to mention what he saw that night."

"So it could have been the killer, driving down there to dump Alexandra's body in the water."

"Exactly. Although we can't be sure, of course. It could have been a couple that just wanted some . . . privacy," Jonny said, raising his eyebrows.

"There are nicer places on a cold, wet night."

"It's out of the way. Nobody around. Definitely not on a night like that."

"Ideal for someone who doesn't want to be seen, in other words," Irene said thoughtfully.

This could be important, she thought.

"Meeting room," she said.

They went along to the main incident room for the investigation into the deaths of the two girls. There was a map on the wall, with red pins marking the spots where Alexandra's and Moa's bodies had been found.

"Store Udds Väg runs along the point that forms the south side of Björlanda marina," she said. "It's pretty wide, which means there's a distance of several hundred meters between Store Udds Väg and the small boat harbor."

Irene quickly measured the distance on the map before she continued.

"Almost four hundred meters as the crow flies. You can drive right down to the water's edge. There are some buildings down there, but very few houses where the road actually ends. If the body was dumped there, that means it drifted . . ."

She checked another measurement.

". . . almost eight hundred meters in five days. We need to

check how that fits in with currents and wind speed. Did this pensioner see who was in the van?"

"No. He said it was too dark and the rain was too heavy. He couldn't even make out if there was one person or two in the front."

"If it was the killer's van, then there was only one. Alexandra was already dead," Irene said grimly.

"Probably. But he's coming in this afternoon to make a statement; I'll try to get him to remember what make of van it was," Jonny said.

Irene told him what Jens had found online and about her own flash of genius with regard to the phonetic alphabet.

"Adam, Bertil, Cesar. Can he really use those names if he's supposed to be a teenager? Nobody's called their kid Cesar for at least a hundred years," Jonny objected.

THE FOLLOWING DAY, Linda Holm arrived in Irene's office immediately after morning prayer.

"I brought us both a cup of coffee. I know you never say no," Linda said with a smile.

She put down the steaming cup in front of Irene, who smiled back and thanked her. Tommy and Irene had worked with Linda while investigating the murder of a young girl a few years earlier. Irene and Linda had met up for coffee occasionally after they wrapped up the case, but she hadn't seen Linda for a few weeks. They were both too busy, and Linda never really let anyone get too close to her. *It suits me perfectly that Linda has a strong sense of integrity*, Irene thought. *It means we don't have to exchange personal confidences, the things we share on a professional level are enough.*

"I actually think I've found something," Linda said, producing a clear plastic folder. Irene could see printouts from an Internet sex site; she recognized the type of page from an investigation into a trafficking-related murder some years earlier. There were pictures and descriptions of the young women currently offering sexual services in the Göteborg area. There was also an indication of which languages the women could speak, shown by the flag of the relevant country—usually Baltic languages, sometimes Spanish or Russian. If it said German or English, the girls often spoke only odd words or phrases that they had picked up from their clients.

"I didn't look specifically for the girl who was killed—Moa—I just checked out the usual pages to see what's happening right now. And I spotted this."

Linda pointed to a Swedish flag next to a link, lolita.se.

"I've never come across this link before, so I clicked on it and a list of contact details came up—all Swedish girls, apparently. Sixteen total. And something tells me these are very young girls. That's where I found this ad."

She passed a sheet of paper to Irene. I'M YOUNG AND CURIOUS. WE SHOULD MEET UP. The address was mimmi.14@hotmail.com.

The picture showed a girl with her face turned away, her body arranged in an unnatural pose. She was wearing nothing but a red see-through bra and panties, her pale nipples clearly visible above the cups of the low-cut bra. Irene recognized her immediately; it was Moa Olsson.

"We found that red lingerie set when we searched her room. She had another pair in black. Moa was wearing the black panties when she was found, and Alexandra was wearing the bra," Irene said.

"I didn't know that."

"No, we haven't told the media. It's something we wanted to keep quiet; it helps us to eliminate the crazies who call up claiming to be the killer. We get at least one a day." Irene sighed.

"And is that the only connection between the two cases?" Linda asked.

"No. We also found the same red nylon fibers on both items—three caught in the clasp of the bra Alexandra had on and five on Moa's panties. We've sent the bra to a specialist lab in the UK, but I think it will be hard to find Moa's DNA on it; Alexandra had been in the water for several days. But if it's possible, they'll find it," Irene said.

"That would make the connection a hundred percent definite."

"Yes. And then there's the killer's MO. The extreme sexual violence to which the girls were subjected is virtually identical. The main difference is that he strangled Moa with his bare hands but used a thin computer cable on Alexandra. We suspect it might actually be a cable from Moa's computer. A small number of straight cuts had been inflicted on Moa's body, while the cuts on Alexandra's body were more numerous and kind of ornate. Moa was hidden in a crevice in a rock, while Alexandra had been dumped in the sea. But we have to remember that Moa was killed first; by the time he murdered Alexandra, he had added more rituals."

"The places where the bodies were found are quite some distance apart," Linda remarked.

"Yes, although we do have a witness statement indicating that the killer might have had access to a vehicle."

Linda nodded, gazing at the picture of Moa.

"So you haven't found Moa's computer?"

"No, it's missing. A laptop."

"So it probably had a wireless connection. All new laptops are set up to work that way."

"You could be right. According to her mother, she used to carry her computer around in a rucksack, which is also missing."

"The killer probably took both."

"More than likely. He knew we'd be able to trace him if we had access to her computer."

"Did she have a cell phone? You can send emails via a cell these days," Linda pointed out.

"That's missing too, as is Alexandra's cell. Once again, the killer probably took it."

"Exactly. He needs to make your investigation as difficult as possible. Perhaps that's why he chose to dump the bodies so far apart."

"Possibly, but in that case surely he shouldn't have made Alexandra put on the bra that matched Moa's panties."

"Right, that seems illogical," Linda agreed. "But who can understand how a killer's mind works?"

"There's always a kind of logic in the sick mind of a killer, though he's usually the only one who understands it."

"These are particularly vile murders,'" Linda said, shaking her head. She waved a hand at Moa's picture with an air of resignation.

"Girls of this age are surprisingly immature. They are incapable of analyzing the consequences of their actions, and are often completely governed by impulse. They might look like smaller mature women on the outside, but on the inside they're still kids."

Irene looked at the picture of the provocative fifteen-year-old, the girl who bought clothes that might possibly suit a girl who hung out in all the smart places on Avenyn in the city center. She couldn't possibly have worn them in her everyday life; they just hung there in her closet, unworn. In the background she could see Moa's bookcase with the cuddly toys, the expensive bottles of perfume, the makeup and the CD player.

She said thoughtfully, "Moa had a difficult upbringing. Her mother took her own life just a few days ago. She was an alcoholic."

"I read about the suicide in the papers. And didn't Moa have a brother who died too?"

"Yes. He was seventeen when he died after crashing a stolen car."

They sat in silence for a little while; eventually Linda spoke.

"Some kids never have a chance."

"No. Moa had a tough time. But Alexandra came from a

well-off family, although as far as we can make out, she wasn't happy. Her parents were in the process of getting a divorce, and she was pretty lonely. She loved horses; she even had one of her own. From a material point of view, she had everything a girl her age could wish for, yet she went looking for a friend online. And ended up in the clutches of the bastard who killed her."

"Poverty isn't always visible from the outside. Even the most apparently solid environments can hide a devastating internal poverty," Linda said quietly. "Loneliness is the most widespread disease we have in Sweden today." She suddenly stood up. "I have to go. See you."

Before Irene had time to reply, she was gone.

TWO DAYS LATER, Jens called Irene again.

"Hi, Jens here."

"Hi. Anything new?"

"Yep. Our killer is using wireless broadband via a satellite connection, probably from a train or possibly a bus."

"Can you trace the train or bus route? Whereabouts was he when he was chatting online?"

"That could take a while; we're just looking into whether it's possible or not. We need to examine the traffic on Alexandra's computer; he might have used the 3G network at some point, in which case we can pin down the area he was in."

"So all we can do is keep our fingers crossed and wait," Irene said with a sigh.

"You've got it," Jens said, ending the call.

Irene sighed again. She was beginning to get that familiar feeling of treading water. She hardly dared think about what might provide the catalyst to get things moving; another murder was a horrible thought, but with every passing day the likelihood increased that the killer would strike again.

THE TEAM WORKED through the list of convicted sex offenders associated with extreme violence. Some had no alibi for one of the murders, but none lacked an alibi for both. Tobias Hansson's story was still doubtful because his only witness was his overprotective mother. In spite of the fact that they had brought him in twice, they couldn't get him to change a thing: he had been at home with his mom, and she confirmed every word he said. And there was no real evidence against him; he didn't even have a driver's license.

They were still very interested in the dark-colored van, but unfortunately the elderly witness had become less and less certain of the make and model during his conversation with Jonny Blom. Jonny had started by showing the man a picture of a Renault Kangoo. It was too small, the man insisted, but it might have been a similar model. But bigger. Jonny produced a picture of a Ford Transit; too big. The only conclusion they reached was that it was a dark-colored van, somewhere between a Renault Kangoo and a Ford Transit in size. Jonny had let out a loud groan, which didn't exactly make the witness feel more comfortable. He couldn't remember if the vehicle had rear windows or not. Nor did he recall if there had been anything written on the van, although he might possibly have noticed "something white on the side," which could have been an inscription or a logo.

This meant they were looking at thousands of possible vehicles within a radius of only fifty kilometers of Göteborg. Medium-sized vans are commonly used within companies, which means that several people could have access to the same van. It was virtually impossible to speak to everyone who might have had access to a dark-colored van at the relevant time.

At the beginning of June the police made a public appeal through the media, asking anyone who had seen a van or car in the area around Store Udde during the hours of darkness on Walpurgis Night to get in touch. Several calls came in, but none of them led anywhere.

They also checked whether any of the men on the list of sex offenders could have had access to such a van. They contacted every car hire firm in the Göteborg area to find out whether any of these men might have hired a van at the relevant period, but the result was negative.

Moa Olsson's father was found; he was working as a gardener in a park in Malmö, having gained a place in a methadone program. These days he had a stable family life with his new wife and five-year-old son. He told the police he had never gotten in touch with Moa after walking out when she was a little girl. "The years went by, and suddenly it kind of seemed too late," he had said.

He was right; it was too late.

The department was snowed under with work. The investigation into Moa's and Alexandra's deaths was a priority, but there were constant interruptions as new crimes came in. The gang war escalated, with another car bomb and an armed attack on an apartment in Angered. The only good news was that there were no more fatalities in those incidents; the three they already had were more than enough.

Suddenly it was almost midsummer, and the holidays were approaching. Efva Thylqvist was due to go on vacation the day before Midsummer's Eve. At morning prayer that same day she had news for the team.

"We will be getting a replacement for Birgitta Moberg-Rauhala. I don't have a name yet, but he or she will be with us in August."

The announcement was so unexpected that no one could think of anything to say. In the silence that followed, the superintendent got to her feet and wished them all a good summer. She would be away for four weeks.

Irene had a week left to work before her vacation began. She and Krister were going over to London to visit her good friend DCI Glenn Thomson and his family; he worked for the Metropolitan Police.

THE MURDER WEAPON was certainly old, and had seen better days. Sven Andersson weighed the pistol in his hand. The note attached to it said *Tokarev M1933*. There was also further data on the weapon: *7.622mm caliber, ammunition 7.62x25 (7.62 Tokarev) with flange. Function: semiautomatic with short recoil. Locking lugs all around the barrel. Length 195mm, weight 0.82kg, barrel 114mm with four right-facing grooves, 8-round detachable box magazine.*

They had received both the report and the pistol from ballistics the previous day. Test firing had shown that the bullets found in Mats Persson's body had come from the Tokarev. The forensic pathologist had found traces of gunpowder around two of the entry wounds. It was estimated that the shots had been fired from a distance of no more than a meter. One bullet had gone straight into the heart and would have killed Persson instantly. There were no fingerprints on the gun.

At first Sven Andersson and Leif Fryxender had been optimistic: if the murder weapon had been found, then it shouldn't be too difficult to trace where it came from. The results of their research had been depressing. The pistol lacked any distinguishing marks, apart from the five-pointed star and the letters CCCP on the butt. There was, however, a serial number on the back at the left-hand side. The four Cyrillic letters and the four-digit number confirmed that it was Russian and had been manufactured in 1937. Further research revealed that this particular model had been mass produced, not only in the Soviet Union but also in Hungary, Yugoslavia and the People's Republic of China, particularly following Germany's invasion of the Soviet Union in June 1941. The murder weapon was pre-war, so it was almost certainly of Russian origin.

Leif Fryxender went back through the archives looking for a report of a stolen Tokarev M1933 around the time of Mats Persson's disappearance in 1983, but without success; reports of stolen goods from such a long time ago no longer existed in any archive.

As far as the Cold Cases Unit's investigations were concerned, there was no rush. Their clients were long dead, and would remain that way. But Andersson thought the unit's existence was important; a killer shouldn't feel safe until the statute of limitations is up. It is completely ridiculous that the statute of limitations for homicide is only twenty-five years in Sweden; in other countries it is significantly longer. No doubt some bright spark in a position of responsibility had worked out that it was an easy way of massaging the statistics on unsolved murders.

Sven Andersson snorted loudly and dropped the pistol back in the box, then pushed the box into a corner with his foot. He was about to start his well-earned vacation, and he had no intention of giving the mum—Mats Persson a single thought over the next four weeks.

Blue-grey thunderclouds hung low over the city. The air was still and heavy.

IRENE HAD A headache, which was unusual for her. If the storm would only break, the pressure behind her eyes would surely ease. She was sticky with sweat. Her short-sleeved cotton blouse was plastered to her back. Only two days to go until her vacation. It felt like an eternity. Not that she was short of something to do; the work was piling up on her desk. She just hoped nothing else would happen; neither she nor the department would be able to cope with that.

AN AGITATED TEENAGER dragged her thirteen-year-old sister along to the police station in Partille. She wanted the girl to tell the police what had happened the previous evening, the Tuesday after midsummer.

Their story could have ended there at the small local station, but the female officer who took their statement realized how serious it was. She decided to pass it on and called police HQ on Skånegatan. The call was immediately put through to Irene Huss.

WHEN IRENE WALKED into the station at Partille, she noticed that everything was back to normal following the attack in the fall. The station was always unmanned at night, and the shooting had taken place on a dark November night.

That had been the prelude to what was now an all-out war involving several gangs—with and without motorbikes.

The female officer introduced herself as Åsa Nyström. She had provided coffee and a fresh pastry for the older sister. The thirteen-year-old was sitting there with her arms and legs crossed. The can of Coke and the pastry on the table in front of her hadn't been touched.

Emma Lindskog was twenty years old and worked at Bokia in the Allum shopping mall. Her younger sister was named Lina. Emma did the talking while Lina stared sullenly at the floor from under her fringe.

Irene was slightly surprised by Lina's attitude. The plump girl was wearing skintight jeans and a black crop top, leaving a wide gap to show off the glittering stone in her navel. One red sandal flapped against the sole of her foot as she nervously waggled it up and down. Her eyes were heavily made-up, and she was wearing a thick layer of foundation, despite the fact that it was summer. Admittedly there hadn't been a great deal of sunshine so far, but most people avoid wearing too much makeup in case the sun were to break through. Lina didn't seem to be a fan of that approach. Nor was she prepared to rely on the sun to lighten her hair; instead she had taken matters into her own hands and doused it in peroxide. The result was a dirty-white lifeless mess, but in order to mitigate the impression of a tangle of steel wool, she had added strands of bright pink and blue. She reminded Irene of her daughter Jenny's most extreme punk period.

Everything passes eventually, Irene thought as she smiled at Lina.

The effort was wasted. Lina gripped her upper arms even more tightly and hunched her shoulders. If she had been a tortoise, she would have retreated completely inside her shell.

Her sister looked sensible and mature. Her hair was dyed

black and cut in a short, trendy style. Her makeup was beautifully applied, and the thin yellow summer dress showed off a
slim, toned body. Her toenails were dark red, and she was
wearing high-heeled gold sandals.

"Emma, Lina—could you please tell Inspector Huss what
you've just told me?" Åsa Nyström began.

Lina snorted and shifted uncomfortably on her chair. The
line of her compressed red lips looked like an angry scar.

"I'm on vacation, but I promised Mom and Dad I'd look
after . . ."

Lina's snorts had almost reached hurricane force. This was
a girl who didn't think she needed anyone looking after her.

Emma ignored her. " . . . Lina. She's only thirteen . . ."

"Fourteen!"

That was the first word Lina had uttered since she walked
into the station. Irene tried another encouraging smile, then
turned her attention back to Emma.

"Thirteen. She'll be fourteen next month. Our parents are
visiting our grandparents in Kalmar; Grandpa had an operation. They'll be home tomorrow."

"Do you have any other siblings?" Irene asked. She shouldn't
really have interrupted Emma, but she wanted to get an idea of
the family setup.

"No. Just Lina. We're seven years apart. Anyway, I happened to hear her chatting to a friend on her cell yesterday
afternoon. She was outside on the patio, but the door wasn't
closed . . ."

"It so was! You pushed it open!" Lina hissed.

At least she's saying something; that has to be progress, Irene
thought. She kept her gaze fixed on Emma, who took no notice
whatsoever of her sister's outburst.

"Lina said she was going to meet this guy she'd found
online. She said they were crazy about each other. He was
going to pick her up at the bus stop in his car at seven o'clock.

Then she tells her friend he's seventeen! Hang on, I thought—how can he be driving if he's only seventeen?"

"It was his brother who . . ." Lina exploded, before clamping her lips tight shut again.

"We had something to eat at about six, and I kept an eye on Lina. At five to seven she set off, and I followed her. She didn't see me. There are some tall bushes by the bus shelter, and I went and stood behind one of them. At exactly seven o'clock this big van pulled up. Lina went over and the door opened. I didn't know what to do, so I yelled. As loud as I could!"

"What did you yell?" Irene asked.

"'Lina! No! Don't get in!' Or something like that."

If looks could kill, Emma would have been stone dead by that point. Lina didn't say a word, she just glared. But Irene could see the glimmer of tears in her eyes.

"What happened?"

"He slammed the door and took off like a bat out of hell," Emma said.

"Did you see what he looked like?"

"No. The windows were dark, and I was kind of behind the van and off to the side."

"Can you describe the van?"

"It was dark blue."

"What make?"

"I don't know—I'm rubbish at that kind of stuff. I'm going to learn to drive in the fall."

"Did you see the number?"

"No, I was just thinking about Lina, how to stop her getting in . . ."

"Was there anything written on the van?"

Emma thought for a moment. "I think there might have been some white letters on the side, but I couldn't see properly from where I was standing."

"Anything on the back?"

"No."

So it was only Lina who had seen the driver. Irene stole a glance at the sullen figure hunched in her chair. It was important to take things slowly.

"Lina, when you got in touch with this guy online, were you on snuttis.se or a similar website?"

No reaction. Lina kept her gaze fixed on the floor.

"Did he call himself Filip, Gustav, Helge, Ivar, Johan, Kalle, Ludvig, Martin . . ."

Lina suddenly looked up. Irene stopped as she picked up a flash of surprise in her eyes.

"So it was Martin."

The girl clamped her lips even more tightly shut, but Irene could see that she was growing anxious.

"He sent you a picture of himself, didn't he?" Irene said.

Thank goodness she had had the foresight to slip the photograph of Pablo Eros into her purse. Without a word she placed it on the table in front of Lina, who gasped and took a deep breath.

"How . . . how come . . . how do you . . ."

"Is this the guy you were going to meet?"

Lina nodded reluctantly, unable to tear her eyes away from Pablo's smile.

"But he said he couldn't come and pick you up himself, so his brother would come instead?"

Lina nodded again. She was staring at the picture as if she had been hypnotized. Irene thought about what she should say next. She couldn't afford to lose the girl now, but at the same time Lina had to understand that Irene was telling her the truth.

"I don't have psychic powers. I was able to come up with the name he used because he follows a certain pattern. I know of other girls this guy has been in contact with, and . . ."

"You're lying! He's mine! We . . ."

Lina broke off and her face closed down once more.

Goddamn kid! Irene pulled herself up as soon as the thought crossed her mind. That was exactly the problem: Lina was just an immature kid in a young woman's body.

"Lina, listen to me. The guy in the van is the one who's been chatting with you. The guy in the picture doesn't exist. I can prove it if you . . ."

"Prove it then, you . . . bitch!"

The tears welled up, dissolving the black eyeliner. It looked as if thin streams of lava were pouring down her cheeks.

"For goodness sake, Lina—she's a police officer!"

"Like I care!"

By now Lina was sobbing and sniveling. Åsa Nyström got up and handed her a bundle of paper tissues, then bent down and gave her a quick hug.

"He fooled you. He's a cunning bastard."

Before Lina had time to protest about the embrace, Åsa was on her way back to her seat.

"Lina, the guy in this picture is an Italian actor named Pablo Eros. The photograph is twelve years old. He died two years ago. I can understand why you fell for him—he's really hot," Irene said.

Lina didn't seem to be listening.

"The driver of the van was the person who contacted you online. He's done it before—told girls he's the good-looking guy in the picture, then arranged to meet them and said his brother will come and pick them up."

Irene paused to allow her words to sink in.

"Things didn't go too well for those girls. Your sister saved you."

Lina rubbed her eyes and tried to pull herself together. "So what . . . what happened to . . . to them?" She blew her nose.

Irene waited until she had finished, then answered as calmly as she could. "He raped them. And we know that he killed at least one of them."

In spite of the fact that Lina's makeup now bore a close resemblance to army camouflage, Irene could see that her face had lost its color.

"You're lying," Lina whispered, but without a trace of conviction.

"Unfortunately I'm not, Lina. And the girls who believed his lies were older than you. You shouldn't feel dumb. He's very, very clever. This man is extremely dangerous. He's a murderer."

The room fell completely silent, apart from the frantic buzzing of a fly, banging into the window over and over again in a futile attempt to escape. In the distance Irene could hear the rumble of the approaching storm. Soon the blessed rain would come and wash away the oppressiveness of the still air. She felt as if her headache was already beginning to ease.

"We're trying to catch him before he has time to rape and possibly kill more girls. Will you help us?" Irene asked. She held her breath and didn't let go until Lina nodded, almost imperceptibly.

"WE'VE PUT TOGETHER a facial composite with the help of Lina Lindskog. She's the only person who's actually caught a glimpse of our guy. He called himself Martin in his dealings with her, which means she ought to be number thirteen," Irene said.

Her colleagues looked attentively at the picture projected on the wall. They saw a slim clean-shaven face, shadowed by a dark blue cap pulled down over the forehead. The eyes were hidden by dark aviator sunglasses. The hair that was visible looked greasy and light brown. The nose was straight, the lips narrow. It was difficult to imagine a more ordinary appearance. He could be anywhere between twenty and forty.

"I've checked all the guys on our list; the only one who resembles the composite is the one who killed himself almost two months ago," Irene informed them.

"How long had he been in touch with Lina?" Tommy asked.

"Nine weeks. He can certainly tell when they're ready. Lina would have gone anywhere with him. She was crazy about him," Irene replied, wondering if the others could hear the sadness in her voice.

Lina had been utterly devastated. But she wasn't stupid; she had realized that she had been fooled. She had marched off to the bathroom and washed off her ruined makeup. Then she was ready to help with the composite. Irene had brought the sisters to HQ, and with the help of Lina's description and a specialist computer program, a police expert had constructed the image of the man who had groomed her.

It hadn't been easy, because to a thirteen-year-old, anyone over eighteen is ancient. In fact, Lina had confided to Irene, the only thing that had worried her had been Martin's age—seventeen. She had mentioned it to him, but he had simply dismissed her concerns and told her that age is irrelevant when it comes to love, which had made Lina forget her reservations.

All the time Lina was talking, Emma had sat beside her, gently stroking her younger sister's back.

Afterward Irene had taken the girls down to the café and bought them ice cream. With her face scrubbed clean of makeup, Lina appeared extremely young and vulnerable. As she sat there licking her cone, she looked like exactly what she was: a little girl. When Irene thought about what could have happened if Emma hadn't been on her guard, she felt a hard knot in her stomach.

It was Monday, August 4. Over the past few days it had finally gotten a little warmer; otherwise the summer weather had been pretty bad on the west coast, which was unfortunate for those who had taken their vacations in June and July. Even though this applied to Irene and Krister, they had spent a lovely week in England and a decent fortnight in the cottage in Värmland. Irene hadn't felt fully rested until the last week, and would have liked a few more days before she went back to work.

"It seems as if the bad guys have taken some time off too. July has been quiet; let's hope things stay that way in August," Efva Thylqvist said, smiling at her team.

Fredrik Stridh and Tommy Persson were absent; they still had another week off. However, a young woman whom Irene had already met had joined them.

"May I introduce Åsa Nyström, who will be standing in for Birgitta for the time being," the superintendent said.

Åsa smiled and nodded to everyone around the conference table. Irene hadn't paid all that much attention to her when they met in Partille three and a half weeks earlier; now she saw a woman aged about thirty, with curly chestnut hair and greenish-blue eyes. She was quite tall and looked muscular. She had a round face and a wide mouth that looked as if it smiled easily, revealing deep dimples. She could be described as attractive, but not classically beautiful.

"Perhaps you'd like to say a few words about yourself?" Efva Thylqvist suggested.

Åsa Nyström got to her feet and looked at her new colleagues. "Okay, so my name is Åsa Nyström, and I'm thirty years old. As you can hear from my accent, I was born and bred in Göteborg. When I graduated from high school . . ."

She paused for effect, a mischievous expression on her face.

". . . I had no intention of joining the police. It wasn't even on my radar. My family tends to go for artistic professions. I wanted to be an actress, so I applied to drama school and got in! I spent three years training, and then . . ."

A look of resignation played across her face.

". . . then I realized I'd gotten it completely wrong. I just didn't enjoy trying to imitate reality in front of a select few night after night. And I also realized nobody was going to ask me to play the leading lady."

She placed one hand coquettishly at the back of her neck, pouting and fluttering her eyelashes. Then she slowly rolled up one sleeve of her shirt and showed off an impressive bicep. She grinned as the others started to laugh. *This girl certainly isn't shy,* Irene thought. *And I wonder how she got those muscles.* A scar was clearly visible just above Åsa's left eyebrow.

As if she had heard Irene's unspoken question, Åsa continued.

"I started kickboxing when I was fifteen. That was in 1993, and women's boxing wasn't very common in Sweden. Maybe I was already looking for a challenge back then. It took three years at drama school for me to realize what I really wanted to do: I applied to the police training academy as soon as I finished."

"You've already requested time off later in the year; is that because of your kickboxing?" Efva Thylqvist asked with genuine interest.

"Yes. I've got a four-day training camp in September, and the world championships in October."

"Wow! How often do you train?"

"Five to seven times a week."

Efva Thylqvist seemed to be weighing up the team's newest recruit. Irene felt the look on the superintendent's face didn't bode well.

"Do you have time to fit in anything else, apart from work and training? I see from your file that you're married; you must have a very understanding husband. What does he do?"

There was a flicker of something in Åsa's eyes, but Irene thought she was the only one who had noticed.

Åsa's voice gave nothing away as she replied. "He's a musician. But we're in the process of getting a divorce."

Irene had the feeling that things were going badly wrong. This was no longer a presentation on Åsa's part; it was more like an interrogation. But Thylqvist seemed totally oblivious to what she was doing.

"Which is also an artistic profession, of course. What kind of music does he play?"

"Hard rock. He's the drummer with Hell's Metal Warriors."

Thylqvist's face stiffened. "Perhaps you could tell us something about your career so far."

"When I'd finished training I moved back to Göteborg. I drove a patrol car around Frölunda and Hisingen for a while. I liked being out and about, but I felt like I should be doing something else, so I applied to cover the summer vacation in Partille. And now I'm here." The dimples appeared once more as she steadily met the superintendent's gaze.

Efva Thylqvist smiled back, but without much warmth. She turned to Irene. "You've got the biggest office, and you're used to sharing. I thought Åsa could move in with you."

"No problem. It gets a bit lonely all the way down there," Irene replied calmly.

If Thylqvist picked up the little dig, she showed no sign.

"Excellent," she said with a brief nod to Åsa Nyström.

• • •

WHEN THE TWO women reached what was now their shared office, Irene had to ask a question. "Did you know you were coming here when we met in Partille?"

Åsa smiled. "No, but I had applied. They called the following day and told me I'd gotten the job."

"What a coincidence! And I'm so pleased to have some company again."

"Again?"

"Yes. Tommy Persson and I shared this office for many years, but now he's Thylqvist's deputy, so he's got his own office next door to her."

Irene made a huge effort not to let her tone of voice give away what she really felt, but the look Åsa gave her made it clear that it hadn't worked. Or perhaps Åsa was an excellent judge of character. Irene wasn't sure this was the kind of new colleague she would have wished for.

"Is your ex really a hard rocker?" she asked, changing the subject.

Åsa grinned. "No, he's a saxophonist. He plays jazz."

She assumed a serious expression and said loftily: "Which is also an artistic profession, of course."

THE ATMOSPHERE WAS gloomy in the Cold Cases Unit's office. Sven Andersson and Leif Fryxender had just been informed that their colleague Pelle Svensson needed a heart bypass. The angioplasty had revealed that his condition was worse than the consultant had first thought, and the operation was scheduled for the beginning of September. Needless to say, he wouldn't be returning to work in the meantime.

"He won't come back at all," Andersson stated.

"I think you're right," Fryxender agreed.

They both knew that Svensson was intending to retire on the same day as Andersson—October 31.

"When do the two new guys start?" Andersson asked.

"October first."

"Good. We need reinforcements."

They gazed in silence at the files and the pile of small boxes marked E.P. SEPT 16, 1941. They had taken over a very strange story. Their eyes were drawn to the transparent evidence bags, each containing three bullets. One bag was labeled 420315 MATS PERSSON NOV 9, 1983. the other 081002 ELOF PERSSON SEPT 16 1941. The Tokarev pistol lay beside the bags.

While looking into Mats Persson's disappearance in November 1983, the investigating officers had managed to access documents from the Second World War. The security service, SÄPO, had looked at the papers first and decided there was no security risk involved in releasing most of the case notes from forty-two years earlier.

Inspector Arne Carlsson, who had led the investigation, had produced an exemplary summary when the search was scaled down in 1985. Andersson and Fryxender had put together their own summary when they took over the old case, and they now had a pretty clear picture of what had happened in both 1941 and 1983.

Elof Persson was born on October 2, 1908, in Katrineholm. His father was a station master. Elof seriously considered a career with Swedish Rail, where his two older brothers also worked.

Young Elof liked the idea of a profession that required a smart uniform. Meanwhile he spent his mid-teens in the freight depot at Katrineholm station, running errands and helping to load the wagons. At the age of eighteen he was called up for military service. He did well, and was accepted to the officer training program. He was very happy in the army, but realized after a year or so that he would never be able to advance beyond the rank of sergeant due to his lack of education. He considered his options and was accepted at the police training academy in Stockholm, where he qualified as one of the best cadets in his year.

His rise was meteoric, and he was the youngest inspector when war broke out at the beginning of September 1939. One month later Elof Persson and a dozen hand-picked colleagues were brought together. They were to begin work with the security service, which had been created by the government back in June 1938 but only became active when war broke out.

The officers were forbidden to tell anyone, including their closest family and friends, where they worked and what their job entailed. Anyone who broke the rules was summarily dismissed.

In spite of the difficulties, Elof immediately felt at home. He approached his work in the Surveillance Unit, monitoring suspects, with both enthusiasm and seriousness. These suspects were referred to as "red" and "brown" Socialists in order to distinguish between them. Their basic ideologies were bewilderingly similar, even though Hitler had introduced increasingly vague nationalistic and fascist elements during the late 1930s. However, both groups were firmly anti-Zionist and shared a hatred for homosexuals. After the German attack on the Soviet Union, it became easier to tell them apart, because the reds were clearly on the Russian side, while the browns were with the Germans.

In the fall of 1940 Elof was asked to travel to Göteborg on a special assignment. They were having problems with an Englishman, George Binney. He was responsible for the shipment of steel, machine tools and ball bearings to the Allies. He also tried to support the Danish resistance movement. The Russians were on his side, as were Swedish communists and Torgny Segerstedt, who led the publicity campaign against the Nazis in the daily newspaper *Göteborgs Handels-och Sjöfartstidning*. Against Binney were Georg Wagner, the chief of the German intelligence service, as well as German intelligence officers, Swedish Nazi agents and Norwegian Quislings. There were also a significant number of Swedish officers who sympathized with the Germans, and a good proportion of the Swedish public had a positive view of Hitler, particularly during those first successful years of the war.

The security service wanted to know why Binney had moved to Göteborg, and what his plans were. Elof and his colleagues came up with the brilliant idea of bugging Binney by dropping a microphone down the chimney. A second microphone was fed through an air duct to a vent in the living room.

They soon learned that Binney was planning an operation with the code name "Rubble." Five Norwegian merchant ships were to run the German blockade of the Skagerrak, carrying cargo essential to the war effort, including ball bearings and steel.

During his stay in Göteborg, Elof met a young woman named Marianne Strandberg. She was born and bred in the city, and had just gotten her certification as an elementary-school teacher. When Elof proposed after just a few months, she said yes right away. She was ten years younger than her husband-to-be.

They married at Easter 1941 and moved to Stockholm. Elof had handed over the surveillance work in Göteborg to local operatives; he was needed back in the capital. The couple managed to secure a small one-bedroom apartment on Horns-gatan. They shared a bathroom with two other families on the same floor. Marianne had obtained a post at a school within walking distance, but she was never really happy in Stock-holm. She got on reasonably well with her colleagues at school, but she still felt lonely and was terribly homesick. Elof was often away on secret missions, both during the day and overnight, and it was a long way to Katrineholm where his family lived. They went to visit them only twice during their short marriage.

At the end of July she realized she was pregnant. Only then did she dare to complain about the poor condition of the apart-ment, but Elof got angry and she didn't bring it up again. Therefore, she was very surprised when suddenly, on the eve-ning of September 16, he said: "Trust me, darling—we'll soon be able to afford a much bigger and better place to live." He had laughed at her astonishment, which soon turned to delight. They had been standing just inside the door; Elof had put on his overcoat, ready to set off on yet another secret assignment. He hadn't said as much, but Marianne had stopped asking where he was going. He had pulled his hat well down with a nonchalant gesture and added: "They call them-selves the net. The net! Have you ever heard such nonsense?

A disgusting creature is about to get caught in his own net, I can promise you that!" With those words he had opened the door and disappeared into the wet and windy night. That was the last time she saw him alive.

A neighbor had called the police at 10:54 P.M. His bedroom window on the first floor looked out onto Hornsgatan. A minute or so earlier he had heard several shots in the street. The patrol car arrived eight minutes later. The two officers found a man in the doorway, covered in blood. He appeared to be dead. He had been shot in the chest and in the middle of the forehead. The neighbor came outside once the police were on the scene and said he thought the deceased was herr Persson, who lived on the same floor. The police knocked on Elof Persson's door just as Marianne was about to go to bed. She pulled a coat on over her robe and accompanied the officers downstairs, where she identified the man who had been shot as her husband. At that point she had broken down, and was taken to Sabbatsberg Hospital.

That same night, September 16, the security service and the police launched an inquiry into the murder of Elof Persson. They didn't find the murder weapon at the scene. Other neighbors who had heard the shots came forward. None of them had seen the perpetrator. The street lamps hadn't been on because of the blackout. The killer had gotten away under cover of darkness and rain.

On the morning of September 17, the Hårsfjärden disaster took place. Three of the Swedish navy's four destroyers were anchored in Hårsfjärden. The torpedoes on board the destroyer *Göteborg* exploded; this was immediately followed by a similar explosion on board *Klas Horn*. Burning oil then caused the fire to spread to her sister ship *Klas Uggla*. All three vessels sank, with the loss of thirty-three lives. A further seventeen sailors were injured. The catastrophe would have been even more serious if the majority of the crew had not been on shore leave.

It was still the worst incident in Swedish territorial waters during the entire war.

One of the security service's most comprehensive sabotage investigations of the Second World War began straightaway, working closely with the naval authorities. All available resources were brought in. At first it was thought that a bomb might have been dropped from a Swedish plane by mistake while on a training exercise, but there were also several other theories. The cause of the catastrophe was never established.

But the following morning, the inquiry into Elof Persson's death was overshadowed by the Hårsfjärden disaster, and the murder was never solved.

Marianne Persson moved back to Göteborg straight after the funeral, and her son, Mats, was born in March 1942. Marianne got a job at Nordhem School, where Mats eventually became a pupil. After graduating from Levgrenska High School, he attended the School of Business and Economics, and while studying there he met Barbro, who was training to be a physiotherapist. They married in 1969 and had two children, Peter and Anna. Mats worked for a large accountancy firm and seemed happy.

His mother, Marianne, never remarried. She continued to work full-time as a teacher until her retirement in 1982. Just before Christmas 1983 she suffered a major stroke and died a few days later.

After the funeral Mats cleared out her apartment, but didn't feel up to sorting anything or throwing things away. He moved the family Volvo out of the garage and put the rest of his mother's furniture in there before carrying boxes and bags down to the cellar. When he had finished, he broke down.

He was diagnosed with severe depression, and his therapist suggested that he start looking for information about his father. He felt that Mats's reaction to the loss of his mother indicated that he was also upset that he had never known his late father. Mats started to go through his mother's things, listlessly sorting through boxes without much hope of finding something that would tell him more about his father.

During the late summer of 1983, he spent more and more time down in the cellar. Sometimes he would bring papers upstairs and lock himself in his study. According to both Barbro and his children, he was obsessed.

At the end of October, Mats had said something about a breakthrough, that the final piece of the puzzle might be within reach. When Barbro had asked him what he meant, he had smiled and said cryptically, "It's still top secret. I have to get permission from SÄPO." The police were unable to find any indication that Mats Persson had contacted SÄPO. Which was perhaps not entirely unexpected. However, given that SÄPO appeared to be cooperating fully, and handed over a considerable amount of material from the investigation into Elof's death in 1941, the police were inclined to believe their assurances.

Had Mats been imagining things? Had he been affected by some fresh psychosis? The only indication that something might be amiss was the fact that Mats had disappeared while looking into his father's life and death.

On the evening of November 9, 1983, Mats had hurried into the city library on Götaplatsen just before it closed at six o'clock and picked up some books he'd ordered. Before he left he had leaned over the counter and whispered conspiratorially to the librarian, "They've always thought they were protected by the net, but I'm onto them!" Then he walked out.

Once he had left the city library, he might as well have gone up in a puff of smoke. There was a statement from a person who had been standing outside the theater; a man had hurried past her, heading around the corner toward the back of the building. Bearing in mind where Mats Persson's mummified body had been found twenty-four years later, the witness could well have been right; the demolished building on Korsvägen was barely three hundred meters from the library.

The books Persson had ordered were H.-K. Rönblom's *The Spy Without a Country*, Stig Wennerström's *From Beginning to End*, and John Barron's *KGB: The Secret Work of Soviet Secret Agents*. This particular choice of books had interested SÄPO, but when they went through them they couldn't find any link to the murder of Elof Persson. The retired air force attaché Stig Wennerström had been arrested by the Swedish security police under sensational circumstances in 1963, on suspicion of spying on behalf of the Soviet Union. He was convicted and sentenced to life imprisonment, and stripped of his military rank. This was twenty-two years after the murder of Elof Persson.

SÄPO concluded that Mats Persson had been confused, and during the course of his research had become fascinated by spies and their activities. With regard to the limited investigation into the murder of Elof Persson, there were a number of questions that had never been answered. Marianne had kept a log of the times Elof was working. When this was compared with the service reports Elof had handed in, there were many discrepancies—nights and certain days when he had been free according to the security service, yet Marianne's notes indicated that he had been away. During the spring of 1941 this had happened only occasionally, but during the summer and early fall it became far more frequent. The investigating officers had assumed that he was doing another job on the side, but there was no evidence to support this assumption. Marianne had dismissed the idea.

There was yet another mystery with no apparent explanation. Elof had deposited six thousand kronor in a bank account in two installments, three thousand each time. This amounted to almost two months' salary. The first deposit was made in the middle of July, the second almost exactly a month later. No money had been paid into the account in September.

Marianne had no idea where the money had come from. When the case was closed, it was decided that the young widow would be allowed to inherit the money.

The police spent a long time wondering what Persson could have meant during that last conversation with his wife. She had interpreted his promise of a larger apartment to mean that he would be getting a raise, perhaps even a promotion. However, his employers made it clear that this was definitely not the case. Nor could they work out what he meant by his talk of "the net." Marianne had thought he was talking about some kind of spy network or something similar, and the security service had also leaned toward that theory. However, they were never able to verify it.

When Mats Persson went missing, he had his wallet with him. His bank account was monitored following his disappearance, but it was never touched, which led the police to believe at a fairly early stage that he must be dead. His family hadn't noticed any signs of deepening depression, but still the conclusion was that he had probably taken his own life. There was nothing whatsoever to suggest that he had fallen victim to crime. Not until his body was found walled up in a chimney on the first sunny day in May 2008.

Shot three times, just as his father had been forty-two years earlier.

Sven Andersson had found the three bullets that killed Elof Persson in a small tin inside one of the cardboard boxes. According to the ballistics report, they were 7.26mm caliber. Andersson was taken aback; he read the report three times before he asked his colleague to take a look. Leif Fryxender picked up the sheet of paper and read through it. Slowly he put it down, and their eyes met.

Fryxender had taken the bullets and the gun down to the lab himself, and now the results had arrived. All six bullets had been fired from the old Tokarev pistol.

THE TWO REMAINING members of the Cold Cases Unit had each armed themselves with a mug of coffee and a wrapped pastry from the canteen. Andersson's pastry was sugar-free; it looked both smaller and drier than his colleague's. Leif Fryx-ender pressed PLAY on the small cassette player, and Tommy Persson's voice filled the room:

"... DCI Tommy Persson. Today's date is Monday, May twelfth, 2008. Are you okay with me recording this interview?"

"Yes ... that's fine. I realize it must be difficult to write everything down. Where shall we start?"

"Let's begin with your name and date of birth."

"Barbro Linnea Persson-Melander. I was born on July third, 1945, so I'll be sixty-three this summer."

"Unfortunately I have to ask you to revisit what actually happened before your husband ... your husband at the time ... disappeared. The original investigation was conducted as a missing persons case; today we know that he was murdered."

[Silence.]

"Murdered ... I can't believe it! Who'd want to murder Mats? He was so kind and ... inoffensive. It's ... I just can't process it."

"What did you think had happened to him?"

"I thought . . . I thought he'd gotten confused, maybe lost his memory and was wandering around somewhere . . . at least that was in those first few days. When I started to realize that he was gone . . . suicide seemed the most-likely explanation. But then again, it didn't."

"Why not?"

"His depression had lifted—in fact, he was almost manic. That last day he was kind of . . . feverish."

"Did he seem as if he'd come across a secret?"

"Yes . . . well, it was more as if he was going to find out about something. He seemed . . . full of anticipation. I remember he was pacing around the house when I got home at four thirty."

"And he never told you what was making him feel that way?"

"No. When I asked what was going on with him he just said he was close to a breakthrough, and that the final pieces of the puzzle were within reach."

"I believe he mentioned SÄPO as well?"

"I can't remember his exact words . . . it's a long time ago . . . but I think he said the material was still top secret, and he'd have to get permission from SÄPO."

"Permission to do what?"

'I've no idea. I was only half-listening to him . . . I was so sick of hearing him go on about his father and the secret police tracking down spies."

"Could he have arranged to meet someone?"

"That's what I've been wondering since I heard . . . that he's been found . . . how did he end up in that place?"

"You didn't know anyone who lived in the vicinity?"

"No."

[Brief silence.]

"What actually happened when his mother died?"

"My mother-in-law never regained consciousness after her stroke; she passed away after three days. Mats was so strong when it happened and immediately after her death. When the funeral was over he went to clear out her apartment, and when I got home one day there was a rented truck outside our house. Mats had filled our cellar with bags and boxes. I couldn't believe it—I wondered what the hell he was doing. I mean, I thought he was supposed to be clearing the place out and sorting her stuff, but apparently he'd just boxed it all up. I was furious—I stormed off to ask him for an explanation, but I couldn't find him anywhere. I remember searching the whole house . . ."

"And where did you find him?"

"In Anna's playhouse in the garden. He was curled up on the floor, shaking. I couldn't get through to him at all. In the end a neighbor helped me get him indoors, and the following day he was admitted to a psychiatric clinic."

"Did you go through the boxes while Mats was away?"

"No. I couldn't bear to look at them."

"So nobody touched them?"

"No."

"And when did Mats start to sort through them?"

"In August '83. His therapist had told him to have a look to see what was in his father's papers. After only a few weeks he was completely obsessed."

"Did he tell you what he'd found?"

"He talked about nothing else! He got in touch with his father's family in Katrineholm, and wrote down the family history. He'd found a number of documents relating to Elof's service record—he'd been in the army from the start—and Mats contacted various authorities."

"Did he ever tell you that he'd come across some kind of secret?"

"No, except for what he said on that last day, about SÄPO and the material being top secret. Then he took the bus into the city; he said he was going to look around for a new camera. I can't actually remember whether he mentioned going to the library. The police asked me about that when he disappeared, and I've thought about it since then."

[Brief silence.]

"When did you move to a new house?"

"When I moved in with Frank in '89. We didn't get married until '94. I wanted to wait ten years."

"But Mats was declared dead before then?"

"Yes of course, but you can't imagine . . . every time the doorbell rang . . . the hope . . . and at the same time the fear . . . that it would be him."

[The sound of rustling papers, Barbro blowing her nose discreetly.]

"Are you okay to carry on?"

"Yes, I'm fine. It's just a reaction to . . . actually knowing. You wouldn't believe what a relief it is to finally find out what happened. To be able to bury him. The kids have gotten their dad back. At long last they have a grave to visit. And I hope I will find peace in my soul too."

[Brief silence.]

"What happened to all the boxes when you moved?"

"My son, Peter, took some of them. He was nineteen at the time, and I guess he wanted to save anything that might provide some kind of clue. We got rid of everything else."

"Does he still have them?"

"I don't know. I've never asked what he did with them."

"In that case I'd like to thank you very much for . . ."

Sven Andersson pressed the STOP button.

"We need to contact the son."

Leif Fryxender nodded.

"I wonder what happened to the books he'd ordered. Because he had them with him when he left the library," he said thoughtfully.

ON JUNE 22, 1941, German forces launched an offensive against the Soviet Union: Operation Barbarossa. Finland saw an opportunity to regain the territory they had lost to the Soviet Union, and allied themselves with Germany in what came to be known as the Continuation War. Germany requested permission to send the Engelbrecht Division, consisting of almost fifteen thousand fully equipped troops, through neutral Sweden. The Swedish parliament was deeply divided on the issue; the heated debate went on for four days and was later dubbed the Midsummer Crisis. Prime Minister Per Albin Hansson then stated that King Gustaf V was threatening to abdicate if Germany was not allowed to transport troops through Sweden, and faced with this threat parliament acceded to the request, opening up a transit route from Norway to Finland via Sweden.

The Engelbrecht Division's journey across Sweden ended on July 12 without incident. The only thing that happened in association with the transportation was that five wagons carrying German ammunition exploded at Krylbo train station on July 19. Suspicions of sabotage were later confirmed.

During this period of political tension, Elof Persson was working in Stockholm. His role within the security service was to monitor individuals who were suspected of cooperating with the Soviet Union. His office was responsible for running counter-espionage operations against NKVD,

Russia's civilian intelligence bureau, along with its military counterpart RU; they also monitored the activities of Comintern and Swedish communists. All Russians living in Stockholm were kept under surveillance in order to map their network of contacts.

According to his wife, Marianne, Elof Persson had been talking about a "net" minutes before he was killed. The conclusion reached by the investigating officers in both 1942 and 1983 was that Persson had been murdered by someone who worked for the Soviet Union and was involved in some kind of espionage network. Perhaps Persson had unwittingly exposed an agent who was significantly more important than he had realized. The security service interpreted the expression "a disgusting creature" as referring to a traitor, which meant that Persson's comment probably implied that he was talking about a Swede. However, these were merely hypotheses with no underlying evidence.

When SÄPO went through what was left of the material from the summer of 1941 in 1983 and 1984, they were unable to find any report submitted by Elof Persson that suggested that he was on the trail of an unknown agent. He had spent most of that summer keeping the Intourist travel agency in Stockholm under surveillance, principally following two NKVD officers by the names of Viktor Starostin and Vasily Siderenko. They were employed at the agency as a cover, and were watched around the clock. Their telephone calls were also bugged, and every single person they contacted was meticulously noted. There wasn't the slightest indication that Elof Persson had had any personal dealings with the Russians, nor with anyone else mentioned in the copious reports on the activities of Starostin and Siderenko.

THE REMAINDER OF the Cold Cases Unit had gone through all the old case notes relating to Elof and Mats

Persson; there were documents from the Second World War and up to the mid-1980s. They had read certain passages several times, without getting much further than their predecessors had done sixty-seven and twenty-four years ago.

"Elof must have been running his own race," Leif Fryxender said eventually.

He took off his glasses and massaged the deep indentation on the bridge of his nose. Sometimes he wished he could wear contacts. It wasn't that he hadn't tried; the whole family had ended up on their knees in the bathroom, searching for his lenses. They had found only one; the other had mysteriously disappeared. After that Leif had decided that contacts weren't for him; his blink reflexes were too strong.

"I expect you're right," Andersson muttered, trying to suppress a yawn. He was sick and tired of all these old documents.

"So in order to solve the murder of Mats Persson, we have to solve the murder of his father," Fryxender said slowly.

"And how are we supposed to do that? It happened sixty-seven years ago!" Andersson exclaimed, suddenly coming to life.

"But we've got something they didn't have in 1941," Fryxender said with a cunning smile.

"Like what?"

Fryxender's smile grew broader.

"The murder of Mats," he said, looking as if he'd just come up with a solution to global warming.

"The murder of . . . What the f—"

"We know that Mats said he'd found something out on the day he disappeared. He said he was close to the solution and talked about SÄPO. We know which books he'd ordered from the library. There could be something useful in the boxes his son kept. And we know that Mats and his father were shot with the same gun. Either it was the same killer or, which is perhaps more likely, the person who killed Mats had access to the same gun."

Andersson tried to feel as optimistic as Fryxender sounded, but he couldn't quite get there. The whole case seemed impossible to crack.

"I've arranged to see Peter Persson this afternoon. Let's hope he still has the boxes; if so I'll ask him if we can go through them."

Andersson wasn't looking forward to going through yet more boxes. That was the worst aspect of his new job, all those boxes of old garbage he had to rummage through. On the other hand, both he and Leif had gotten pretty good at it: rooting through a load of crap and finding the tiniest fragments of gold.

PETER PERSSON LIVED in a residential area not far from the old church in Örgryte. The houses had all been built during the first half of the twentieth century, and most bore the signs of recent or ongoing renovations. The gardens were large, with impressive fruit-laden trees. Roses and an array of early autumn perennials filled the beds with glorious color. Even though Sven Andersson had lived in Göteborg all his life, he had never been in this part of Örgryte, either for private or professional reasons. It was no more than half an hour by tram from the area around Masthugget where he had grown up, but the class divide between the two parts of the city made the journey much longer—virtually unachievable, in fact.

Andersson recognized Mats Persson's son as soon as he opened the door. He bore a striking resemblance to the passport photo they had obtained of the deceased, and he also matched the description: slightly above medium height, slim build, with fine blond hair. Andersson and Fryxender knew that Peter Persson was thirty-eight, but he looked older. He was casually dressed in blue jeans and a blue-and-white-striped polo shirt.

He politely invited them in, leading them straight through the house and out onto a large glassed-in veranda. The sliding doors were pushed back to let in the afternoon sun and a cooling breeze, which carried with it the heavy scent of over-ripe berries and summer apples from the garden. The cane chair creaked alarmingly as Andersson sat down. On the glass-topped matching table there was a tray laid out with coffee, cups, milk and sugar. To Andersson's disappointment the only accompaniment was a plate of Ballerina cookies. *I'd better stick to coffee since there's nothing but sugar bombs*, he thought crossly.

When Fryxender had accepted a cup of coffee and a cookie, he started by asking whether Peter Persson still had the boxes his father had left behind. It turned out that he had.

"Did you take all the boxes?"

"No, only those that seemed interesting. The ones that contained paperwork, that kind of thing."

"And have you ever gone through them?"

"No. I've only lifted the flaps and peered inside, nothing more," Peter said, sounding slightly apologetic. He remained silent for a little while before continuing. "I think I brought the boxes when I moved out because I was angry with my mother. She wanted to burn the lot. I was thirteen when my father disappeared, and I missed him . . . somewhere deep inside I always hoped he'd turn up one day. I felt as if my mother was betraying him somehow. But that was the reaction of a teenage boy. I realized a long time ago that meeting Frank was good for her."

Suddenly he laughed.

"Perhaps you can tell that I've worked through my father's disappearance? I was in therapy for a few years—and I married my therapist. Erika and I have two kids, a boy and a girl. She went to pick them up; they'll be back at any moment, and I can promise you that will be the end of the peace and quiet!"

"In that case perhaps we should go and take a look at the boxes," Andersson suggested.

Peter led the way back through the living room with its contemporary décor. The fact that most of the furniture and the walls was white suggested that the children couldn't be all that young, Andersson thought. The place felt cold and unwelcoming, if anyone was interested in his opinion.

The boxes were in a storeroom that had once been a pantry off the cellar: ten banana boxes piled on top of one another.

"Is it okay if we take them down to the police station?" Fryxender asked.

"Sure. Erika will be delighted."

Ten more goddamn boxes to go through, Andersson thought gloomily.

It took two trips in the car to transport all the boxes. They stacked them along the wall, then started to work through them one by one. First of all they simply put to one side anything that didn't seem relevant. Nothing was thrown away; even the material that was discarded initially would be checked later. Then they began to look more closely at anything that seemed even vaguely interesting. It was time-consuming, but they were experts.

After two weeks they had finished examining the contents of all the boxes; it took another five days to revisit everything they had put aside at the very beginning.

It was Sven Andersson who found it. On the back of an A5 notepad someone had written in pencil: *Rönblom H.-K., The Spy Without a Country.*

And underneath, in the same neat handwriting: *Stig Wennerström, Carl-Johan Adelskiöld, Oscar Leutnerwall.*

"Well, we know who Stig Wennerström was. And Adelskiöld is the old guy who died in the fire. In the building where we found Mats Persson! But who the hell is Oscar Leutnerwall?" Andersson said.

"Mmm . . . the name sounds vaguely familiar . . . No, I can't remember. But we'll find out!"

"I've made contact with him."

There was something in Åsa's tone of voice that made Irene look up from her keyboard, a tension she hadn't heard before.

"Sorry?"

"I've made contact with Adam. Or Gustav. Or Kalle. Or Mr. Groomer."

"What! You've . . . How the hell did you do that?"

"My nephew's old computer. He got a new one because the memory on the old one was too small. The kid plays these incredibly advanced games . . . anyway, I asked if I could have the old one, and my brother agreed to let me use their broadband. For a while, at least."

"Their broadband?"

Irene realized she sounded like a simpleminded echo. Åsa nodded eagerly.

"That was the key. I'm sure our Mr. Groomer has a trace function so that he can see who he's exchanging messages with. If he checks out the Nyström family in Böö, he'll find that it consists of two parents and two children: a thirteen-year-old boy and a fifteen-year-old girl."

The dimples deepened as she added: "What he doesn't know is that the children's aunt lives just a few kilometers away in Kålltorp. And that she's a cop. So I laid out my bait on snuttis.se. And he took it!"

Irene was lost for words.

"I've asked Jens to try to trace him now that we have a little more material than we had before."

"What's he calling himself?" Irene finally managed a coherent sentence.

"X-man. Something tells me he's gotten as far as Xerxes. But he's using a different picture, a blond guy who looks familiar; I think he might have been in some high school soap that was on TV in the mid-90s—which today's teenagers won't have seen, of course. He claims his real name is Micke—we've heard that name before!"

"It definitely sounds like him. How long have you been in touch with him?"

"Two weeks. He thinks he's chatting to a fifteen-year-old girl called Ann. There you go—meet Ann!" Åsa said, tossing a photograph on the desk.

"But . . . you can't expose your niece to the danger of . . ."

Åsa interrupted her with a laugh. "That's not my niece, that's our secret weapon."

A very young girl was looking shyly into the camera, an uncertain smile playing on her lips. Her long black hair was parted in the center, framing her delicate features. Her almond-shaped eyes were free of makeup.

"How old is she?" Irene asked.

"Twenty-six."

"Twenty-six? No way!"

"I've known her since she was a baby," Åsa replied patiently.

"And she knows everything?"

"Everything she needs to know. And she's happy to help."

Irene gazed at the photograph of the pretty teenage girl. Who wasn't a teenager at all. Åsa filled in the background on the girl and her family.

The Björkman family had three daughters, Li, An and My. The oldest daughter Li was a familiar face in Göteborg; she was a journalist and a regional news reporter on TV4. An, the middle daughter, had been Åsa's best friend since they were kids. She was four years younger than Li, and worked as a nurse at the Queen Silvia Children's Hospital. Both girls came from Korea.

The girl in the picture was My, the youngest. She had been adopted from Thailand, and was a dancer specializing in musical theater. She had trained in London and had worked there for a few years. She had just returned to Göteborg, and in a few weeks she would be moving to Copenhagen to appear in a production of *Cats*. Although she was a rising star when it came to the international musical scene, her face wasn't known in Sweden.

"The best thing is that My is less than one and a half meters tall—147 centimeters! She's tiny. She often plays the role of a child or a teenage girl. Plus she's a top level competitor in kickboxing. She's won several prizes at straw weight."

"Straw weight? How much do you have to weigh for that class?"

"Next to nothing!"

Åsa was positively shining with enthusiasm, and Irene had to admit that My could definitely play a fifteen-year-old if necessary.

"So how far have you and X-man got?" she wondered, her expression serious.

"You mean has he asked me for sexy pictures? Do bears crap in the woods? Of course! I imagine he can't believe his luck in finding such a naïve, easy target. I've only sent him a fairly innocent topless shot of My . . . I mean Ann."

"Topless! But . . ."

"It's a still. She has her hands cupped over her breasts and looks pretty upset. Ann is supposed to be shy, remember. When I joined the site I said I was fifteen and I'd only just moved to Göteborg from Jönköping. I was about to start ninth grade—well, I've already started because the schools went back last week. But when we first started chatting I didn't know anyone, and I was very lonely. Plus I'm adopted so I look different, which can make things difficult. Shy, lonely and desperate to make contact just about sums Ann up."

"And that hooked Mr. Groomer."

"I can't tell you how many dirty old men were tempted by little Ann! Some of them get straight down to business, telling me how much they'll pay for a blow job, a few hundred for nude pictures, a thousand for full sex and so on."

Åsa grimaced in disgust.

"I'm just thinking about my daughters, how worried I used to be when they were teenagers, hanging out with friends at night, going to parties, music festivals . . . but the Internet is even more dangerous for kids, no matter what time of the day it is," Irene said.

"Absolutely."

Irene thought for a moment, then said, "We have a problem."

"What's that?"

"We have to inform the boss."

"She'll say no. Not because it's a bad idea, but because it comes from us," Åsa stated baldly.

She looked worried.

"But we have another boss. A male boss," Irene said with a cunning smile.

Åsa also broke into a smile when she realized what Irene meant.

FOUR DETECTIVES WERE sitting in DCI Tommy Persson's office. At Irene's request, none of the other officers in the department had been called to the meeting, which meant that Efva Thylqvist was not present either. Tommy had listened in silence as Åsa explained how she had managed to contact Mr.

Groomer. When she started talking about My Björkman, Irene could see that Tommy was finding it difficult to keep his opinions to himself. However, he succeeded in controlling himself until she had finished.

"Absolutely not! We can't use a civilian as bait!" he said firmly.

At that point the fourth person in the room cleared his throat, indicating that he had something to say.

"We've mapped all communication and checked the times of bus and train departures. He's chatting online on the X2000 route between Göteborg and Malmö. He takes the seven o'clock train down to Malmö and comes back on the one that leaves at five in the afternoon. On a few occasions he chatted to Alexandra in the morning, but mostly we're looking at evenings between five and eight. On Sunday evening the train leaves an hour later, so then he chats until nine. Never on Mondays or Tuesdays, very rarely on Wednesdays. Mainly Thursdays, sometimes Fridays, often on the weekends," Jens reported.

"Is there any kind of pattern when it comes to the weekends?" Tommy asked, showing an interest in spite of himself. Obviously he wanted to catch the killer just as much as the others did, even if he didn't agree with their methods.

"Nope. He doesn't chat every weekend; usually it's every other, but it can be two in a row."

"Can we trace him?"

"That's tricky. He buys a card with a single-use code. It doesn't allow for pauses or interruptions. One hour costs around seventy kronor, two hours ninety."

Jens realized the others had no idea what he was talking about. Patiently he explained. "You buy a card in the restaurant car; there's a code on it that you use to log in."

"And is this card only valid during that particular journey?" Irene asked.

"No, you can use it on a second journey."

"Seems kind of expensive," Åsa said.

Jens gave a wry smile. "He's clever. The chances of us finding him are very small. I think he uses this method only with the girls he's intending to kill."

"You mean he separates his contacts? Decides right from the start who's going to be his next victim?" Åsa exclaimed.

"He can easily sit at home surfing the net on his own computer. He could be in touch with hundreds, maybe thousands of girls. It's not against the law to contact teenagers online."

"He's got it all worked out. He uses a stolen computer and publicly available broadband to chat to the girls he's picked out. Which makes him almost impossible to track down," Tommy said, thinking out loud.

He considered the situation for a moment, then eventually he said, "So what's the plan?"

Irene quickly ran through what she and Åsa had worked out. The idea was for Åsa to carry on chatting for a while longer before suggesting a meeting.

"It would have to be somewhere with plenty of people around—a café, for example. Our decoy will be My Björkman, pretending to be fifteen-year-old Ann. The customers around her will be plainclothes police officers," Irene explained.

"I can get into Åsa's nephew's computer, which means we can sit here chatting to this guy," Jens offered.

"Does that mean I can carry on using the computer?" Åsa asked.

"Sure. You won't even know I'm there."

THERE HAD BEEN no difficulty in getting a hold of Oscar Leutnerwall; he was in the phone book. Both Andersson and Fryxender had been surprised to find him there. The name listed above was Astrid Leutnerwall, with the same address on one of the streets above Näckrosdammen, but a different telephone number.

According to the information they had found, Oscar Valentin Leutnerwall was born on December 15, 1915. He was the son of a lawyer, Valentin Leutnerwall, and his wife, Siri, née Adelskiöld. The couple also had a daughter, Astrid, and a son who had died of meningitis at the age of only two.

Oscar had pursued a career within the Swedish diplomatic service, and in 1939 he was appointed to a post as attaché with the Foreign Office. From October 1941 and for most of the Second World War, he served in Moscow. After the war he spent a few years at the Swedish embassy in London before returning to Sweden to work in the Foreign Office in Stockholm. He had spent the last ten years of his professional life as Sweden's ambassador in London.

"He retired twenty-five years ago!" Fryxender exclaimed, sounding impressed.

"Personally I'll be glad if I make it to the first of November," Andersson muttered.

"He worked until he was sixty-eight," Fryxender said,

looking down at the sheet of paper giving Oscar Leutnerwall's personal details and list of awards.

"His cousin didn't."

"No. He retired at sixty-two."

Fryxender picked up the other sheaf of papers on his desk.

Carl-Johan Henric Adelskiöld was born on October 23, 1917. Fryxender had also managed to confirm his initial assumption that Carl-Johan's and Oscar's mothers were sisters. Carl-Johan had been an only child. He had followed in his cousin's footsteps and read law at Uppsala. He completed his studies quickly and started work at the Foreign Office in 1941. Around Christmastime he was sent to join Oscar in Moscow, where he remained until the end of the war in 1945. He returned to Sweden, then served in various embassies and legations around the world. A gifted linguist, Carl-Johan had spent the last five years of his professional life as Sweden's *chargé d'affaires* in Berlin. When he retired in 1980, he moved back to his hometown of Göteborg and into one of the apartments in the building on Korsvägen, which he had inherited from his parents several years earlier.

"The cousins have quite a few things in common," Fryxender said, placing the two sets of papers neatly beside each other on his desk.

"You mean they both worked for the Foreign Office?"

"Yes, let's start there. They both went to the Foreign Office straight after university. They were both sent to Moscow. They were both there during the war. Do you know who else was in Moscow in 1940 and '41?"

Andersson thought for a moment before he came up with the obvious answer.

"Stig Wennerström."

"Bravo! He was air attaché."

"What does that entail?"

"I've no idea. It's a military title. But that's not important.

The interesting thing is that the cousins and Wennerström were in Moscow at the same time."

"So the point of contact between them is Moscow."

"Exactly."

"But where does Elof Persson come into all this? He was in Stockholm," Andersson pointed out.

Fryxender wasn't about to be put off by his colleague's objection.

"I've checked with SÄPO and the Foreign Office. Wennerström, Oscar and Carl-Johan were in Stockholm on September sixteenth, 1941!"

"Are you trying to tell me that Wennerström shot Elof Persson?" Andersson asked dryly.

Fryxender ignored his sarcastic tone.

"Maybe. Or it could have been one of the cousins. All three of them were still alive at the time when Mats Persson was murdered. Even while Wennerström was in Russia there were reports that he was suspected of engaging in intelligence activities for a foreign power, as it was called back then—spying for the Germans, to put it simply. His behavior was causing concern; he was asking questions about things that had nothing to do with him. His mail and telephone calls were monitored in 1943, but there was never any proof, and the surveillance was canceled. They didn't catch him until twenty years later. I'm wondering whether Elof Persson might have gotten wind of something. Seen something. Perhaps the cousins were involved in some way."

Andersson needed time to digest all this information about Stig Wennerström, the spy.

"Did either of the cousins actually know him in September 1941?" he asked.

Fryxender looked noticeably less pleased with himself when he realized where Andersson was heading.

"Hardly. He was older, and a high-ranking officer in the air force," he admitted reluctantly.

"In which case there is no connection between the cousins and Wennerström at the time of Elof's murder."

"Well, no, but the cousins . . ."

". . . hadn't even been to Russia! One of them had just finished university, for Christ's sake, and the other one was still at the Foreign Office. The only thing we know for sure is that all three of them were in Stockholm in September. That's the only point of contact. But we have no evidence to suggest that Elof Persson and the cousins ever had anything to do with one another. Or that Persson met Wennerström. Or that the cousins met Wennerström."

Fryxender's enthusiasm had vanished. He frowned and thought for a moment. "In that case we need to look for something that proves the link. We need to find whatever Mats Persson found. We need to find those books," he said eventually.

"And we have to speak to Oscar Leutnerwall, if that's even possible. The guy is over ninety."

"Mmm. Actually, the cousins had more elements in common. Neither of them ever went on to have a family of their own, perhaps because they moved around so much when they were young. And they both came back to their hometown when they retired."

"They stuck together."

"Although they can't have seen that much of each other during their professional lives. They never served in the same country at the same time, apart from those early years in Moscow."

Andersson didn't even attempt to suppress a sigh. Moscow. The war. Spies. Murder. Sixty-seven years ago. He sighed again.

ANDERSSON STILL WASN'T sure whether it was Oscar Leutnerwall himself he had spoken to on the phone. If so, he definitely wasn't some gaga old man. The lively voice on the other end of the line could have belonged to a guy half his age.

They were in the car on the way to Nedre Johanneberg to speak to Oscar. They could have walked from police HQ, but wind and rain had swept in across the city, and Andersson's asthma was making its presence felt. It was the first sign of the approaching fall. At least when the cold, wet winter arrived at the beginning of November he would be able to deal with his asthma in peace. November 1 was the date he could begin to call himself a pensioner. He was facing the prospect with mixed feelings.

"Hang on in there! We're getting reinforcements on October first," Fryxender had said several times. Two new investigators would provide a much-needed boost for the Cold Cases Unit. It was a pity that he would only have the opportunity to work with his new colleagues for a month, but at the same time Andersson felt as if he had served his time with the Göteborg police. During November and December he was planning on taking things easy, maybe doing a little work on the house. Between Christmas and New Year he and his wife, Elvy, were traveling to Thailand, which he was really looking forward to. He had never been to Asia. Following their summer vacation in Bohuslän, Elvy hadn't gone back to work but had decided to retire. She still missed her job in the cake shop sometimes, in spite of the fact that she had worked there for thirty-seven years. Or perhaps that was why. She missed the contact with her colleagues and with the customers. That was what worried Andersson. What if he found he wanted to come back to work?

"I've spoken to someone at the library. They can't check whether a particular book disappeared or was returned twenty-five years ago; it's impossible. The data is saved for a maximum of three years," Fryxender informed him, jerking him out of his reverie.

"Three years? What's that got to do with anything?"

"Because we didn't find the books in the aperture with Mats Persson's body. The gun was there, and so were his clothes and his wallet. It just occurred to me: What if the killer took the books back to the library?"

"Why would he do that?"

"To get rid of them."

It actually sounded pretty logical, Andersson thought. All you had to do was place the books discreetly on the returns desk and slip away.

As USUAL IT was difficult to find a parking spot in Nedre Johanneberg. After driving around the area for a while Andersson eventually found a space on Lennart Torstenssons-gata. The rain lashed their faces as they struggled along into a strong headwind. All the wet leaves torn down from the imposing trees made the sidewalks treacherous.

They were heading for an apartment block on the slope leading down to the pond known as Näckrosdammen and the park beyond. Some of the plumpest ducks in Göteborg live in the slimy waters of the pond; in the summer its surface is com-pletely covered with pink and white water lilies. During the late spring and summer, students and other residents of the city often sunbathe on the huge lawns between the pond and the university library.

Today the park was deserted, and there were worrying creaking noises from overhead as the wind tugged at the old trees. Andersson and Fryxender hurried down the hill toward Oscar Leutnerwall's apartment.

Impressive buildings entrenched behind high brick walls lined both sides of the street. Shiny metal plaques by the gates revealed which companies conducted their business behind the walls, although often there was only an uninformative name or a set of initials. A couple of the buildings housed free schools. Even if the interiors were buzzing with the activity of

modern life, their showy façades stood as a monument to a
bygone age.

Andersson thought back to his own upbringing in Masthugget, in a "governor's house" so typical of the city of Göteborg. A family of four had lived in a one-bedroom apartment,
with an outdoor toilet in the yard. They had no running hot
water. The building burned down the year Andersson started
school; no one was hurt, so no one was sorry to see the dump
disappear. The family relocated to a house on Fjärde Lång-
gatan, where they had two bedrooms and a kitchen, hot and
cold running water, and their very own toilet with a hand
basin. Andersson remembered his mother weeping with joy
when they moved in.

Leif Fryxender stopped in front of a sturdy iron gate set in a
high wall made of liver-colored bricks. There was an intercom
with three buttons beside the gate. A small brass plaque next
to the top button had the initials o. l. engraved on it; the
middle button clearly belonged to a. l., and by the bottom
button a large, shiny plaque informed visitors that the law firm
Leutnerwall & Leutnerwall resided on the ground floor.

Fryxender pressed the top button. After a few seconds the
speaker crackled into life; it was impossible to make out what
the person on the other end said, but Fryxender leaned closer
and introduced himself and Andersson. There was a buzzing
sound, and the lock on the gate clicked. Fryxender pushed it
open, the hinges protesting loudly. *A little oil wouldn't go amiss;
on the other hand, nobody's going to sneak in this way,* Andersson
thought.

The courtyard was paved with cobbles in an intricate cir-
cular pattern. The lawn was edged with luxuriant rhododendrons, which would no doubt provide a blaze of color when
they flowered in the spring. With a stab of envy Andersson
noticed that the magnolia at one end of the building must be
at least twelve meters tall. His own was no more than two

meters, and seemed to be fading away in spite of all the care and attention he lavished on it. When he retired he would be able to devote more time to his garden. He would damn well make sure that magnolia flowered!

The heavy oak door was also locked, with a slightly more modern intercom beside it. Fryxender pressed the button marked O. LEUTNERWALL, and the door immediately buzzed. Andersson opened it and they entered the building.

There were three doors on the ground floor, all adorned with huge brass plaques advertising the law firm, which seemed to occupy the whole floor. Next to the stairs leading to the upper floors was a small elevator.

"You take the elevator," Fryxender said.

Andersson suddenly became aware that he was wheezing slightly, and nodded gratefully. That goddamn wind would be the death of him.

The elevator wouldn't have been much use to anyone suffering from claustrophobia, but Andersson decided he didn't have much choice, and bravely stepped inside. He closed both doors and the elevator began to ascend with painful slowness. As Andersson stepped out, Fryxender reached the top of the stairs; he wasn't even out of breath.

Oscar Leutnerwall's apartment boasted tall double doors in some kind of dark wood, with beautiful frosted windows with a Jugendstil pattern. The light was on in the hallway, and Andersson could see a shadow through the glass. The door opened before he had time to knock.

A woman was standing there; they couldn't see her face because the light was behind her, but both men noticed the sheen of her platinum blonde hair that fell softly around her shoulders. She rested one hand on the door frame and struck a pose that reminded Andersson of the film stars of his youth.

"Welcome, gentlemen. Oscar told me he was expecting visitors. Do come in."

Her voice was husky, and didn't sound young. As she stepped back to let them in, the light struck her face, and Andersson actually heard himself gasp.

She was slim and beautifully attired in a dark blue dress, a short jacket and black high-heeled shoes, with a double rope of pearls around her neck. Her makeup was skillfully applied, if a little too thick. But it couldn't hide the fact that the face belonged to an old woman.

She held out a slender hand, the crooked fingers laden with sparkling diamonds.

"Astrid Leutnerwall," she said with a smile.

Her dazzling white teeth shone against the bright red lipstick. So this was Oscar's sister. *Jeez, she's ninety!* Andersson was stunned by the thought. A quick glance in the mirror in front of them revealed that Fryxender had been struck by the same realization. Her handshake was surprisingly firm.

She gestured toward a closet door. "You're welcome to hang up your wet coats. Don't bother taking off your shoes—it's a terrible modern habit. Typical of the Swedes. Nobody would expect you to remove your shoes anywhere else in Europe."

They both took off their wet outdoor clothes and hung them in the closet, which had oval mirrors in gilded frames set in the double doors. Astrid Leutnerwall led the way into a large living room, where wine-red leather sofas and black armchairs were grouped around a smoked glass coffee table, with brightly colored Persian rugs beneath. Two matching leather chairs stood on either side of the open fireplace, and on the carved table between them were two coffee cups and two large brandy glasses, the amber liquid shining in the glow of the fire.

Large oil paintings adorned the walls; Andersson noted with satisfaction that you could tell what they were meant to be: beautiful scenes from nature in strong colors, overlaid with patches of diffuse, shimmering light. Next to the fireplace was a picture of a woman, sitting with her legs crossed, hands intertwined behind her head. Between her naked breasts hung a necklace made of yellow and black pearls. Despite the strong tones, there was an air of great serenity about the composition.

A man was sitting in one of the chairs by the fire. Carefully he picked up the Persian cat on his knee, stood up, and with a practiced hand draped the cat over his left forearm. The animal gazed at the visitors with its sapphire-blue eyes. Oscar Leutnerwall waited until they reached him, then greeted them with a firm handshake each. The cat let out a low growl.

"Quiet, Winston. These gentlemen are friends. I think."

He gave a charming smile. Andersson noticed that the cat and his owner had the same color eyes.

"I noticed you looking at the pictures; do you like them?" Leutnerwall asked.

The question was directed at Andersson, which worried him deeply. He didn't know much about art, but he instinctively liked these paintings.

"Er, yes . . . they're very nice. They make me feel happy," he ventured.

Oscar Leutnerwall's face lit up. His blue eyes sparkled and he chuckled.

"Exactly! They make you feel happy. Impressed. Reverent. The Impressionists were utterly brilliant. I'm so grateful and pleased that I own these paintings."

"*Were* brilliant . . . Does that mean they're all dead?" Andersson dared to ask.

Oscar Leutnerwall's eyes flashed, and for a brief moment Andersson thought that he was about to burst out laughing.

"Yes, unfortunately. But their art will live forever," he said with a kind tone.

He was just as tall and almost as thin as Fryxender. The halo of white hair was cut very short, emphasizing the attractive shape of his head. Like his sister, Oscar looked twenty years younger than he was. The siblings were quite different in appearance, but they did have one thing in common: that sharp, clear blue gaze. Astrid had a small, neat nose, while her brother had a stronger profile. *Then again, she could have had a nose job*, Andersson thought. He had already noticed that all her wrinkles were horizontal and pointed upward when she smiled. And he was beginning to suspect that she was wearing a wig. *Nobody has hair like that at ninety*, he said to himself as he unconsciously ran a hand over his own bald pate.

Oscar Leutnerwall was also very smartly dressed, in a dark brown wool blazer and beige pants. His shirt was a few tones darker than his pants, while his shoes and belt were also dark brown. The deep forest-green silk tie with matching socks and handkerchief were the icing on the cake. And he was over ninety years old! The only possible hint of his age was a very slight stoop, although Andersson had seen plenty of twenty-year-olds with worse posture.

"Oscar and I have been out shopping. He came along as my adviser; he has such good taste. I've bought a new skirt suit to wear at my birthday party in three weeks' time," Astrid chirruped.

Oscar smiled, his expression tender as he looked at his sister.

"We thought we'd warm ourselves up as the weather is so terrible," he said. "Can I offer you gentlemen a coffee and a drop of Cognac?"

Before Andersson had the chance to speak, Fryxender replied. "Just coffee, thanks."

"Let's sit down," Astrid suggested.

She seemed determined to stay around while they spoke to her brother—although perhaps that wasn't so surprising, bearing in mind that Carl-Johan Adelskiöld had been her cousin too.

The siblings sat down on a sofa with Winston between them, while the two detectives took an armchair each. The cat rolled over on his back and allowed Oscar to rub his tummy; the sound of contented purring filled the room.

There was a plate of small cookies on the table, and the coffee cups were tiny, so delicate they were almost transparent. Andersson was terrified of snapping the thin handle. Clumsily he grasped it with his chubby fingers, and noticed to his annoyance that his pinkie was sticking out.

"You must be pleased that the law firm is still in business," Fryxender began. "It was started by your father, wasn't it?"

Astrid merely nodded in response.

"Was it a close relative . . . or perhaps one of your children who took over for their grandfather?" Fryxender continued in the same polite vein.

"Unfortunately I don't have children, despite the fact that I've been married three times. I'm the lawyer; I specialize in company law. And I still have a significant number of clients; a couple of them have been with me for over sixty years."

Astrid raised her perfectly plucked eyebrows and smiled, clearly amused as she contemplated Fryxender's embarrassment. Suddenly Andersson realized why she had stayed; it was very simple. Oscar Leutnerwall had his lawyer with him.

"You're right, our father started the firm and he built this house," Oscar said. "It happened around the time our parents got married, in 1913."

"Oscar took over their apartment when our mother died in 1978. She was ninety-seven, so I guess Oscar and I take after her," Astrid said.

Andersson seized the opportunity. "Your cousin Carl-Johan lived to a good age as well. Ninety . . . such a tragedy that he lost his life in that fire."

Both Oscar and Astrid stiffened. After a moment Oscar cleared his throat.

"Terrible . . . It was just . . . terrible. Poor Calle." His eyes shone with tears, and he removed the meticulously folded handkerchief from his breast pocket.

"Oscar and Calle were very close. They were more like brothers than cousins," Astrid explained, glancing anxiously at her brother.

"Did you grow up together?" Andersson asked.

"You could say that. He really was like a younger brother, and he was my best friend." Oscar dabbed at the corners of his eyes. Astrid grimaced and took over:

"Calle's father lost everything in the Kreuger crash in 1932, when the whole stock market went under. For once Uncle Henric made a sensible decision: he shot himself in the head. He was our uncle by marriage. Our father signed the house on Korsvägen over to Aunt Vera, and she immediately reverted to her maiden name, Adelskiöld, which was also our mother's maiden name of course. She and Calle lived there for free, and the rent from the other tenants provided her with an income. She also had Henric's pension, so she was reasonably well off, and Calle was able to finish his studies," she said without a trace of sentimentality.

Fryxender nodded and turned back to Oscar.

"It seems as if you and your cousin followed the same path— you both studied law, then you both worked for the Foreign Office. And you both served in Moscow . . ." He left the sentence hanging in the air.

Astrid started to chuckle, and exchanged an amused glance with her brother.

"Uncle Leopold!"

Oscar smiled. "Calle had an uncle who was one of the highest-ranking officials in the Foreign Office. He put in a good word for me when I applied as soon as I graduated from the university, although I would probably have got the job anyway; I had a first-class degree. Calle, on the other hand . . . Uncle Leopold had to pull a few more strings on his behalf. But

Europe was at war, and there was a shortage of embassy staff. And of course Moscow was exciting for two greenhorns, with a certain amount of danger in the air."

"Did you meet Stig Wennerström when he worked at the embassy there?"

"No," Oscar said firmly.

"Did you meet him during the summer of 1941?"

"No."

"Had you met him previously?"

"No, absolutely not. Even if we'd been working in Moscow at the same time, I very much doubt that we would have gotten to know each other. He was almost ten years older than me, and he was a military attaché. He would have had far more important things to do than to spend time with the underlings at the embassy. Wennerström was recalled to Sweden in the summer of '41, and he didn't return to Moscow. I arrived at the beginning of October, and Calle in December that same year. So we never met the future master spy."

"So both you and Calle were in Stockholm at the time of the Hårsfjärden disaster?"

"Yes. It was terrible. Total chaos."

Oscar Leutnerwall had confirmed what they already knew: Stig Wennerström, Carl-Johan Adelskiöld and Oscar had all been in Stockholm when Elof Persson was murdered.

Oscar picked up the beautiful silver coffeepot to top off their cups. The lid was shaped like a gentle wave, while the knob and handle were made of dark polished wood.

"What did you and your cousin do in Moscow?"

"We worked at the embassy, dealing with a range of issues involving Swedish interests—usually private individuals or business matters."

"So you were never what we might refer to as spies?"

"Never. It was more the military personnel attached to the embassies who went in for that kind of thing."

"Like Stig Wennerström?"

"Like Stig Wennerström."

"So you and Wennerström never met in Stockholm during the war?"

Fryxender maintained the same calm, neutral tone, but Andersson could actually feel the tension emanating from his colleague. His own palms were sweating.

"No. If I'd bumped into him on the street, I wouldn't have known who he was."

"What about your cousin? Did he know Wennerström?"

Oscar shook his head.

"No. He would have told me, certainly when the Wennerström affair hit the headlines. Calle would never have been able to keep something like that to himself."

"And after Moscow you both had glittering careers. I assume that the years in Russia were extremely beneficial?"

"Being in Moscow during the war was very educational. We learned a great deal."

"Did you and Calle keep in touch?"

"We called each other now and again, and exchanged Christmas and birthday cards. But we could go for two or three years without meeting up."

"But you both moved back to Göteborg after you retired?"

"Yes—we had our apartments here, after all. Aunt Vera lived to the age of ninety-four. Calle had the place renovated after her death, and moved in a few years later. He loved that building."

There was a brief pause as they remembered what had happened to the building and its owner. Andersson thought about what had been found in the cellar after Carl-Johan's death.

Fryxender broke the silence. "Did you and Calle ever meet a man named Elof Persson in Stockholm during that last summer, before you went to Moscow?"

Oscar frowned. "Elof Persson . . . Not as far as I recall. The name doesn't ring any bells."

"What about Mats Persson?"

"Mats Pers—but wasn't that the name of the man they found walled up in the . . . I saw the name in the paper. Neither Astrid nor I have ever known anyone named Mats Persson. We discussed it when we read the article, but I've been wondering ever since why he ended up in Calle's cellar," Oscar said.

"We've never known a Mats Persson," Astrid confirmed.

"So who's Elof Persson?" Oscar asked, giving Fryxender a sharp look.

"Mats Persson's father."

The siblings looked puzzled when no explanation was forthcoming.

Eventually Astrid spoke up. "And why are you asking questions about him?"

"He was murdered too."

In the stillness that followed they could all hear Winston, purring away contentedly.

Once again Astrid was the first to speak. "When?"

"In the fall of 1941. In Stockholm."

"And why would you think that Calle or I knew this Elof Persson?" Oscar asked.

"Your names came up, along with Stig Wennerström's name, in the papers Mats Persson left behind. He had been doing some research of his own, trying to find out the truth behind his father's death. Unfortunately it looks as if he found it," Fryxender said dryly.

Oscar and Astrid stiffened. Neither of them moved or said anything for a long time.

Eventually Oscar cleared his throat. "And what was the truth?"

"We're not quite sure, but obviously it was dangerous," Fryxender replied.

"I imagine this Mats had been reading too many spy stories from the Second World War," Astrid said firmly. "Maybe he'd just jotted down the names of some of the people who worked at the Swedish embassy in Moscow in 1941."

Oscar looked pensively at his sister. "I think Astrid is on the right track. As I said, Calle and I never met Wennerström during the war, or afterwards. We might have said hello at some reception or other during the '50s, but I have no recollection of that. We just didn't have any contact with him."

"And I've never met him either. Which is perhaps regrettable—he was a very handsome man," Astrid said.

"In that case I'd like to ask you a few questions about Carl-Johan Adelskiöld. Who was he? What was he like?" Fryxender presssed.

"We were almost the same age, and we often played together when we were children. And of course we saw a lot of each other when we were growing up—no one was as much fun as Calle! He was tremendous company, the heart and soul of any party," Astrid said with a smile.

"And did you keep in touch over the years?"

Astrid's expression grew serious and she chewed her lower lip. Before she could work out what to say, her brother leapt in:

"Astrid finds this difficult to say, but Calle had problems with alcohol from an early age—while he was a student, in fact. His father was a drinker, and unfortunately Calle inherited the trait."

Astrid lowered her head and nodded almost imperceptibly.

"Did that affect the amount of time you spent together?" Fryxender asked.

Astrid nodded. "Yes. He could be unpleasant at times. Not often, but occasionally when he'd had too much to drink. He and my husband, Harald, fell out at a New Year's Eve party, and I didn't hear from Calle for several years—not until Harald and I divorced, in fact, when he sent me a congratulations card. And

I forgave him—that's the way things were with Calle. You couldn't stay angry with him for too long. There was something about him . . . something sweet and childish . . . vulnerable, perhaps."

Fryxender turned to Oscar. "So you and Calle were in and out of touch during your careers. But you re-established contact when you both retired?"

Oscar answered with a smile. "Of course. We spent a lot of time together in those first few years. Astrid and I would take him to the theater or restaurants, to art exhibitions and concerts. Calle was a keen opera fan."

"I often asked him over to dinner," Astrid said. "The three of us would meet up in my apartment at least every other Sunday. Oscar's a really good cook, but we couldn't come here because Calle was allergic to cats. And it was no good going to Calle's place—he hardly had enough kitchen equipment to boil an egg!"

Fryxender considered what he had heard, then asked, "You said you spent a lot of time together in those first few years. Did something happen to change that?"

Oscar sighed deeply before he answered. "You could say that. Calle's drinking problem got worse and worse. He became very moody; he didn't want to go out and socialize. For the last ten years he lived more or less as a recluse."

"But you called round to see him now and again?" Andersson chipped in.

"Of course. He needed help with practical matters, shopping and so on. He had a cleaner once a week, and she did his laundry as well. Unfortunately she left last Christmas, and we didn't manage to find a replacement before . . . before the fire," Oscar said.

He sounded tired and upset. It was clear that the conversation was taking its toll.

Fryxender exchanged a glance with Andersson, who

realized that they were approaching the tricky stuff. He felt his heart rate increase. It was important to register the siblings' reactions now. If they tried to hide something in order to protect their cousin, he needed to spot it.

Fryxender's approach was deceptively calm as he asked, "How do you think Mats Persson's dead body ended up in Calle's cellar?"

Both Oscar and Astrid fixed him with a sapphire-blue gaze.

"How many times do you think we've asked ourselves that very question?" Astrid countered.

Andersson noticed that the atmosphere in the room suddenly seemed more highly charged. Oscar and Astrid were preparing themselves for awkward questions.

"Mats Persson was murdered on November ninth, 1983. Your cousin was living in the apartment at that time. Did he ever say anything that could explain the presence of Persson's body in the cellar?" Fryxender went on.

Both siblings shook their head decisively.

"We've given the matter a great deal of thought. He never said anything. Not one word!" Astrid insisted.

"It occurred to me . . . Perhaps Calle never knew that Persson had been walled up," Oscar said slowly.

"But that's impossible—he was always home!" Astrid objected.

"True, but he wasn't always *compos mentis*. When he was drinking he could be virtually unconscious for several days."

Oscar sounded serious; he really was making an effort to be constructive, Andersson thought. Before anyone else had time to speak, he asked, "You mean someone could have sneaked in with the victim and walled him up, without your cousin knowing anything about it?"

"I think that would have been entirely possible," Oscar replied calmly. He leaned back on the sofa and began to massage his temples with his slender fingertips. "My memory isn't what it was . . . but I think Calle had the old boiler changed in the early '80s. It could well have been summer '83. I do remember he had it done in the summer. The chimney breast was also redone at the time. But Calle was just the way he was, and I don't think he ever . . . Well, I know he never sorted out the cellar after the builders had gone. I'm sure there were bricks and mortar lying around."

"So someone could have gotten into the cellar and walled up this Persson without Calle noticing! If, as you say, Calle was in the middle of one of his drinking bouts," Astrid said.

"Or else it was Calle who shot Persson and walled him up," Andersson said.

"Why would he have done that? He didn't even know the guy," Oscar said wearily.

"Are you absolutely sure of that?"

"Yes. Calle had a very limited social life when he came back to Göteborg. That was the way he wanted it. He was kind of . . . broken."

Oscar fell silent; for the first time he looked as if he regretted what he had just said.

"Broken? In what way?"

Astrid pursed her lips and answered in her brother's place. "He was sacked. Or asked to retire. He'd made a complete spectacle of himself, got as drunk as a skunk at a big reception. And it wasn't the first time."

"That's right. He had to leave immediately. Needless to say he was embarrassed and ashamed. He really only saw Astrid and me. He spent his time in front of the TV, or in his arm-chair with a book."

There was a long silence. Andersson heard a clock strike three somewhere deep inside the apartment. Winston had curled up and was still purring happily as Oscar stroked him.

"You're absolutely certain that no one ever visited Calle? And that he never mentioned Mats Persson's name?" Fryx-ender said eventually.

Oscar nodded.

"But he did have tenants!" Astrid pointed out. "Have you checked to see who was living there in '83?"

Andersson and Fryxender looked at each other; Andersson sighed.

"How do we find that out? Do you know who the tenants were?"

Shaking heads and mumbled apologies. *Back to the goddamn archives*, he thought gloomily.

"I'm afraid you must excuse me—I have to get back to my own apartment," Astrid said suddenly.

She got to her feet and held out her hand in a gracious gesture. For one confused moment Andersson thought she might be expecting him to kiss the back of it, but Fryxender rescued him by leaping to his feet, grabbing her hand and shaking it firmly. He smiled at her, his eyes twinkling behind his thick glasses. Astrid Leutnerwall smiled back. It seemed as if nothing could shake that lady's composure.

Oscar Leutnerwall also stood up and accompanied them to the door.

"Please don't hesitate to get in touch if anything comes up that you think I might be able to help you with," he said.

Well, you could try telling us the truth, Andersson was tempted to say. Even though the siblings had given the impression that they were answering honestly and openly, he had the feeling that they were hiding something. And who would be more adept at concealing the truth than a career diplomat? Possibly someone who had been a lawyer for sixty-five years.

"Can anyone swap shifts with me this weekend?" Fredrik Stridh asked during the afternoon coffee break on Wednesday.

The whole team was there, apart from Hannu Rauhala and Efva Thylqvist. Hannu was at home because his son was ill, and the superintendent was at one of her innumerable meetings.

Two weeks earlier Fredrik had become the father of a little miracle named Agnes. Everything had gone well, and Fredrik had been like a positive ray of sunshine around the department ever since. Mother and baby had now been home for a while, and Fredrik wanted to take a few days off to spend with his little family. He had plenty of time to take, but unfortunately the gang war had escalated again following the summer lull, with two cases of serious assault and another car bomb. The car owner had survived; his injuries were serious but not life-threatening, and he was still in intensive care. Fredrik's temporary placement with the special unit monitoring the gangs was looking increasingly permanent.

"I'm on duty next weekend, and I'm too old to work three weekends in a row," Jonny Blom said quickly. He didn't look too upset about this sudden descent into old age; in fact, he was only a year or so older than Irene and Tommy.

"I can't help you either, I'm afraid. Jenny's found an

apartment in Malmö and I said I'd drive her down there. Krister's working, so it's just me and Jenny. We've hired a huge trailer, about the size of a horse box," Irene said.

Katarina and Felipe couldn't help because they were in the process of moving themselves. To the astonishment of her parents, Katarina had gained a place at the teacher training college in Göteborg. She wanted to teach sports, Spanish and Portuguese at high school; she had picked up Portuguese during her three extended trips to Brazil. Felipe had finally gotten into Chalmers University of Technology to study architecture; this had been his fourth application, and he had almost given up hope. At the same time they had managed to find an apartment in a privately owned house in Kålltorp. They would be renting the whole of the top floor—two rooms with a kitchen, shower and toilet. The rent was very reasonable, and in return they were expected to cut the grass and clear the snow. The lawn was no more than fifty square meters, and the stretch of sidewalk they would have to clear wasn't very long, so they felt like they'd won first prize in the housing market; none of their friends had been so lucky.

Irene was pleased for them. At last things had started to fall into place, after several years of living for the moment. They definitely hadn't been wasted years; the young couple had worked and traveled a great deal, gaining job experience and getting to know other countries and cultures. It seemed to Irene that they had matured into two responsible adults.

Tommy's voice brought her back to reality. "I was on duty last weekend. How about you, Åsa?"

"I've promised to look after Elliot from Friday evening until Monday morning. My weekend is fully booked, in other words."

"And who's Elliot? A dog, a cat, a budgerigar . . ."

Tommy smiled at Åsa, full of sympathy that as a newly single woman she felt the need to fill her lonely weekends with something like looking after someone's pet.

Åsa leaned forward and whispered loudly enough for everyone in the room to hear. "Elliot is the man in my life."

Tommy couldn't hide his disappointment. In order to smooth over his embarrassment, he forced a smile and said in a casual tone of voice, "Oh, so you've already found someone new?"

"New? Not exactly—we've known each other for five years."

"Five years! No wonder your old man had had enough and wanted a divorce!" Jonny snorted, staring at Åsa with renewed interest. She beamed at him.

"Wrong. Thanks to Elliot I stayed in our marriage for longer than I would have if he hadn't been around," she said calmly.

"I guess a love triangle can be fun . . ." Jonny said, raising his eyebrows meaningfully.

"Hardly. Elliot is eight years old. He's my ex-husband's son." Åsa turned to Fredrik. "Have you checked with Hannu? He might be able to work the weekend, since he's home now."

Fredrik's gloomy expression lifted. "Good point! I'll give him a call."

He knocked back the last of his coffee and rushed out of the room. Irene realized she had her fingers crossed, hoping that Hannu would be available.

ON THURSDAY MORNING Irene was on board the X2000 train that departed from Göteborg at 6:55, destination Malmö. In order to make the best use of her time she had brought some paperwork with her. With the cooperation of Swedish Rail's ticket office, she had been given a seat right at the back of the very last carriage, and the same applied to her return journey on the express leaving Malmö at 5:55 P.M., when Jenny would be with her. They had made the arrangements at the last minute the previous evening, when Irene found out that she was traveling to Malmö on Thursday. The idea was that Jenny

would come home with her and spend Friday loading her possessions into the trailer and throwing away anything she didn't
want to take with her, which meant they would be able to
leave early on Saturday morning.

Irene was planning to go through the whole train at least
once on the way down, and the same again on the return
journey, discreetly trying to see if there were any men in the
twenty-to-forty age group chatting online. If she spotted
anyone, she would memorize the carriage number, seat number
and description. If possible she would take a picture with her
cell phone. If he had booked his seat they would be able to find
out his name from the central ticket office because virtually
every ticket is purchased using a credit card these days. The
man would be unable to deny that he had been on board
because Irene would be a witness.

She expected to find several men who fit the profile, so she
had a tiny notepad and pencil in her pocket. Jens had offered
to lend her a palmtop, but she had refused, thinking that would
make life too complicated. Jens would be keeping an eye on
the Internet while Irene was on the train, to see if X-man tried
to get in touch with shy little Anna. If he started chatting with
her, Jens would contact Irene so that she could take a walk and
look for someone who might be of interest.

She didn't have high hopes. Tommy Persson and Efva
Thylqvist had come up with the plan, but it felt like a shot in
the dark. At best it might give the police a face or a name to
look out for when they switched to plan B. Tommy was probably trying to avoid plan B at all costs. He still wasn't convinced, but the only alternative he had come up with so far was
the train journey. However, he had tentatively begun to outline plan B to Efva Thylqvist. He realized it was essential to
make the superintendent believe she had been involved in the
proposal right from the start. My Björkman might be a brilliant
actress who could convincingly play a shy fifteen-year-old, but

Tommy didn't want to be left holding the baby if something went wrong.

Irene was well aware that she wasn't at her best in the mornings, so she had brought along a thermos of strong coffee. Even the aroma as she unscrewed the lid made her feel better.

Three cups of coffee and two ham sandwiches later she was beginning to feel almost human. She looked at her watch and decided to start her walk through the train in exactly one hour. Until then she would plow through the paperwork she had brought with her; she rarely had time to sit down and tackle everything that piled up on her desk.

When she had finished her hour of admin, Irene started her patrol, moving slowly along the aisle. The carriages were almost full, and several of the passengers had their laptops open on the table in front of them. The train was lurching from side to side, so she didn't have to pretend that progress was difficult and was able to take her time. Whenever the train rounded a bend she took the opportunity to lean a little further to check a screen. Some people were watching films, while others were busy with documents that looked as if they were work-related. Several were chatting online or writing emails. Irene paid particular attention to this category; she stopped in the area between carriages to jot down the relevant seat numbers and a brief description. To be on the safe side she included women at first, but quickly decided to ignore them. Mr. Groomer was definitely a man.

She reached the end of the train and slipped into the toilet cubicle to check her notes before returning to her seat.

The train was made up of five carriages, of which one was first class. There were thirty-two men using computers on board, twenty-seven of whom fell into the relevant age bracket. She had been able to establish that at least twelve of them were writing emails or chatting, but it could have been as many as twenty. The uncertainty arose because of a problem the police hadn't foreseen: eight of the "interesting" men were using various types of palmtop or cell phones with an Internet connection. It had been impossible to see what was on the tiny screens.

Irene took out her cell and called Jens.

"Hi, Jens. Any activity?"

"Nope."

She put her phone away, feeling disappointed. He might not even be on the train. Or maybe he was reading. Or sleeping. In spite of her doubts, she made her way back just as slowly, then checked her notes once more. Nothing new. At the same time, she realized that if this exercise was to have had any chance of succeeding, they would have needed at least three investigators. But they had neither the manpower nor the money for that. She sighed, and closed her eyes for the final stretch of the journey.

Thirty minutes later the train reached Malmö Central.

Jenny was waiting on the platform, her blonde hair shining in the sun. She waved and made her way through the crowd of disembarking passengers. As Irene hugged her daughter, she took the opportunity to take a look around. Everyone who was getting off the train seemed just as stressed and focused as you would expect; no one attracted her attention for any reason. Either her gut instinct wasn't working today, or Mr. Groomer wasn't there. She decided to forget about him until she was on her way home.

Jenny had taken both Thursday and Friday off; they had agreed that Irene would help her clean her student room, then they would go and see the new apartment. They were going to have lunch at Jenny's school, which was open to the public on certain days.

It was a fine day, with a gentle breeze blowing in off the Sound. The trees were only just starting to turn yellow, and the roses were still glorious in the beds around the station. It felt as if Göteborg were a couple weeks ahead when it came to the onset of fall. South of the Halland Ridge, a feeling of late summer still lingered. Irene slipped off her jacket as they walked toward the bus stop; her thin cotton top was warm enough in the mild weather.

IT DIDN'T TAKE long to clean the room and pack Jenny's few belongings into two suitcases and a few paper carrier bags. Irene called a cab; she thought they'd earned it.

"Limhamn. Järnvägsgatan," Jenny said to the driver as they got in.

She fumbled in her wallet and found the address of her new apartment. She gave the driver the number, then sat back and relaxed.

The cab pulled up outside a large white functionalist-style building, surrounded by an extensive garden full of slightly over-grown shrubs and trees. Irene noticed that the large vegetable plot seemed to be pedantically well tended. She paid and they got out. They walked through the open gate and up to the house; Jenny fished a key out of her purse and unlocked the door.

"There's an intercom system too," she said. The name plate next to the top button was blank; soon it would say J. HUSS.

As they stepped inside, one of the doors on the ground floor flew open and a short man with a huge belly appeared. His bald head appeared to be resting directly on his shoulders, with no neck in between. In order to compensate for the lack of hair on his head, he was sporting a splendid mustache peppered with grey.

"Welcome!" he exclaimed, beaming at them.

They shook hands and introduced themselves; it turned out that the man was Jenny's landlord. She and Irene made their way upstairs; Jenny unlocked her door and proudly waved Irene inside.

The apartment was light and fresh. The wooden floor had recently been polished and varnished, and the walls and ceiling were painted white. There was a huge picture window and a glass door that led to a balcony. The small kitchen had an unusual triangular window.

"Isn't it fantastic?" Jenny was glowing.

"Yes. You're going to be very happy here," Irene replied, and she was sure it was true.

THEY WERE BACK at Malmö Central in plenty of time for their train. Irene bought an evening paper, some bananas and two bottles of mineral water. Well equipped for their journey, they boarded the train, which seemed to be full, and found their seats. Only then did Jenny ask the question Irene had been expecting all day, but had hoped to avoid.

"So why did you actually come down today, Mom?"

Irene quickly signaled to Jenny to lower her voice. She looked around the carriage; she could see four men working on computers, two of them palmtops. She recognized one of them from her morning trip. He was sitting diagonally opposite, and was about thirty years old. She had noticed his tall, toned body and his thick, well-cut bright red hair. His eyes were an unusual shade of green; Irene wondered if he was wearing colored contact lenses. He was dressed with casual elegance in a white polo shirt, light brown linen jacket and dark jeans. Irene knew he was Danish; he had been chatting on his phone when she passed his seat during her morning patrol. However, that didn't mean he couldn't be Mr. Groomer; then again, his handsome appearance was nothing like the facial composite they had put together.

She could only see the back of the other man using a palmtop. He had a bald patch in the middle of his blond hair, and was getting on for forty. Irene was sure he hadn't been on the early train, but she would take a closer look at him when she went through the train in an hour or so.

"I was supposed to be seeing a colleague this morning, but unfortunately she couldn't make it. She had some kind of bug, but I was already on the train when she called. So I thought you and I could spend all day together instead of meeting up after lunch. That's why I called and asked you to come to the station."

Irene thought the explanation sounded flimsy at best, and that the tension in her voice was obvious as she delivered the lie, but Jenny seemed to accept it. She simply nodded, opened her mineral water and picked up the newspaper. Before long she was munching a banana, absorbed in the music-review section.

Then Irene's cell rang.

"Hi, it's Jens. He's online now."

Irene glanced around, but couldn't see anything unusual.

"Has he just started?"

"One minute ago."

Irene could feel her pulse rate increasing. She ended the call and tried to look calm. The Dane had been tapping away ever since he boarded the train twenty minutes ago, and the same applied to the other users in her carriage. Of course Mr. Groomer could have been elsewhere on the net and only just entered the chat room where he was hoping to get a hold of little Ann.

Irene turned to Jenny, keeping her tone light. "I'm going to get a coffee. Would you like some tea or . . ."

"No thanks," her daughter mumbled without looking up.

Irene set off. Her mission was the same as this morning: to make a note of the carriage number, seat number, brief description. She put a little dot beside the ones she recognized from the morning, even though she wasn't sure that was relevant, since Mr. Groomer hadn't been online at the time. But it was best to keep things in order.

When she had gone all the way through the train, she

locked herself in the toilet in the front carriage and quickly read over her notes.

Twenty-nine men between age twenty and forty were using their computers right now. Nine of them had palmtops or cell phones with a wireless connection. Of the twenty laptop users Irene had been able to eliminate eleven who were watching films, playing games or working on documents of some kind. Seven of the others were writing emails. She didn't know what the remaining two were doing; they were in first class, and she couldn't see their screens.

She decided to focus on the eleven men whose activities on the net she couldn't identify. It was likely that Mr. Groomer wouldn't want any of his fellow passengers to see what he was chatting about; two of the eleven were in her carriage: the red-haired Dane and the guy with thinning hair. Before leaving the cubicle she called Jens.

"Is he still there?"

"Yep. He's suggesting they get together."

"When?"

"We haven't got that far. Ann's not too sure. Says she'd like their first meeting to be in a café, somewhere like that."

"Who's chatting, you or Åsa?"

"Me. And I'm a smart cookie." Jens sniggered.

"Good. Call me when he's done."

Now what? Irene thought. *Any one of them could be Mr. Groomer!* None of them bore the slightest resemblance to the composite, but several of them shared certain features with the man in the picture, or elements of the description. So he disguised himself when he went to pick up Lina. *There should have been more of us on the train, goddammit!* She took a deep breath in order to calm herself before she set off back to her seat.

She did her very best to catch a glimpse of the suspects' screens. She leaned right across the seats as the train lurched around a bend, she stopped to rummage in her purse, she knelt down and retied her shoelaces. In the first-class carriage she paused for quite some time to blow her nose. Her efforts produced just one result: it turned out that the blond guy in her carriage was looking for summer cottages in the Falkenberg area. She had no idea what was on the other ten screens.

As she was about to sit down, Jenny raised her eyebrows.

"I thought you'd gone to get some coffee?"

Damn! She'd forgotten all about the coffee.

"They'd run out. They're just brewing a fresh pot. I'll go back in a little while." Irene leaned closer to her daughter and whispered, "I actually needed the toilet, and the one in the restaurant car was busy. I waited and waited, but whoever was in there never came out, so I had to come back here."

That left her with no option but to go into the cubicle at the back of her carriage, but it did give her the chance to check her notes one more time.

Ten suspects. She had their seat numbers, and had taken notes on their appearance. If Mr. Groomer was there, they would find him.

If nothing else, her notes might give the team something to start working on: a name. Perhaps it hadn't been a wasted journey after all.

"YESTERDAY HE USED the Fujitsu. The palmtop. So we can rule out the two laptops, which leaves us with eight names of interest," Jens said.

Everyone except Hannu Rauhala was present at the Friday afternoon briefing; he had agreed to swap shifts with Fredrik Stridh, so would be on duty all weekend.

"When can we have these names?" Tommy Persson asked.

He looked very pleased with the results of Irene's surveillance. Even if none of the eight men were on any of their databases, the team would take a close look at them. The chance to follow up on specific names always felt like a breakthrough in an investigation.

"Not before the beginning of next week," Jens replied.

"In that case we'll just have to be patient," Superintendent Thylqvist said, smiling sweetly at Jens. She made a point of looking down at her wrist and her designer watch, which had no numbers on its face.

"I have to leave very shortly, but I'd just like to say that this has been a very positive week. We might not have found Mr. Groomer, but he should be among those eight names. So next week we can put all our efforts into—"

She was interrupted by an insistent signal from the internal telephone.

"Hello? Is anyone there?" asked a female voice.

"We're in a meeting," Efva Thylqvist replied sharply.

"Okay. I'm calling from reception. There's a Denzel Washington look-alike down here. He's got a little boy with him; they're looking for an Inspector Nyström. Do you have anyone of that name with you?"

"Shit! It's Jason!" Åsa exclaimed as she leapt out of her seat. She ran to the door and shot out.

Efva Thylqvist cleared her throat, then spoke into the telephone. "Inspector Nyström is on her way down."

The room was utterly silent as she ended the call. After a few seconds she put into words what everyone was thinking. "A Denzel Washington look-alike?"

Å s a ' s f a c e w a s bright red when she returned ten minutes later, accompanied by a little boy who gazed around with great big eyes. When he saw all the grown-ups looking at him he was embarrassed at first, but he quickly straightened up and gave a sharp salute.

"Police cadet Elliot Abbot reporting for duty!" he said in a clear voice, before breaking into a big smile that spread all the way to his big hazel eyes. *What a charmer*, Irene thought. *And he knows it.*

"I'm so sorry. They weren't supposed to be here for another hour . . . Jason made a mistake with his ticket . . . his plane leaves at six, not seven . . . they have to check in an hour beforehand, and . . ."

Åsa didn't know what to say, which was definitely unusual for her. Irene had never seen her so off balance.

"It's fine. Perhaps you'd like to show our new recruit around the place," Tommy said, smiling at Elliot and Åsa.

Efva Thylqvist had gone off to her meeting, and in her absence Tommy was in charge of the department. He picked up the plate of cinnamon buns and offered it to the boy.

"Would you like one?"

"Yes, please," Elliot said politely, picking up one in each hand just to be on the safe side. He took a big bite, and crumbs went everywhere as he announced, "I'm going to be a cop, just like Åsa. But Dad doesn't want me to."

Tommy nodded. "You stick to that decision," he said, winking at the boy.

"I will," Elliot said, winking back.

He took another bite of his cinnamon bun and beamed up at Åsa, who followed him out of the room murmuring yet more apologies, her cheeks still on fire.

"So Jason is a Negro and the kid is a half-caste," Jonny stated. "I have to admit our temporary replacement is full of surprises."

As much as Irene disliked Jonny's word choice, she couldn't argue with the fact that Åsa definitely had hidden depths. She was an international kickboxer, and was a member of the Swedish national women's team. Irene knew from experience how difficult it is to combine a demanding training regimen with a working family life. That was why she had withdrawn from competing in jiujitsu after the birth of the twins. Perhaps that was why Åsa's marriage to Jason had broken down? She had never said a word about the divorce or her ex-husband, and Elliot's name had only come up in conversation a couple of days ago. She had to agree with Jonny Blom for once; Åsa was certainly full of surprises.

WHEN IRENE GOT back to her office, Elliot was sitting at Åsa's desk, drawing. As far as Irene could see he was working on a picture of a cop car with flashing blue lights. A figure with curly dark hair was at the wheel—a figure that bore a strong resemblance to the artist himself.

Åsa was standing with her back to him, gazing out of the dirty window. She was on her cell, and seemed to be listening intently. After a moment she said, "I'm stuck here with Elliot, but Irene's just arrived. She can come down. Okay."

She ended the call and turned to Irene, tension etched on her face.

"Jens called. Mr. Gr . . . is chatting again."

"Who's Mr. Grr?" Elliot asked immediately.

Åsa gave him a loving smile. As Irene walked out of the door she heard Åsa's reply. "He's just a bad-tempered guy—that's why we call him Mr. Grr. But he doesn't work in this department, so we don't need to bother about him. Do you know how to play solitaire on the computer? Look at this . . ."

Åsa would certainly have her hands full with Elliot over the weekend, but Irene had a feeling she had no objection to his company. It was obvious that she loved the little boy. She had referred to him as "the man in my life," and any guy was going to find it hard to compete with Elliot.

WITHOUT A WORD Jens pointed to the screen. Irene sat down beside him and began to read.

x-man: have you decided if you want to meet up?

Ann: of course i do.

x-man: how about next friday or saturday?

Ann: friday is better.

x-man: ok.

Ann: there's a café at the central station opposite the bookshop. they do the best hot chocolate ☺

x-man: sounds perfect ☺ i've got your cell number. will try to get a new cell next week. only problem is i might have hockey training on friday—can you do saturday instead?

Ann: nope, babysitting.

x-man: i've got an away game the following weekend, so that's no good. i want to see you NOW ☺

Ann: i want to see you too.

x-man: i just thought—my bro can pick you up on friday. he's got a car, he can come and get you before he picks me up.

Ann: so what's his name?

x-man: fredde.

Ann: and he's driving? how old is he?

x-man: 25.

Ann: have you got any other brothers or sisters?

x-man: nope.

Ann: big age difference.

x-man: he's ok though. cool guy.

Ann: i'd rather meet you.

x-man: and i want to see my girl of course! will try
    to come to the station.

Ann: four o'clock?

x-man: too early—six o'clock.

Ann: we eat at half seven, that won't give us
    enough time.

x-man: we can go for a pizza, ok?

Ann: ok.

x-man: can't wait to see you for real! ☺

Ann: me too.

x-man: gotta go. Xx

Ann: Xx

"We couldn't put it off any longer; he's starting to push hard. Little Ann can't keep on turning him down or he might just give up. We know he's probably grooming other girls at the same time," Jens said.

Irene read through the conversation again.

"In exactly one week. We might have tracked him down before Friday; if not, we have to be ready to implement plan B. Anything from the banks yet?"

"It takes time; we won't hear anything until Monday afternoon at the earliest. I'll be in touch as soon as we have the first name."

"Excellent! Then what?"

"I'll run the credit cards and names against journeys between Göteborg and Malmö, check whether any of them match up with Mr. Groomer and his chats with the girls. We've got his conversations with Alexandra and Ann, so we know exactly when he was online. If he was booked on the train at those times, that becomes interesting. Once could be a coincidence. Twice is suspicious. Three times . . ."

He grinned and made a victory sign in the air.

"Is it really that simple?"

"Sure. No problem—with a little help from my friends in the ticket office at Swedish Rail!"

It would save an enormous amount of time if they could find a travel pattern that matched Mr. Groomer's contact with his victims. Although little Ann was still only a potential victim, Irene corrected herself.

IRENE WAS FEELING confident as she left the department a few hours later. Computers really are a fantastic tool when it comes to investigating people's activities. We leave an electronic trail everywhere: debit and credit card payments and withdrawals, the use of season tickets on public transport, swipe cards for various doors and gates, e-tickets on trains and flights and so on. And most people are blissfully unaware of what's going on. It is possible to work out a fairly detailed picture of an individual's habits—and vices!—without him or her having a clue!

SVEN ANDERSSON AND Leif Fryxender had spent many hours trying to track down the residents of the building on Korsvägen in 1983. They had eventually come up with a list of names: Signe Kjellberg, Staffan Molander, the Workers' Educational Association—known as Arbetarnas Bildningsförbund or ABF—and Carl-Johan Adelskiöld. ABF had rented the offices on the ground floor from 1978 to 1985. A call to ABF produced the names of five women who worked on the admin side of the organization. Three of these women had since passed away, and the remaining two were both over eighty years old.

Signe Kjellberg had rented a three-room apartment that she had shared with her sister Rut. They had lived there since 1960, but in May 1983 Rut had died at the age of seventy-eight. On October 1 that same year Signe moved into an assisted-living facility. The Kjellberg sisters were hardly relevant to the investigation, but interestingly their apartment had been under renovation when Mats Persson was murdered on December 9.

Two trainee nurses had lived in the third apartment: Staffan Molander and Per-Olof Wallin. Staffan had been twenty-two and Per-Olof thirty at the time. The rental agreement had been in Molander's name from 1982 to 1984.

Andersson and Fryxender decided to split the work between

them. Andersson would take Staffan Molander, while Fryxender would try to get a hold of the two elderly ladies from ABF.

After some difficulty Andersson finally managed to track down the right Staffan Molander. He was working as a senior charge nurse in a post-operative care unit at Sahlgrenska University Hospital. He told Andersson that it would be difficult to find somewhere in the unit where they could talk undisturbed, so they arranged to meet in the café by the main entrance.

STAFFAN MOLANDER CAME rushing in a few minutes after the agreed time. He apologized, and sank down on the chair opposite Andersson, puffing and panting. The superintendent had already bought two cups of coffee and two Mazarin cakes; his own was sugar-free, of course. It was obviously the right choice because Molander thanked him profusely and devoured his cake in no time. He was slightly below average height, but slim and toned. His highlighted hair was thinning on top but was well-cut and styled. He looked fit and tan against the white coat he wore over his white T-shirt and jeans. On his feet he had white clogs.

After outlining the details of the case, Sven Andersson got straight to the point.

"We'd like to know if you or Per-Olof Wallin saw or heard anything that could be linked to the murder," he said.

Molander sat in silence for quite a long time, considering the question carefully before he spoke. "It's hard to remember after so many years. But Perra . . . Per-Olof and I were together for almost two years. We split up in the summer of '84. I moved in with my new partner, and Perra moved to Stockholm. He died in September '94."

AIDS, Andersson thought.

"The Estonia disaster," Molander said, compressing his lips

into a narrow line. His blue-grey eyes darkened as he looked at Andersson.

"Did either of you see or hear anything unusual on November ninth, 1983?" Andersson continued blithely.

"Not that I can recall. Things were a little . . . turbulent back then. We argued all the time. I used to take off and stay over with a friend when things got really bad."

"What did you argue about?"

"Perra was pathologically jealous."

Could Mats Persson have been gay? Or did he swing both ways, bearing in mind that he was married? Was that why he had snuck off to the house on Korsvägen? And been murdered in some dramatic relationship tangle?

Andersson was quite overcome by this unexpected train of thought. He sat there with his mouth half-open, his vacant gaze fixed on the ice-cream display at the other end of the room. Under normal circumstances he was an extremely methodical person who didn't allow himself to be swayed by anything but the facts, but this was a burst of creative imagination!

Suddenly he became aware that Molander was talking to him.

"Hello! Anyone home?"

"Sorry—I just had a thought."

Andersson looked at the man opposite with renewed interest.

"Did you or Per-Olof have . . . relations with Mats Persson?"

Molander looked surprised at first, then he tilted his head to one side. "I've had *relations* with lots of people, but not with Mats Persson. I can honestly say I never met the guy, and I'm sure Perra didn't either."

"You don't think Per-Olof might have arranged to meet up with Mats Persson?"

"Why would he have done that?" Staffan countered immediately.

"I don't know . . . Maybe you'd taken off after an argument and he wanted to make you jealous, so—"

Staffan interrupted him: "No chance."

"How come?"

Andersson was reluctant to give up on the new hypothesis that had begun to take shape in his mind.

"Perra liked really young guys. I was starting to get close to the borderline. He wasn't a pedophile, absolutely not, but he wanted them between eighteen and just over twenty. Twenty-five at most. And as far as I remember, this Mats Persson was around forty. There's no way Perra would have gone for someone that old," Staffan said with utter conviction.

"And what about you? Did you go for older guys?"

"Age has never been important to me. I'm only interested in good looks and good sex," Staffan replied with a smile. Then he became serious once more. "I saw a photo in the paper of that poor guy who got killed, and I can tell you there was nothing about him that would have turned me on. I was twenty-two, for God's sake!"

Reluctantly Andersson had to admit that there was something in what Staffan Molander said. And when he thought about it, he realized there was a weak link in his brand-new theory: How could Staffan or Per-Olof have gotten a hold of the pistol that had been used to kill Elof Persson in 1941? No, it just didn't work.

"So you never saw Mats Persson visiting someone else in the building, maybe walking around outside . . ."

"No. I've got an excellent memory for faces. The only time I've seen him was in that photograph in the paper a few months ago," Staffan said firmly.

Andersson considered his next question.

"What was your landlord, Carl-Johan Adelskiöld, like? As a person, I mean."

"He was a nice old guy. He mostly kept to himself, but he was never unfriendly in any way. He invited us for coffee and Cognac once. But it never happened again."

Andersson pounced on the snippet of information, sensing possible discord. "Why's that?"

Staffan shrugged. "I don't know. The age difference, maybe. I mean, we returned the invitation—mulled wine and gingerbread cookies at Christmas. He came along; there were quite a lot of people there. But he didn't stay long, said it was too noisy. But the truth was that he'd knocked back a hell of a lot of wine."

He fell silent, and seemed to be wondering how to go on.

"Calle . . . he wanted us to call him Calle . . . had a bit of a drinking problem. To be honest, the guy was an alcoholic. Sometimes he was in a really bad way," he said seriously.

That fit with what Oscar and Astrid Leutnerwall had said. Andersson decided to change the subject.

"As we understand it, the boiler in the cellar was changed in the summer of '83, and apparently the builders left piles of bricks and sacks of mortar down there. Do you remember if that was the case?"

"I've no idea. I never went down there, not even when I moved out. The few possessions I had were in the apartment, and I had a little washing machine in the bathroom. I believe there was a laundry room in the cellar, but as I said, I never went down there."

"What about Per-Olof?"

"Hardly. We used our own washing machine and hung the laundry on a drying rack over the bathtub. The Kjellberg sisters did the same thing."

Sven Andersson realized there was something very obvious that he had forgotten to ask. "Did Adelskiöld know that you and Per-Olof were . . . gay?" He could hear his hesitation over the last word; it annoyed him that he couldn't just come out with it in a natural way. Staffan gave him an amused look before he replied.

"He never asked us, and he never said anything. To be honest, I don't think he cared as long as we behaved ourselves and paid the rent."

Andersson nodded and moved on. "Did you notice whether Adelskiöld had visitors?"

"I guess he must have, but I only remember one occasion. There was some kind of musical event at Liseberg, and a man and a woman came to see Calle. I think he said they were relatives."

"Do you remember when this was?"

"The summer of '83. I spent that whole summer working as a junior nurse at Vasa Hospital; when I got home that day I bumped into Calle and his relatives by the front door. They were just on their way out."

Oscar and Astrid Leutnerwall, Andersson thought.

It seemed as if Calle Adelskiöld had lived a pretty reclusive life in his house on Korsvägen. From choice, according to his cousins. So that he could please himself and drink in peace, if you listened to Staffan Molander. All three of them were probably right.

IT WAS POURING as Andersson parked the car. These days it was almost impossible to find a space within walking distance of police HQ; the whole area was more or less under construction.

Andersson was soaked to the skin by the time he reached the station. He swiped his security card and headed toward the elevators. As he was waiting, a large puddle formed around his feet. *A wet but pretty useful day*, he thought.

In spite of the fact that he had only recently left the hospital café, he went straight to the nearest coffee machine as soon as he had removed his sodden outerwear. He took two mugs along with him; Fryxender usually enjoyed a coffee during their conversations.

As expected Andersson found his colleague in the Cold Cases Unit's office. He relayed the key points of his conversation with Staffan Molander. When he had finished, Fryxender gazed thoughtfully at him, then let out a gentle sigh. He didn't comment on anything Andersson had said, however, but went on to report on his own investigations.

"One of the old ladies can't talk. She's in assisted living, and apparently she has Alzheimer's. So that just left one."

"And where was she?"

"In Sydney. Australia."

"What the hell is she doing there?"

"That's where she lives. Both her daughters are over there, so she emigrated fifteen years ago. Wise decision," Fryxender said, nodding toward the window. "She doesn't have to put up with this crap weather. I managed to get a hold of her phone number and called her late last night. She was having breakfast. There's a time difference."

"I know that," Andersson said. His colleague could be pretty long-winded, but there was no point in trying to hurry him along; Leif Fryxender proceeded calmly and methodically, at his own pace.

"Her name is Margit Olsson and she's eighty-four years old. Sharp as a tack. She remembered Carl-Johan Adelskiöld very well, and confirmed what we already knew: that he was seen under the influence, but very rarely. Otherwise she and the other ladies who worked at ABF regarded him as a pleasant gentleman who kept to himself. She can't remember anything in particular happening during 1983, except for the boiler being replaced. She said they were working all through August, and made a hell of a noise. But"—Fryxender paused and took a swig of his coffee—"she did actually remember one thing. She worked late on the last day of August 1983. She's certain of the date because she didn't go in the following day; her car had been stolen, and that happened during the night of August thirty-first. As she was locking the office, she saw one of the young guys who rented one of the apartments come in with an older man. They went in together without noticing her. She said they were making out. It was pretty dark, and she only saw them for a little while by the light of the lamp above the front door. The older man was smartly dressed; she couldn't recall anything else."

"Smartly dressed? But it wasn't Adelskiöld?"

"No, she would have recognized him. She thought this guy was between forty and fifty."

"The only person we're aware of in this investigation who was the right age at the time is Mats Persson," Andersson pointed out. As he spoke a feeling of triumph began to grow inside him. It was just as he'd thought! It could be down to those two fairies and their unnatural behavior!

"It could have been anybody. All we know is that one of the guys brought home an older man," Fryxender said calmly.

"Well, it wouldn't have been Per-Olof Wallin. According to Molander he always went for younger guys. Nothing over twenty-five.

"It must have been Molander!" Andersson exclaimed. "He told me he's only interested in appearance and sex. No . . . good looks and good sex, that's what he said! He's obsessed with sex!"

"Sounds to me as if those are the criteria most people apply," Fryxender said dryly. He thought for a moment, then continued. "We'll have to speak to Staffan Molander again. It's probably a good idea if I see what he's like as well."

Andersson shrugged. He knew exactly what he thought.

"I've been thinking about the pieces of the puzzle that don't fit," Fryxender said. "Whichever way you turn them, they just don't fall into place. In fact, they don't even seem to belong to this particular puzzle.

Since he wasn't quite sure what his colleague was talking about, Andersson simply made vague noises of agreement.

"For a start, there's this business of Stig Wennerström. As far as the time frame goes, he could fit in, but from a purely factual point of view, he doesn't. We know he was active as a spy during the Second World War, so it's possible that Elof Persson picked up a clue back in 1941, which he somehow revealed to Wennerström, who made sure he was taken care of. Elof Persson's last words to his wife about some group calling themselves 'the net' could refer to a network of spies."

"That sounds reasonable to me," Andersson said. "There must have been spies everywhere in Stockholm during the war."

"Absolutely. But Wennerström was in Moscow until the summer of '41. There were already indications that he was showing an interest in things that didn't concern him. Elof Persson was killed in the middle of September, barely three months after Wennerström's return to Sweden. It's hardly likely that within such a short time Persson would have come across something the security services didn't already know about. They didn't put Stig Wennerström under surveillance until the fall of '43, remember. If you read the documents from back then, it seems as if the master spy was keeping a very low profile during the summer and fall of 1941. There's nothing to suggest otherwise."

"So what about the books?"

"The ones Mats Persson borrowed from the library . . . I've thought about them a lot, and I think they're just another red herring. Okay, so they were about Stig Wennerström and spying and the KGB, but it's unlikely that Mats Persson believed Wennerström had murdered his father. He was probably just interested in spies and the war. The books he ordered from the library were an inside view of the everyday lives of spies."

Andersson wasn't quite so convinced. "I rest my case," he muttered, like the old Perry Mason fan he was.

"Take Stig Wennerström out of the picture," Fryxender continued, "and it doesn't change one iota. The master spy doesn't belong here. Nor do the books."

"So what about the cousins?" Andersson asked.

"They're definitely a part of the puzzle, but they don't really fit in with the idea of a network of spies—for the simple reason that they were too young. They'd just graduated, and neither of them had been working for the Foreign Office for long. The only thing I've found out that's politically interesting is that they both belonged to the National Student Society while they were at university; it had very close links with the pro-Nazi National League of Sweden."

"So they were both Nazis?" Andersson exclaimed with renewed interest.

"Hmm . . . in the security service reports they're referred to as 'brown socialists.' This was before the war, remember, and the brown socialists had a considerable amount of support at the universities and among the Swedish public in general. And both Calle and Oscar left the organization as soon as they'd finished their studies."

"Could Elof Persson have stumbled on a network of Nazi spies and not had time to inform the security service?" Andersson speculated.

"There's one thing that contradicts that idea: the money he had in the bank. Two deposits of three thousand kronor, paid in during July and August. Six thousand kronor was a lot of money in those days. And he'd told his wife they were going to be able to afford a bigger apartment, which suggests he was expecting more."

Andersson realized where Fryxender was going with this.

"Blackmail," he said.

"That's what I'm starting to think. It could explain why Elof was killed; blackmailers always live dangerously."

"Maybe he found evidence that would expose Wennerström!

He definitely would have had contacts who could shut Elof Persson up for good!"

"Possibly, but as I said, I don't think so. The security service didn't find a single piece of evidence to prove that he was working as a spy in 1941, even though they'd been tipped off. I'm sticking to my view that Wennerström doesn't belong in our puzzle."

There was something in what Fryxender said. He was a skilled analyst, and Andersson had learned to respect his ability to draw logical conclusions.

"Any other pieces that don't fit in?"

"The rug," Fryxender said, leafing through the piles of paper on the desk in front of him. He found the folder he was looking for. "I read through the forensic report again this morning," he said. "We're looking at a very fine authentic Persian rug, made at the beginning of the twentieth century. It's just over two meters long, but not as wide. The measurements suggest that it was a so-called runner, a rug suitable for a hallway. All the blood that was found on it came from the murder victim, which suggests that either Persson was standing on the rug when he was shot or the killer quickly laid him down on it. We're talking about a large quantity of blood; Mats Persson died on that rug. In fact, you could regard the rug as the scene of the crime."

Andersson sighed. They'd gone through all this hundreds of times already.

Fryxender ignored his colleague's disapproval. "Needless to say, the rug was covered in dust and dirt from the demolition of the chimney breast, but forensics still managed to find quite a lot of other traces. Cigar ash, textile dust, soil, hairs from several different people, and"—he paused dramatically and caught Andersson's eye—"cat hair! From a long-haired cat!"

"And? We knew that right from the start. It's not exactly news," Andersson said wearily.

"But there was something we didn't know when we got the report on the rug; we didn't know that Oscar Leutnerwall owns a Persian cat!"

Fryxender might be long-winded, but he had always given the impression of being well balanced. Never before had he shown any sign that he'd totally lost the plot, but Andersson assumed that kind of thing could happen quickly and with no warning.

"No goddamn cat lives to the age of twenty-five," Andersson said, keeping his tone neutral.

"Obviously I don't mean that the hair came from the cat he has today. What I mean is that *he owns a cat*. He's a cat person."

"So?"

"We could try to find out if he had a cat twenty-five years ago. We know Calle Adelskiöld didn't, because he was allergic. But if Oscar had a cat back then, there's a good chance that the rug belonged to him!" A smile lit up Fryxender's thin face.

"So?" Andersson repeated; he still didn't get it.

"That would mean that Mats Persson was killed in Oscar Leutnerwall's apartment, then moved to Calle's cellar where he was walled up in the aperture next to the chimney breast."

Andersson contemplated this new scenario, then shook his head.

"I don't think so. It's impossible to drive right up to the building; you have to park at the bottom of the steps on Eklanda-gatan. No one could have carried a body in a rug all that way without being seen! Besides which the goddamn rug was too small to roll the body in; they'd have had to use it like a hammock."

Fryxender looked slightly deflated. He thought for a little while, then said, "You're right. It's more likely that Persson was killed in the building where he was found, then carried down to the cellar. Whoever did it knew about the big wood store next to the chimney, and that there was enough space to put a body in there. The killer also knew that bricks and mortar had been left in the cellar. If it wasn't Calle or Oscar, then that leaves us with Staffan Molander and Per-Olof Wallin."

"There you go; we're back on the same track," Andersson said with satisfaction.

"But we've already pinpointed a major problem there: how could Staffan or Per-Olof have gotten a hold of the Tokarev pistol that was used to murder Elof Persson during the Second World War?"

That was the crux of the matter. They both sat in silence for a long time, brooding on what appeared to be an insoluble mystery.

"They couldn't," Andersson stated eventually.

"No. Plus they didn't have a motive."

"Jealousy."

"Possibly. We'll bring it up when we speak to Staffan Molander. He told you he'd never met Mats Persson; maybe he'll change his story when he's had time to think about it."

"Otherwise we're back with Calle and Oscar," Andersson said.

"The thing that really points to the cousins is the fact that they were around when both Elof and his son were killed. They might have been young when Elof died, but they were still adults. And they could have had access to the gun."

"But something's not right," Sven Andersson insisted.

Fryxender fixed his gaze on his colleague through his thick lenses. "You think we're on completely the wrong track."

"Yes. No. Maybe not. But there's something we're not looking at in the right way. It's one of those pieces of the puzzle you were talking about—it doesn't fit!"

"Or we're trying to force it into the wrong place."

"Exactly." Andersson nodded, his expression gloomy.

"In other words, business as usual," Fryxender said, breaking into a grin.

By Thursday morning the weekend's optimism had faded significantly in the department. None of the men who had been using computers on the train had a travel pattern that synced with Mr. Groomer's activities. The only individuals with a criminal record were a notorious speed freak who had lost his driver's license two months earlier and another guy who had lost his due to drunk driving. All the men were commuting for work, which was why they had been on the train a week earlier.

To Irene's surprise, the red-haired Dane turned out to be a male stripper. This aroused quite a lot of interest; those who work with sex in some form are always worth looking at when investigating sex crimes. However, it turned out that he was part of the elite division when it came to stripping; all his performances were listed on his website. He appeared mostly at exclusive restaurants or bars and large private parties, along with other male dancers. According to his busy touring schedule, he had only performed twice in Sweden this year: once in Stockholm, and once the previous week at a restaurant in Göteborg. In front of a packed audience of enthusiastic, screaming women, according to the newspaper review reprinted on his homepage.

No, the young Dane wasn't Mr. Groomer, and none of the seven others from the train seemed to fit the bill. They had all been interviewed by the police; they had been able to account for their actions on the relevant dates, and had been able to provide proof of their whereabouts. Most of them had been at work or on their way home when Mr. Groomer was chatting. None of them had been on the train between Malmö and Göteborg at the times in question. Mr. Groomer was online so frequently that it would have been extremely difficult for someone to hide all the trips every week.

"How did he do it?" Irene challenged Jens, who merely shook his head.

"You must have missed him," Efva Thylqvist said, staring coldly at Irene.

"No. I moved slowly. I checked if there was anyone in the toilets. And if anyone had been in there when I went past the first time, he would have been in his seat by the time I went back."

"Maybe he was in the restaurant," Tommy suggested.

"There was nobody in there working on a computer. Too many people, and it's too noisy. The guy behind the counter was run off his feet; the train was full," Irene said firmly.

"And there's no freight car on the X2000," Hannu chipped in.

"Well, he must have been somewhere," the superintendent insisted. She looked at her team and said: "What do we do now?"

There was a long silence, then Tommy cleared his throat:
"Plan B."

THEY ONLY HAD Thursday and Friday. By six o'clock on Friday evening, everything had to be in place. My Björkman was contacted and arrived in the department an hour later. Less than five feet tall, slender and fine-limbed, from a distance she really didn't look a day over fifteen. She sailed elegantly into the conference room in high-heeled knee-high boots, a black leather jacket, black skinny jeans and an emerald-green sweater. Her waist-length dark hair tumbled down her back like a shining waterfall. Her almond-shaped eyes looked big in her slim face, but as soon as My began to speak, the impression of a young girl disappeared completely. Her voice was surprisingly deep and pleasant, her drama training obvious.

"I've known Åsa all my life. She's my sister's best friend, and we've had a lot of fun together. I understand you're trying to track down a killer; if I can help, I'm happy to do whatever it takes."

She made the offer as if it was the most natural thing in the world, but the superintendent didn't look convinced.

"I'm not sure about this. We're not allowed to use civilians as bait. If something goes wrong . . ."

"I'll take the responsibility," Tommy said before Efva Thylqvist could come up with any more objections. He avoided meeting Irene's gaze. "I was the one who put the idea to you, and I'm the one who's discussed it with Irene and Åsa. You've been doubtful about this plan all along, but we still want to try it. This is our only chance of catching him, and we have to pick him up before he kills again. He's not going to stop until he's caught, and it's now four months since the last one."

Thylqvist appeared to be considering his words.

"Fine," she said eventually.

Before anyone had the chance to ask her to be more specific about what they had actually agreed on, she was gone.

"If this goes wrong she'll deny all knowledge," Jonny said laconically.

Nobody contradicted him. It was obvious that the chief didn't want to be the one in the firing line if things didn't work out.

TOMMY GATHERED EVERYONE involved in the operation in the conference room. Including My Björkman, there were seven of them.

"We need more people," Jonny said.

"I'll try to get some help from the armed response unit; I'll contact them as soon as we're done here."

"Why not call them now, then we'll know how many of us there'll be?" Irene suggested.

Tommy went to make the call. Åsa looked at My and asked: "Are you still sure you want to do this? You don't have to, nobody would . . ."

"I know what I'm doing. I'm in," My replied firmly.

Her voice didn't betray the slightest hint of nerves. Perhaps that was because she didn't fully appreciate the risks inherent in the operation in which she would play a key role, Irene thought. She herself felt a growing sense of unease. She could understand the superintendent's hesitation. But time was short, and there was no plan C or D.

Tommy looked pleased when he returned after a few minutes.

"Good news—they're giving us a full team of six."

He moved on to the strategy for catching Mr. Groomer.

"My will be sitting inside Café Expresso. It's directly opposite the bookshop, and it has two exits. Two officers will be posted at each exit—armed and in plainclothes, obviously. I want two officers inside the café sitting pretty close to My. As soon as Mr. Groomer turns up, you grab him. Just make sure it's really him."

The armed response unit would be stationed by the Nils Ericson Terminal, in constant contact with the team inside the café.

"It's essential that he doesn't suspect they're there because of him, otherwise he'll take off right away, so they can't be too close," Tommy said decisively.

Irene understood his reasoning, but she would have felt better if the heavy mob had been a lot closer. So far the killer had proved himself capable of great guile.

They went over the plan several times. Finally Tommy turned to My. "It's thanks to you that we're able to make contact with this guy. Just promise me you'll stay in your seat and do nothing."

"Absolutely. But you guys have to remember to play along. You mustn't give any sign that you know me. He could be standing outside watching me. I have to behave like a shy fifteen-year-old on my first blind date. And the longer it takes before he turns up, the greater the risk that he's out there watching the café."

She spoke calmly and apparently with no fear. Irene felt a shudder run down her spine. What if something went wrong . . .

Sven Andersson called Staffan Molander and explained that he had a few more questions. Molander was unavailable after work because he already had plans, so they arranged to meet in the hospital café at three o'clock.

Staffan Molander was already sitting at a table when they arrived. He was wearing exactly the same clothes as last time, his tan was just as perfect, his hair equally well-groomed.

"Sorry, I didn't know there would be two of you—I'll go get another cup," he said with a smile as he shook hands with Leif Fryxender.

He hurried over to the counter. Andersson noticed that there were already two cups of coffee and two Mazarin cakes on the table; the paper wrapper around one cake showed that it was sugar-free. It was thoughtful of Molander to remember that he was a diabetic, but it was probably because he was a trained nurse.

"There you go," Molander said when he returned. "Help yourselves. I guess this must be important since there are two of you."

Fryxender spoke before Andersson had the chance to reply. "We still don't know if this is important; that's why there are two of us, so that we can evaluate any information that emerges during the interview."

Molander nodded; he seemed perfectly calm.

"We've found a witness who worked in the building where you and Per-Olof Wallin rented an apartment from Carl-Johan Adelskiöld. On August thirty-first 1983, this witness saw something interesting. A young man who lived in the building came home late that night, accompanied by an older man. The witness thought this older man was aged somewhere between forty and fifty."

Molander nodded, as if to confirm that he had heard what Fryxender had said.

"My first question is: Were you the young man?"

"August thirty-first, 1983 . . . Yes, that was me."

"And who was the older man?"

Molander's expression was serious as he carefully considered his reply.

"That has nothing to do with what happened to that poor guy almost six months later."

"We think there might be a connection. Who was he?"

Molander's face had lost its color beneath the tan. It was clear that he hadn't expected the conversation to go in this direction.

"What makes you think the identity of the man is in any way relevant to your investigation? This was long before the murder."

He was beginning to sound distressed.

"Because we suspect that the man you were with was Mats Persson!" Fryxender barked.

The change was instant. Slowly the color returned to Molander's cheeks, and he managed a faint smile. "So that's what you think! That the guy who was murdered was . . . No. No! You've got it wrong. I told you I'd never even seen Mats Persson when he was alive. Nor afterward, for that matter!" he snapped.

But Fryxender wasn't giving up. "You don't know what we think. So let me ask the question again: Who was the man?"

"Just a guy I met up with a few times. It was nothing serious, just a summer flirtation."

"But you still maintain that it wasn't Mats Persson."

"Absolutely. It wasn't Mats Persson."

"So who was it?"

Staffan Molander leaned back in his chair and took a deep breath, just as his cell phone rang.

"Excuse me," he said, taking the phone out of the pocket of his white coat. He glanced at the display and answered cheerfully: "Hi there! No, I haven't forgotten . . . half past five at the earliest. I don't finish work until five . . . but you can have a shower and get changed while you're waiting."

He was smiling as he listened to the person on the other end of the line.

"Sure, but only if he asks his mom. It's fine by me, and I'm sure Dad won't mind either," Molander said, ending the call.

Andersson realized he was staring at Staffan Molander like an idiot. What kind of weird relationships did this guy have?

"My son. I've got to pick him up from hockey training, and his pal wants to come home with us," Molander said, clearly amused by Andersson's obvious confusion. "I'm not as promiscuous as you think. I've been in a steady relationship for many years. But you'd already decided on your opinion of me, and you just wanted your prejudices confirmed. I thought it would be a pity to disappoint you."

To his chagrin Andersson could feel himself blushing. The worst thing was that Fryxender had noticed it too, with an amused smile. His colleague turned his attention back to Molander.

"Since no crime is involved, there's no reason not to reveal this man's identity. Whoever he was, we need his name," he said implacably.

Molander sighed and began to fold the paper wrapper from his cake over and over again. In the end it resembled a small

oval ball, at which point he raised his head and looked Fryxender straight in the eye.

"I haven't told you or Superintendent Andersson a single
lie. But maybe I haven't told the whole truth. I said I bumped
into Calle with a man and a woman when I got home from
work one afternoon toward the end of August 1983. They were
going to Liseberg. What I didn't tell you was that something
clicked when the man's eyes met mine. I carried on seeing him
for a few weeks after that first encounter. It was Calle's cousin,
Oscar Leutnerwall."

"WHAT THE HELL do we do now?" Andersson wondered.

"I've no idea. It wasn't Mats Persson who was seen with
Molander, so it's got nothing to do with his death. But it does
involve Oscar Leutnerwall, and I'm sure he's mixed up in all
this one way or another."

Andersson and Fryxender were sitting in their office, trying
to think constructively.

"We don't know whether Calle Adelskiöld has anything to
do with the murder of Mats Persson, but I feel as if we ought
to take a closer look at him," Fryxender continued. Let's find
out as much as we can about Oscar and Astrid Leutnerwall
and their cousin. Who knows, something might come up."

Fryxender looked pleased at the thought of rummaging
through all those old files. Andersson didn't share his enthusiasm, and sighed loudly. *Less than six weeks to go until I retire,*
he thought.

THEY WENT INTO the newspapers' databases, and also
contacted SÄPO to ask for more information. After a great
deal of hesitation they were allowed access to a number of
documents containing details about Calle and Oscar during
their careers in the Foreign Office.

In 1946 Carl-Johan Adelskiöld had gotten engaged to a girl

by the name of Greta Bergman. She was twenty at the time, he was twenty-nine. Two years later the engagement was broken off. There was a note stating that Greta Bergman married a doctor the following year. In 1951 Carl-Johan married the operetta singer Lilly Hassel, but the marriage ended in divorce in 1953. There was no reference to any further relationships as far as Calle was concerned.

"Nothing after 1953," Andersson commented.

"And we know that he lived in self-imposed isolation here in Göteborg after his retirement," Fryxender said pensively.

"He was active for a few years after the war, then that was that. No women after the age of thirty-six. Which is weird," Andersson mused.

"I agree. According to Oscar and Astrid, he was good company."

"Oscar, on the other hand, had plenty of women. Which is also weird, considering he's gay," Andersson said, holding up a photograph.

It was taken in 1948 and showed a young couple on their way into a theater premiere. The woman was strikingly beautiful; she was wearing a long black gown that clung to her voluptuous curves. A white mink stole was nonchalantly draped around her shoulders. The caption beneath the picture read: "The enchanting actress Kerstin Dahl, 28, arrived with her very good friend the diplomat Oscar Leutnerwall, 33. The couple has been seen together on a number of occasions recently, and rumor has it an engagement may be imminent. It would be hard to find a more attractive couple."

Andersson and Fryxender could only agree; the two people in the picture were extremely good-looking. Oscar was a more handsome version of Cary Grant, with his thick dark hair, sharply delineated features and an intense expression in those sapphire-blue eyes. *A heartbreaker if ever I saw one*, Fryxender thought.

"But he had lots of women on the go!" Andersson pointed out.

They looked down at the documents and pictures on the desk. Oscar was posing with beautiful women on a whole range of different occasions. They all looked very happy to be with him as he directed the full power of his smile at the camera, apparently in his element.

"There's one thing all those pictures have in common," Fryxender said slowly. He pushed a few across to Andersson and pointed.

"Look at his eyes. That warm smile never reaches them. His expression is ice-cold. And he never looks at the woman he's with, but straight into the camera."

"Too true. He'd rather be posing with some handsome guy. Those women were nothing but camouflage to hide the fact that he was gay."

"Probably. I don't suppose it would have been acceptable for the charming diplomat with his glittering career to admit he was gay. It was the same for a lot of Hollywood actors back then; they were married and had kids, but all the time they were hiding their sexual orientation."

"Women are always attracted to slimeballs like that."

"Which is strange, when they could have guys like us," Fryxender said in a deadly serious tone of voice. Then his thin face broke into a grin, and Andersson couldn't help smiling too.

IRENE WAS CLUTCHING the steering wheel so tightly her knuckles had gone white. She had to make a concerted effort to stop herself from flooring the accelerator in the old Volvo. It would be pointless anyway because the traffic was already building up throughout the city. The monotonous squeak of the windshield wipers normally made her feel sleepy, but not this morning. Right now the sound was slicing through her brain and stabbing at her nerve endings. And then there was the rain, lashing against the windshield, and the hum of the engine. She drummed her fingers impatiently on the wheel as the car ground to a halt for the hundredth time. The traffic lights on the hill leading up to the hospital were probably the reason, but it could be something else. If she was really unlucky, there might have been an accident. *Please God, don't let it be that! Let me just get there!*

The phone call had woken her just before six. Still half-asleep, she had mumbled, "Hello?" It had taken several seconds for her to realize the call was from Sahlgrenska University Hospital, and that it was about her mother.

"We're keeping her under observation at the moment; the doctors will be examining her at about eight o'clock. The doctor on duty thinks she's injured one arm, but he's not sure if it's a fracture or just a cracked bone. Unfortunately, it looks as if she's broken the other hip—the one she hasn't had surgery on," the nurse had explained.

Irene had suddenly felt wide awake and sat bolt upright in bed.

". . . a neighbor heard her banging on the radiator and shouting for help. She was lying on the bathroom floor," the calm voice had continued.

That was one of the disadvantages of being an only child: you were on your own when something happened to a parent. Krister was always there for her, of course, but she couldn't expect him to sacrifice his work.

She had managed to get a hold of Åsa Nyström, who promised to pass on the message that Irene would be in as soon as possible. It was Friday morning, and later that day plan B would be put into operation. Nothing must go wrong. They hadn't made allowances for an elderly, ailing mother. Irene's only consolation was that Gerd was being cared for in a large ward in the hospital with moveable screens around the beds.

"Help me. Can someone help me?" an old man whimpered behind one of the screens.

"We've given her an injection to help with the pain. The poor soul was exhausted; she'd probably been lying on the floor for quite some time. The home care service had a key, so they were able to let the paramedics in," said the nurse who had taken Irene to her mother.

Irene thanked God that she had managed to persuade her mother to sign up for the care service's alarm system.

"Was she conscious when they brought her in?" she asked.

She had always been terrified that Gerd would have a stroke and end up like a vegetable.

"Oh yes—she knew she'd had a fall and was in the hospital. But she was extremely tired and in a great deal of pain."

"When will they operate?"

"The doctors will decide when they've examined her.

We've sent a note to radiography, so she'll be going down there this morning, then we'll see what the X-rays show," the young nurse said with an encouraging smile.

"Can I give you a call to find out what's happening?"

"Of course—leave it until after one o'clock. You can pick up a card in reception with all the numbers on it, and you can also leave your number, so we can get in touch with you if necessary."

She smiled again and hurried over to the nurses' station. There were more patients and relatives who needed her help.

Back in her mother's ward, Irene edged toward the bed. Gerd looked so frail and tiny. Like a bird. One thin hand lay on top of the faded yellow blanket. Irene stroked it gently and bent down to kiss her mother's pale forehead.

Gerd opened her eyes a fraction and said faintly, "Sweetheart. You came." She licked her cracked lips to moisten them, but to no effect; there was no saliva.

"Would you like some water?"

There was a lump in Irene's throat; she felt so powerless. Her dear mother was lying there, incapable of taking care of herself and entirely reliant on other people. And there was nothing Irene could do.

"Please," Gerd whispered.

Irene picked up the glass of water from the bedside table and carefully inserted the straw between her mother's dry lips.

Gerd sucked gently. "Thank you," she murmured, and closed her eyes. The next minute she was asleep. Irene noticed a red mark above one eye, extending down toward the cheekbone. It was already starting to take on a bluish tone; it was going to be a pretty impressive bruise within a few hours.

As she drove toward police HQ, she called Krister to tell him how Gerd was.

"She's having an X-ray this morning, then the doctors will

decide what to do. The nurse said we could call after one. I gave them your number too in case they can't get a hold of me. Shit!"

The expletive was prompted by the fact that she had to slam on the brakes in order to avoid a group of teenagers who had decided to run across the road even though the light was green.

"Sorry, honey—I nearly hit some jaywalking kids!"

She swallowed hard several times to push her heart back down to its proper place. She could definitely feel it stuck in her throat.

"Anyway, back to Mom: there's another problem. I have to switch off my cell this afternoon. We're being issued with special phones for this operation, and they can't be used for private calls . . . no, exactly. At five . . . before you start work? Fantastic! In that case I'll call at one. Love you."

She made loud kissing noises into the phone to let him know just how much she loved him because he always came through for her. Without Krister she never would have coped with all the practicalities of everyday life.

THEY HAD GONE over plan B in detail that morning, then worked on other cases until lunchtime. Irene called the hospital before she rushed off for something to eat. The nurse couldn't tell her anything because Gerd was still down in radiography.

After lunch they gathered in the conference room; My Björkman was there too. She looked just the same as the last time they had seen her, except now she was wearing black nail polish. Irene didn't really think it was her style; the cerise pink from their first meeting had suited her much better, but it was much more likely that a fifteen-year-old would go for edgy black rather than pink. My seemed completely calm and focused.

Tommy Persson had projected a large sketch of Café Expresso on the wall, and was channeling his inner schoolteacher as he pointed with a laser pen. The red dot bounced all over the place when he forgot himself and started waving his hands around.

"We have to assume that Mr. Groomer is watching the café at all times. It's essential that we act naturally. This is door A; it faces the ticket office. There are a number of tables and chairs just outside. I'll sit down there with a cup of coffee and a newspaper at about 5:40 P.M. Irene will come along ten minutes later, laden with bags as if she's been shopping. She's my shopaholic wife."

This produced delighted giggles from just about everyone in the room, providing a welcome light relief; the tension was palpable.

Tommy smiled at his own joke, then went on. "She will go inside and buy a cup of coffee, then she'll come out and join me, and we'll sit and chat. So we've got door A covered."

He turned to My Björkman. "You arrive on the bus at 5:56 P.M. Åsa will be standing inside the door of the terminal and will follow you to Café Expresso. She will carry on to the table where Fredrik is sitting, near door B. You buy a hot chocolate and sit down at the bar counter in the middle of the café. There's always plenty of room, because everybody wants to sit by the window and watch the world go by. So you and Åsa will arrive last, when all the other officers are in position."

The red dot stopped in the middle of the café on the outline of a long bar counter. Tommy highlighted both ends of the counter.

"Jonny and Hannu will be sitting at either end of the bar, which means that My will have a police officer on either side of her. Jonny will arrive at about the same time as me. He's an ordinary commuter on his way home from work, just waiting for his train. Hannu is a sales rep with a train to catch. Did you remember the suitcase?"

Hannu bent down and picked up a small black cabin case.

Tommy nodded his approval, then moved the red dot over to door B.

"Fredrik will be sitting by door B alone to begin with, then when Åsa arrives at the same time as My, she will do roughly the same as Irene, joining Fredrik with her shopping bags. When Jonny sees My approaching the café, he will use his cell to call Jens. You can pretend you're calling the little woman at home or something."

Tommy cleared his throat. "So to summarize: Jonny and I will take up our positions at 5:40. Irene, Hannu and Fredrik will be in position just before 5:50. My and Åsa will arrive at approximately 5:57. Any questions?"

"What about the armed response unit?" Jonny asked.

"They'll be parked next to the Nils Ericson Terminal, facing the shopping mall."

Tommy opened an anonymous grey box on the table in front of him.

"There you go: cell phones, courtesy of Jens. He will be our central control and will monitor our location. He will also call us if necessary. All the cells are equipped with GPS. Jens has programmed in his own number, plus My, the armed response unit, and the six of us. That means there are only eight numbers in the memory, listed under first names. The armed response unit is under A, of course."

Åsa had a question. "My has some clothes and other stuff with her so that she can transform herself into little Ann. Hannu has his suitcase. Has anyone else brought anything?"

The response was a bewildered silence, then one by one her colleagues slowly shook their heads.

"I thought so. Just as well I've brought along some props and makeup," she said cheerfully

"What . . . ? Surely that's not necessary," Jonny protested.

"But we were supposed to be in plainclothes," Irene said.

Åsa rolled her eyes and sighed theatrically.

"Just consider yourselves with critical eyes. Do you blend in? Does Irene look like Tommy's shopaholic wife?"

Everyone stared at Irene. To her surprise they started to shake their heads again, one after another.

"Exactly! Mr. Groomer isn't going to fall for that. And the rest of you smell like cops from a mile away. I'll sort you out. You have to immerse yourself in the role, feel like the person you're supposed to be," Åsa instructed.

"You should have stayed in the theater," Jonny muttered.

She ignored him and continued. "I'd like to get started right away. Nothing major, but as we know it's the smallest details that make the difference."

Jonny snorted, but said nothing.

Irene couldn't help feeling slightly hurt. What was wrong with a black polo, white cotton cardigan, black prêt-à-porter jeans and black loafers? Okay, so maybe the shoes weren't exactly glamorous. As if she could read Irene's mind, Åsa turned to her.

"I'll start with you."

"Best to tackle the most difficult challenge first," Jonny sniggered.

"In that case you're next," Åsa informed him with a smile. She led Irene back to their office; Irene stopped dead in the doorway, completely taken aback. The place where she had worked for the past nineteen years had been transformed into a dressing room. Åsa had put Irene's lamp on her own desk, so that both sides of the face could be properly lit as the makeup was applied. In the middle she had placed a rectangular mirror. She had moved Irene's desk closer to her own, and it was covered with bags of clothes, shoes, purses and a plethora of makeup.

"Åsa . . . I mean . . . is this really necessary?" Irene said wearily. She could hear how bewildered she sounded.

"Absolutely! You're just out of practice. Sit!" Åsa said,

pointing to the visitor's chair that had been upgraded to a makeup chair.

I can always go and wash it off afterward, Irene thought as she obediently sat down.

"Look at yourself in the mirror. You're only wearing a little bit of mascara. And you've got your hair in a ponytail. It just won't do!"

With practiced hands Åsa began to apply moisturizer, followed by foundation and a little blush high on the cheekbones, then a light dusting of loose powder. Irene sneezed; her face felt stiff and peculiar.

"Bless you! Good job I hadn't started on the eyes," Åsa said. Eyeliner came next, then a little more mascara. Finally she produced a bright red lipstick.

"Here, take this. Don't forget to reapply it later. No serious shopaholic would ever dream of letting the surface crack."

"But I've got my own lipstick—"

"Which is a super-discreet nude pink. Excellent for work. But totally lacking in the glam factor," Åsa stated implacably.

She was right. A very attractive face was looking back at Irene from the mirror; evidently time and skill could work miracles.

"I'm sorry, Åsa, but you're going to have to come into work half an hour earlier from now on," Irene said seriously.

"And why's that?"

"So that you can do my makeup before I start. After this I can't possibly show my real face again."

They both laughed as they started to go through the clothes Åsa had supplied. Eventually she picked out a wide scarlet belt that she cinched around Irene's waist, with a purse to match.

"I can't do anything about the shoes; I don't have any ladies' shoes in a 41."

"To hell with the shoes—can you fix my hair?"

Irene had decided it was great fun being transformed into a

woman who had all the time in the world to wander around town. Åsa combed her hair and twisted it into a chignon, with a casual little tuft at the top.

"Great! That just leaves one thing," Åsa said after examining her handiwork from every angle.

"What's that?" Irene asked anxiously.

"Your jacket."

Irene knew what she meant. Her old reefer jacket was warm and practical, but it had seen better days. It had long since been demoted to a walking-the-dog jacket, but now she didn't have a dog anymore; she just used it when the weather was bad. She had pulled it on this morning as she dashed off to the hospital in the pouring rain.

"I'll go into town and buy a new one. I've been meaning to do it for ages," she said.

WHILE ÅSA TURNED her attention to her colleagues, Irene slipped away to the Nordstan mall. She did a quick tour of the fashion stores looking for a new jacket. Eventually she found a blue three-quarter-length coat that was just beautiful. The fine woolen lining was removable, and the coat itself was water-repellent, which was perfect for such a rainy city, Irene thought contentedly. The best thing was the modern generous cut, which meant that the gun holster on her shoulder didn't show. She just hoped there were no CCTV cameras monitoring the changing room; a woman wearing a shoulder holster while trying on clothes might just raise a few questions.

She decided to wear the new coat and asked the assistant to put the old one in a large bag. It was colorful and shiny, the perfect accessory for a shopaholic.

It was ten past five; no point in rushing back to police HQ. She might as well wait around in the mall. She went into a shoe store, sat down on a stool in a quiet corner and called the hospital.

"We've been trying to reach you; I'm afraid Gerd isn't feeling too good right now," said the nurse, who introduced himself as Per.

"What's happened?"

"She was complaining of chest pains, and an ECG showed signs of arrhythmia, or an irregular heartbeat. We're just taking her down to the cardiac intensive care unit; the doctors want to check her over thoroughly."

"Oh my God—intensive care!" Irene exclaimed, clutching her cell tightly.

"It's just a precaution. She's quite frail because of the fall; her hip is definitely broken and she has a fracture to the left forearm that will require surgery. She's also suffered a concussion; we think she probably hit her head on the toilet when she fell, and has probably fractured her cheekbone. We'll be X-raying her face tomorrow."

"Can I come and see her later on?"

"They're very strict about visits on the cardiac unit; I suggest you ring and check with them first," Per said.

He gave her the number; she could feel her own heart pounding against her rib cage as she ended the call. She immediately rang Krister to tell him about the deterioration in Gerd's condition; he promised to keep in touch with the hospital while Irene was occupied with plan B.

SHE WANDERED AROUND the mall forcing herself to think about something other than the state her mother was in. In Åhlén's department store she bought a new mascara, a tinted moisturizer and a fragrant body lotion that was on sale. The assistant looked a little surprised when Irene asked for two large bags, but she obliged—albeit with pursed lips and a muttered comment about a lack of environmental awareness. Getting into the swing of things, Irene slipped into Lindex and bought panties and tights, once again requesting two bags. Surely five shiny bags would be enough?

She emerged from Lindex and headed toward the pedestrian tunnel leading from the mall to the central station. If she walked slowly, she would arrive just in time. There were crowds of people, all hell-bent on shopping for the weekend. She allowed herself to be carried along. The faces coming toward her came from every corner of the world. You don't have to go to New York or some other world city to realize that you're living in an ethnic melting pot; just visit Nordstan on a Friday afternoon.

Tommy was sitting at one of the small round imitation-marble tables outside Café Expresso, with a cappuccino and a bagel in front of him. He had swapped his usual polo shirt for a dazzling white shirt with a jacket and tie. He was wearing his own reading glasses, and was absorbed in *Industry Today*. With a few simple tricks, Åsa had managed to turn him into a businessman.

Irene went over and placed all her bags under the table. She kissed him lightly on the cheek and said, "Hi, darling. Keep an eye on my bags."

The café was busy, and there was a pretty long line waiting at the checkout. A young girl with bright eyes took the orders, another filled them, and a third took payment; it was a very smooth operation. Irene glanced around discreetly; she spotted Fredrik at a table over by the other door, while Hannu was standing just a few meters away from her, leaning on the counter. He had a latte in a glass cup in front of him, and was speaking quietly in Finnish into his hands-free. Only the police officers in the café knew that he wasn't talking to anyone. If Jens or anyone else should call, all he had to do was press gently in order to answer; he had turned off the ringtone and switched to vibrate.

As far as Irene could see, Hannu had managed to avoid a restyle. However, the little black cabin case now bore a sticky label: NOKIA BUSINESS, SUOMI. So simple, but so effective. Hannu was obviously a Finnish businessman having a coffee while visiting Göteborg.

Jonny simply had a green-and-black-striped GAIS football scarf draped around his neck, which somehow miraculously took away the smell of cop that might otherwise have emanated from him. He was standing at the end of the bar with an Americano and a chocolate muffin. There was a folded newspaper next to his cup, and he was gazing wearily into space. Anyone who noticed him would assume he was an ordinary commuter on his way home for a well-earned rest over the weekend. But Irene knew better; he was looking out for My.

Just as Irene was about to pay for her double espresso, she saw Jonny take his cell phone out of his inside pocket. He keyed in a number and put the phone to his ear. This was the signal that he had spotted My heading toward the café and that the operation to pick up Mr. Groomer was about to enter its active phase. Irene felt her heart rate increase.

"Hi, it's me. I missed the train. It was all down to that bloody Norwegian . . . picky bastard. We were late getting out. No . . . no . . . I'm in the café at Central Station . . . half six . . . Okay . . . What the fuck!"

Irene reacted not to the expletive, but to Jonny's tone. She glanced in his direction, and was surprised to see him staring wide-eyed out of the window.

"He's got her! Shit! Outside! Contact the armed response unit!" he hissed into the phone, clearly shaken.

Irene was already on her way to the door.

"Excuse me! You forgot your coffee and your change!" one of the girls behind the counter called after her.

Tommy got to his feet as she came out, looking around in some confusion.

"There!" Irene yelled as she broke into a run.

Ahead of her Åsa's green jacket and curly hair were just

disappearing through the glass doors leading to the platforms. The area was packed with people hurrying along with their luggage; Irene almost tripped over a suitcase on wheels that someone was pulling along behind them. She could see Åsa pushing her way through the crowd; she also saw a man dressed in dark clothing and a cap turn the corner by the newspaper kiosk. He was moving quickly without actually running. Irene, on the other hand, was running as fast as she could.

As she rounded the corner a dark blue van started up and drove off, with Åsa Nyström racing along behind it. The van had been parked in the platform area, and it sped away with the horn blaring. People scattered immediately; the engine revved as the van screeched away and cut across the old taxi zone. A mail van had to slam on the brakes to avoid a collision.

"Shit! Shit!" Åsa screamed as she realized she would have to abandon the pursuit.

Irene caught up with her, and Åsa yelled, "The car! Come on!"

Without slowing down they ran to the unmarked police car in which Åsa and a couple of the others had arrived. Åsa took out the key and pressed the button to unlock the doors as she ran. They leapt in and Åsa started the engine. Irene was already calling Jens.

"He's got My! In the back of the van," she panted.

"Where are you?"

"Outside the station. In the parking lot . . ."

"Okay, I've got you. Two signals. Who's with you?"

"Åsa. We're in an unmarked car. He . . . Mr. Groomer threw My in the back of a dark blue van and drove off across the parking lot."

"I can see My's GPS signal; they're traveling at high speed toward Nya Allén. Now he's turning right. Heading toward Haga."

Irene switched to speakerphone so that Åsa could hear; she was totally focused, trying to find gaps in the traffic.

"Switch on the radio so everyone can hear," Jens said.

Irene turned on the police radio and managed to dig out a blue light from the backseat. She wound down the window and clamped it on the roof with a metallic click. As the siren began to wail, the traffic moved aside, and they were able to start closing in on the dark blue van, although they were still too far behind to be able to see it. The mature trees of Nya Allén flickered by and the Trädgår'n restaurant was no more than an illuminated façade, a bright flash that immediately disappeared in the gathering twilight.

"Tommy called; he's on his way to me," Jens informed them.

"Have Jonny and the guys taken the other car?"

"Yes, and the armed response unit is following you."

"Is the van still in Nya Allén?"

"Yes. He's just about to pass Haga Church."

"We're approaching the theater."

"The armed response unit has just turned onto Nya Allén," Jens reported.

Åsa didn't take her foot off the gas as they shot across the intersection by the theater.

"Shit!" she yelled as they almost ran down a male cyclist in a white helmet.

"What's going on?" Jens wondered.

"We almost mowed down a militant cyclist who thinks he has the right of way over a cop car on a blue light," Irene said grimly.

It had been a close call, and she could feel the adrenaline pumping through her body. In the rearview mirror she saw the furious cyclist waving his fist in the air.

"Mr. Groomer is continuing toward Järntorget. Crossing the square . . . turning into Andréegatan. Left toward Oscarsleden."

"Can you try to alert patrols to meet him from the other direction?"

"Already done, but there's been a major car accident in Tynnered with several vehicles involved; the place is gridlocked. There are also problems on Backaplan in Hisingen; robbery at a jeweler's store. But we've put out a general call for help."

Åsa's concentration was intense. She hadn't said a word, apart from the expletive when they almost hit the cyclist. They hurtled past Järntorget and out onto Oscarsleden via Andréegatan.

"He's flying. No hold-ups. He's just passed the German ferry terminal," Jens said.

Irene could see the Stena Line terminal for ferries to Denmark on the right-hand side. One of the huge ships was just casting off; it was illuminated by thousands of lights and glowed like a beacon against the black water.

"It looks as if . . . yes . . . he's turning off at Rödastensmotet, up onto Älvsborgsbron."

"Is there no one who can cut him off?"

"A car is on its way from Hisingen. It's on the far side of Brämaregården, but it's doing its best."

Åsa and Irene drove past the German ferry terminal. Åsa unbuttoned her jacket and Irene glimpsed her shoulder holster. She followed suit; she never felt entirely comfortable carrying a gun, but right now she was grateful for the SIG Sauer.

"He's almost reached the bridge."

The Älvsborg Bridge loomed up ahead of them, with a seemingly endless stream of vehicles driving across in both directions. One set of headlamps belonged to Mr. Groomer, but it was impossible to say which.

"He's on the bridge," Jens said. With the next breath they heard him say, "Hi."

Someone had joined him, and after a moment they heard a breathless voice:

"Tommy here. Where are you?"

"On the way to Rödastensmotet."

"Okay, I can see you on the screen. He's no more than four hundred meters ahead of you and Åsa."

Jonny's voice suddenly broke in. "Did you run back to HQ?"

"I took a cab—a quick-thinking driver who realized I was in a hurry. By the way, I brought your shopping, Irene."

She hadn't given her shiny bags a thought. Before she had time to thank Tommy, Jens reported:

"He's turning off . . . down onto Oljevägen, heading fast toward Arendal."

Åsa put her foot down; they were approaching the exit for Oljevägen. It looked as if Mr. Groomer was intending to hide on the industrial estate.

"He's turning left onto Bentylgatan . . . still at speed . . . he's slowing down . . . turning right! There's no road there—it must be a little track leading into Rya Forest . . . the nature reserve . . . he's about seventy-five meters into the forest now. Or whatever the terrain might be—I can't tell from the map." Tommy's tense voice came through the speaker. Åsa followed onto Oljevägen. Irene turned off the siren, but left the blue light pulsating. They were doing 130 when they hit the deserted road; Åsa slammed on the brakes and they took the corner into Bentylgatan on two wheels. For a few seconds Irene thought the car was going to tip right over; the tires squealed, and Åsa was back in control.

Tall oaks and other mature trees rose up on the left-hand side in the nature reserve.

"We're on Bentylgatan. You need to guide us," Irene said.

"Keep going, around one hundred and fifty meters. I'll tell you when you . . . now!"

Åsa stopped the car, and she and Irene peered into the darkness. All they could see were impenetrable thickets of undergrowth.

"Are you sure?" Irene asked.

"Absolutely. You're exactly in line with My's GPS, and . . ."

Irene and Åsa were out of the car before he had finished speaking. Both drew their guns; Irene had brought the flashlight from the car and shone the beam along the side of the road and in among the trees.

"There!" Åsa whispered.

They could just make out fresh tire marks in the tall grass, leading straight into the forest. Without wasting any more words they set off at full speed. The ground was wet and sucked at their shoes; there was a loud smacking noise as they lifted their feet. The acrid smell of damp earth and rotting vegetation pricked at their nostrils. Suddenly they heard the slam of a car door ahead of them, very close by. Irene switched off the flashlight and they both stopped to listen before moving forward in the darkness as quietly as possible. Åsa suddenly stopped and Irene almost cannoned into her before realizing that someone was directly in front of them. Heavy footsteps were moving around in the wet grass, and a cough broke the silence. He must be very close. Perhaps no more than fifteen or twenty meters, Irene thought. A second later a door opened, and the van's interior light shone out into the gloom. It was parked with its rear doors facing them. They could see the silhouette of a man; in his right hand he was holding something that looked like a baseball bat. Irene noticed a small movement from Åsa, and a shot rang out. The man screamed in a combination of pain and surprise as he spun around to try to see who had shot at him.

"Get down on the ground! Police!" Åsa roared as she began to run toward the van. The man turned back and tried to clamber into the van. There was a sudden flurry from inside, followed by a loud thud, and his head whipped to one side. Without a sound he sank to the ground, and a small, slender figure appeared. My stood motionless in the back of the van, looking down at the man lying on the ground.

"Keep still, you bastard! Keep still . . . or I'll shoot . . . I'll shoot . . ."

Åsa's voice broke and Irene heard her colleague start to sob.

"It's okay, Åsa. He's unconscious. I'll cuff him. You take care of My," Irene said, trying to convey a calmness she certainly wasn't feeling.

Åsa let out another sob and rushed over to My. The two friends hugged each other tightly as if they would never let go.

Irene bent down and clicked her handcuffs around the man's wrists. Since he was lying on his back, she secured his hands in front of his body. The side of his chin had already turned bright red. *A clean hit from a kickboxer is no joke, even if she is a straw weight*, Irene thought. She checked his pulse, which was strong and steady. The bullet had hit the back of his thigh, just above the knee. The wound was bleeding, but not excessively. Irene used her cell to inform Jens, and he immediately requested an ambulance. At the same time she heard her colleagues approaching through the undergrowth.

"Over here!" she shouted, waving the flashlight.

The six officers from the armed response unit emerged from the shadows, carrying more powerful flashlights.

"Good evening, ladies! We heard over the radio that you've already parceled him up," commanding officer Lennart Lundström greeted them. Irene gave him a short summary of what had happened, and Åsa came to join them.

"Nice shot," Lundström said.

It was obvious that Åsa had been crying, but the compliment made her face light up. Irene squeezed her arm, but said nothing; it could wait until they were in the car.

Irene went over and peered curiously into the back of the van. A shudder of distaste ran through her body.

The interior was covered in some kind of long-pile nylon carpet: floor, walls and roof—even the inside of the doors in the windowless space. It was highly probable that the red nylon fibers that had been found on both Alexandra and Moa had come from the décor in the van. Irene became aware of an unpleasant smell, just as Jonny and Hannu arrived.

"My feet are soaked," Jonny complained.

Hannu and Irene went over to take a look at their captive. He had started to move his head, and was mumbling something. The cap had fallen off and was lying beside him, with long strands of brown hair attached. The man himself had cropped dark blond hair. He was medium height, and looked fit. Irene thought he was probably around thirty years old. He was wearing blue jeans, heavy work boots, and a dark blue jacket. The perfect outfit for someone trying to pass as a professional driver. She stared at his face, and was absolutely certain she had never seen him before. And yet he had been chatting online from the train she'd been on; where had he been?

It was decided that the armed response unit should take over until the ambulance arrived; they would also wait for CSI, who would deal with the van.

One of the officers walked back to the road with Irene, Åsa and My in order to direct the medics when they arrived. They realized it was possible to drive into the forest by following Mr. Groomer's tire tracks; presumably there was an old dirt road there.

"Could he have some kind of link to this place?" Irene wondered.

"I don't think there's anything to have a link to," her armed response colleague replied.

"No, but he knew he could drive his van into the clearing, so he must have been here before. I'm just thinking he might have brought Alexandra and Moa here too."

IRENE DROVE BACK to police HQ with Åsa and My in the backseat.

"How are you feeling, My?" Irene asked.

"A bit shaken up."

Irene studied her in the rearview mirror. She had pulled back her hair in a loose topknot, and she was wearing no more than a hint of mascara. Her face looked young and naked. She had on a lined grey hooded jacket over a black T-shirt, scruffy Doc Martens and baggy blue jeans. *She doesn't even look old enough to have been confirmed,* Irene thought with astonishment.

"And what about you, Åsa?" she went on.

"I feel a bit shaken up too. I've shot elk, deer, hare, you name it. But I've never shot a human being before. It was . . . terrible!"

"It was a clean hit. You're a good shot," Irene commented.

They spent the rest of the journey in silence.

WHEN THEY GOT back to police HQ, Irene excused herself and went straight to her office. Åsa's props and makeup were still there, but she had put back the desks and returned Irene's lamp to its rightful place.

Irene called the cardiac intensive care unit and spoke to a nurse who informed her that Gerd would be staying with them for a while. Her condition was serious. It wasn't possible to operate on either her fractured arm or her broken hip until the irregular heartbeat was under control because they couldn't risk anaesthetizing her. Irene asked if she could call back later, and the nurse assured her that would be fine.

As she made her way to the meeting room, Irene felt both distressed and excited. When she reached the open door she took a deep breath and decided to put her anxiety to one side for the time being; the important thing now was to focus on Mr. Groomer.

"I've ordered pizza all round," Tommy said as soon as he caught sight of her. Only then did she realize how hungry she was. It was almost nine o'clock, and she hadn't eaten since lunchtime.

"I think we'll start by asking My to tell us exactly what happened," Tommy said with an encouraging smile. As if My were a young girl. It was easy to forget that she was a grown woman of twenty-six.

"I guess all that dressing up was a complete waste of time," Jonny said, glaring at Åsa.

"Don't say that. He didn't suspect a thing," My said.

"He must have. He grabbed you practically as soon as you got to the station!" Jonny protested.

"Not because he suspected anything. He just didn't want to show himself in the café. I think he was hanging around just inside the doors leading into the station. I didn't see him; I just felt his hands on my shoulders all of a sudden. He was strong, and he quickly pushed me toward the van. He kept on talking about 'my brother Micke.'"

She drew quotation marks in the air. Tommy raised a hand and interrupted her.

"Let's just back up a little. Try to remember exactly what he said from the time he got hold of you until he threw you in the back of the van."

"He grabbed my shoulders and said: 'Hi! I'm Fredrik, Micke's older brother. Micke's at ice hockey training and he asked me to pick you up. We don't have much time because all the guys are going to McDonald's after training; Micke wants you to meet his pals.' When we got to the van he opened the back doors and said: 'Jump inside and I'll take you to him.' He more or less threw me inside and slammed the doors. It was pitch black. He drove fast, and the van was lurching from side to side. I sat down on the floor. The smell . . . there was a horrible smell in there."

No one spoke for a little while after My had finished.

"I think you're right. Of course he didn't want to come into the café. Too many people," Åsa said.

"What did you see?" Tommy asked her.

"Unfortunately, it turned out that I was on the wrong side of the concourse. I saw My come in from the Nils Ericson Terminal, then suddenly this guy appeared from behind a pillar and bundled her away. I set off after them, but of course an entire school class came along at that precise moment. And then all these other people were in my way . . . I got a bit stressed, to tell the truth. By the time I got to the van he'd already started it up and was driving off. But I'm not sure he realized I was chasing him; there were so many people wandering around and—"

She was interrupted by a call from reception to say that the pizza delivery guy had arrived, and could they please come and collect all these boxes!

They took a break to eat. Irene tried Krister's cell, but he didn't pick up. It was Friday night, so he was probably busy at work. She left a message asking him to call her when he had time.

When they had finished the pizzas, Tommy asked My if she would mind leaving the room for a little while; he and Hannu would then take her statement. My nodded, and Åsa took her along to the office she shared with Irene.

As soon as Åsa returned, Tommy told her that she must write down exactly what had happened, from the minute she saw My being hustled out of the concourse to the point where she fired the shot. Monday morning would be fine, he assured her. Åsa nodded, compressing her lips into a thin line.

"Irene, I'm going to need a detailed report from you on what happened out there in the forest."

Irene knew this was essential for Internal Affairs; any shot fired at another person by a police officer on duty has to be investigated.

"The van is a '96 Chrysler Voyager. It's registered to a Mattias Eriksson, who bought it in December last year," Tommy went on. "He's twenty-nine years old and lives in Malmö. He's probably the individual who has now been taken to the hospital. He is refusing to answer any questions, and won't even give his name. They will be treating the bullet wound tonight; apparently there was no damage to the bones or major blood vessels, only to the muscle. He will be transferred to the custody suite tomorrow."

"Do we know anything else about him? Any previous?" Jonny asked.

"Jens has put together some notes."

Jens nodded and looked down at the papers in front of him.

"Born in Malmö in 1979. Unmarried. No children. He's on our records; he was questioned twice last fall, the first time following a complaint that he had exposed himself to a group of eleven-year-old girls outside Fågelros school. The second time he was accused of sexually molesting two underage girls in Biskopsgården. They were eleven and twelve years old, but neither of them was able to pick him out or provide a detailed description. He denied everything, and was released due to lack of evidence."

He put the sheet of paper to one side and picked up another.

"He moved to Göteborg eight years ago to study at the Chalmers University of Technology, but dropped out after less than one semester. He was unemployed for a while, and since then he's had a series of casual jobs at places like McDonald's and various stores. Last fall he started work as a conductor on the trains. He doesn't have a fixed timetable, he just covers wherever necessary, but from Thursday to Sunday he's usually on the X2000 between Göteborg and Malmö. At the moment he's registered at his mother's address in Malmö; he moved back there in November last year."

"Hang on, he can't possibly chat online while he's working," Irene said. "Those trains are packed."

"Not while he's working, no. But he's got plenty of time when he's on his way back to Malmö after his shift. Or up to Göteborg to start his next shift from here. Central Station in Göteborg is a terminus, which means that all trains traveling further on have to turn around after stopping here. Railroad employees travel free to and from work," Jens explained.

"I need coffee!" Irene exclaimed.

While she was waiting for the machine she tried Krister again, but without success. She left another message asking him to contact her.

When everyone had a cup of coffee, Tommy took over once more.

"We need to work out a strategy for the investigation. Fredrik and Jonny are working over the weekend. Contact our colleagues in Malmö and ask them to visit Mattias Eriksson's home address; we'll assume he's the person we have in custody. Maybe they can find out a little more about him. Meanwhile, I'd like you to try to get him to talk, if possible. If not we'll wait until Monday. I don't think it will do any harm to let him soften up in the cells for a day or two."

Jonny held up his hand.

"Why did he kill the girls here? If it is this Mattias Eriksson, he lives in Malmö," he pointed out.

"He wanted to put some distance between himself and the crimes," Hannu suggested.

"Okay, but where was the car?" Jonny went on.

The most likely answer was the obvious one: in a garage. They agreed to look into whether Mattias Eriksson had access to a garage somewhere in Göteborg.

"The next question is where he was on the train when he was chatting to little Ann last Thursday," Irene said.

"You definitely didn't see him?" Tommy asked.

"Absolutely not," she replied firmly.

"Tricky one," Fredrik said, attempting to suppress a yawn.

Tommy gazed at his weary team and glanced at the clock.

"Almost ten. I suggest we leave it there. We'll take My Björkman's statement before we drive her home, and forensics will examine the Chrysler over the weekend. On Monday we'll come back with renewed energy, and let's hope we can nail this guy."

HER MOTHER WAS dead.

Irene understood that, but she couldn't accept it. Gerd's body was lying there in front of her in the neatly made hospital bed. On the bedside table a candle burned in a wrought-iron holder, and next to it the nurses had placed a Bible and a book of psalms. Gerd's face was smooth and peaceful in the soft glow of the candlelight. She looked different somehow; several years younger, in fact. Death had freed her from all her pain. There was no mistaking the fact that the soul had departed, leaving only the shell behind. The essence of Gerd was no longer there.

And yet Irene couldn't get her head around the idea that she was gone forever.

Krister gently squeezed Irene's left hand, while on the other side Katarina clutched her right hand in an iron grip. They were standing by the bed to say their last goodbyes. Irene's head felt completely empty. What do you say at a time like this? What do you do? She could feel the tears beginning to well up. The outline of her mother's body in the bed became blurred, unreal.

"Oh, Mom . . . Why did it have to end like this?" she whispered.

The flame flickered, then grew still once more.

"I think . . . I think Grandma is happy. She'd had enough of her life. She wasn't enjoying it anymore. She'd come to the end," Katarina said, her voice trembling. She loosened her grip on Irene's hand and patted her grandmother's pale cheek.

"Sleep well, darling Grandma. I love you. And I'll miss you. Thank you for everything."

Deep down, Irene knew that her wise daughter was right. Gerd had lost both the ability and the will to carry on fighting. They had been so close, Gerd and the twins. And now she was gone.

BOTH IRENE AND Krister had worked all through Friday evening. The restaurant had been very busy, and Irene had had her hands full with plan B. They had gotten home shortly after eleven. Irene had called the cardiac unit; the nurse had told her that Gerd had been given medication to help with the arrhythmia, along with pain relief. She was now sleeping peacefully, and they were welcome to visit her the following day.

They were both worn out, and had gone to bed at around midnight. Before she fell asleep Irene said to Krister that she was going to call the hospital first thing and ask if she could visit in the morning.

But that didn't happen. The telephone rang at two thirty. A large blood clot had formed in the left ventricle of Gerd's struggling heart. It had made its way through the major blood vessels to her brain. It had all happened so fast. The hospital called Irene and Krister and told them to come in, and they in turn called Katarina; she had asked them to let her know if anything happened to her grandmother.

None of them had gotten there in time.

Irene understood that there was nothing they could have done. The clot had been unusually large, and Gerd had been weak. And yet she still felt guilty. It was totally irrational, but she couldn't shake it.

She hadn't been at her mother's side when death came.

IRENE HAD SPOKEN to Tommy on Sunday and told him that Gerd was dead. He had known Gerd and expressed his sorrow and his condolences. He had also understood that she couldn't concentrate on her account of what had happened out in the forest, but Irene had promised that it would be on his desk by Wednesday at the latest.

On Monday morning Irene went to work as usual. The very thought of staying at home and going over and over what had happened stressed her out.

The weather was cold and clear, one of the first really crisp fall mornings. Soon there would be more. Sammie had loved days like this; he would get really frisky during his morning walk, something that rarely happened otherwise. He didn't really come to life until later in the day—unless there had been a heavy snowfall, which was one of his favorite things. This year he wasn't around anymore, which meant that now no one in Göteborg was looking forward to the approaching fall and winter. *I'm getting old; everyone close to me is dying,* Irene thought.

That morning she would contact a funeral director and start making the practical arrangements. Then . . . well, she didn't really know. She felt as if there was a black, gaping hole inside her. Presumably it was the shock; everything had happened so fast.

Was that true? She and Krister had talked about how Gerd had obviously lost her sparkle over the past two years. She had felt that she was a burden, and had hated the fact that she could no longer cope on her own. The dizziness, the fear of falling again, the isolation in her apartment and the loneliness had taken over.

"And there was nothing I could do," Irene said out loud as she drove along.

Or was there? That was where the feeling of guilt came into the picture. If she was honest, she knew that she always put work first. She could have visited her mother more often, taken her out and . . . no, that wouldn't have worked. Gerd had consistently refused all attempts to get her out and about. You can't force a person if they don't want to do something. Gerd had made her own choices.

Katarina was probably right; Gerd hadn't been enjoying life anymore.

There was some small consolation in the thought that she had felt she'd come to the end.

Katarina had called Jenny in Malmö on Saturday. The girls had wept together on the phone for a long time, and Jenny had decided to come up on the train that afternoon.

It was good to have both her daughters at home on Saturday evening. Krister had made a delicious vegetable soup, with chocolate mousse and a tropical fruit salad for dessert. To Irene's surprise, they had all eaten with a good appetite. They had sat up late, talking about Gerd, remembering the good times and laughing. Irene had felt as if Gerd was very close; she had always had a great sense of humor, and loved it when people were laughing. Of course she would have wanted her nearest and dearest to have happy, funny memories of her.

THERE WAS AN air of tense excitement in the department. Irene could feel the vibrations in the air as soon as she walked in. She went into her office and took off her jacket; Åsa had obviously been in over the weekend because all the bags were gone. For once Irene was early, and she strolled along to the coffee machine and decided to pour herself two cups right away; it was that kind of morning.

Efva Thylqvist and Tommy Persson were waiting in the meeting room already. The others drifted in one by one.

"I'm delighted to inform you that we have arrested the man who killed Alexandra Hallwiin and Moa Olsson," the superintendent said once everyone was seated. "The red nylon carpet inside Mattias Eriksson's van is full of DNA traces from both girls. Either he didn't manage to clean it, or he didn't bother to try. Forensics found strands of hair, a broken nail, pubic hair, semen and blood. There was a hunting knife and a video camera in the driver's cab. He filmed his victims. And we know what he used the knife for . . . Ladies and gentlemen . . . we got him!"

She looked at her colleagues around the table with a triumphant smile. Åsa and Irene exchanged glances; it was clear who would be taking the credit for the successful outcome of plan B!

Tommy took over. "The suspect is definitely Mattias Eriksson.

He hasn't said a word, but his mother identified him. She visited him in custody yesterday, but he wouldn't speak to her either. She was devastated; she couldn't believe that her son was being held on suspicion of homicide. Poor woman— she was crying so much it was impossible to talk to her. Apparently she brought him up on her own, more or less; his father died in a car accident when Mattias was four. His mother never remarried or formed another relationship."

Tommy paused and took a sip of his coffee as he leafed through his papers.

"I feel sorry for people," Åsa said quietly to Irene.

"What the hell are you talking about?" Jonny snapped.

"That's what Indra's daughter says in Strindberg's play . . ." Åsa began, but she fell silent when she realized that Tommy was ready to carry on.

"The mother insisted that Mattias didn't own a car. He'd borrowed one from a friend occasionally, but he didn't need a car; after all, he always traveled by train. The only interesting thing we got out of her was that Mattias stays over in Göteborg now and again, if the time between shifts is too short to make it worthwhile traveling back to Malmö. She didn't know where he stayed, but assumed it was with a friend. We haven't managed to find an address for Mattias here in Göteborg."

"Biskopsgården," Hannu said.

He was a man of few words, but when he did say something, it was usually well thought out.

"You think that's where he stays?" Tommy asked.

"Yes. That's where he lived when he was registered in Göteborg. That's where he was accused of molesting young girls last fall."

"And it's not far from Rya Forest," Åsa commented.

"In that case I suggest we start by concentrating on Biskopsgården and the surrounding area. We're looking for a small apartment or a rented room," Tommy said.

"With a garage," Hannu added.

"Exactly. The van can't have been left outside in a general parking lot over such a long period. He must have had a place where he could fix it up, both before and after the murders. It would have taken him a hell of a long time to cover that whole area with the nylon carpet, and he also kept things in there that he didn't want to lose—the video camera, for example," Tommy said.

"I wonder what that business with the carpet is all about?" Jonny chipped in.

"You can see it in the filming he did . . . he arranged the girls in different positions. This guy is definitely not right in the head," Tommy said seriously.

"So you've seen these films?" Jonny asked.

"Yes, and I wouldn't recommend them to anyone of a sensitive nature. He filmed the girls after they were dead, and thank God they were! He's one sick puppy."

"So he doesn't torture them to death; he gets off on the rituals involving the dead body," Fredrik concluded.

"Yes, and it's a good thing we picked him up before he managed to lure any more girls into his trap," Tommy said.

Irene's thoughts turned to Lina Lindskog. If her older sister hadn't suspected something, there would have been three mutilated bodies on film. The fact that he had failed on that occasion had given them a few months' respite and the chance to step up their investigation. And it was Åsa who was responsible for the eventual breakthrough.

Irene decided to speak up. "Let's give credit where credit is due; it was Åsa who managed to make contact with Mattias Eriksson online, which enabled us to start closing in on him. Åsa has been a key player in this investigation."

To Irene's satisfaction, Efva Thylqvist looked less than happy. Praising other women wasn't her strong point. She was saved by the internal telephone. A deep male voice came through the speaker:

"Håkan Matsson from the custody suite here. We've got a problem. The suspect has hanged himself in his cell. We're trying to revive him; the ambulance is on its way."

Everyone in the room leapt to their feet and rushed toward the door.

"Stop!" Efva Thylqvist yelled. She hadn't moved; her face was deathly white.

"Tommy and I will go. The rest of you stay here."

Without waiting for a response she left the room, with Tommy right behind her. The rest of them returned to their seats.

"It can't be true! How the hell could that happen? The guards down there are so damned careful about taking everything away after last year's record suicide figures. And now . . . fuck!"

Jonny slammed his fist down on the table, expressing exactly how they were all feeling.

"I need more coffee. Anyone else?" Irene said, getting to her feet. She couldn't stay in that room. The coffee was just an excuse to escape and move around.

As soon as they appeared in the doorway, the expression on their faces said it all.

"He's dead," Efva Thylqvist informed them tersely.

"Oh my God!" Åsa exclaimed.

"Calm down. The shot you fired didn't kill him," Jonny said; it almost sounded as if he was trying to reassure her. Åsa glanced at him in surprise, but didn't say anything.

"He used the bandage around his thigh to hang himself. Apparently some bright spark at the hospital had used a wide dressing that wound around his leg. No one in the custody suite saw it when they booked him. Mattias Eriksson was a smart guy; he had covered it with an elasticized support stocking that looked completely smooth, according to the custody officers. And of course none of them looked underneath. The hospital notes said he would need a clean dressing in a week's time," Efva Thylqvist said icily. Something told her colleagues that there had been hell to pay down in the custody suite. Superintendent Thylqvist had no intention of letting a shadow fall over the Violent Crimes Unit due to negligence elsewhere.

The gloomy atmosphere in the meeting room had nothing to do with any sense of grief over the death of Mattias Eriksson. Everyone present realized what the media would do with the story of the murder suspect who had been shot by the police, then died in custody. Things were going to get uncomfortable.

Efva Thylqvist seemed to be thinking hard. She looked down at her hands, pressing down on the surface of the table. The pink mother-of-pearl nails were the perfect length, the slim fingers unadorned by rings. Suddenly she looked up and her gaze swept around the table.

"We have to find Eriksson's hideout in Göteborg."

Without another word she got up and walked out.

"We'll meet back here at three o'clock," Tommy said, hurrying after her.

"Some people have a poodle. Others have a DCI," Jonny murmured.

IRENE MANAGED TO get an appointment with the funeral director the following day. To her surprise it turned out they were open in the evenings, so she arranged to go over there at six o'clock. The kindly woman on the phone suggested that Irene take a look at their website beforehand, so that she could take her time to consider the options that would be discussed at the meeting.

"You can even bury people online these days," Irene said to herself with a sigh.

For pity's sake, I've started talking to myself! Yet another sign of aging, she thought. Her father had done the same thing.

THEY HEARD FROM their colleagues in Malmö, who had searched Mattias Eriksson's mother's house on the outskirts of Tullstorp. Mattias had lived in the basement; the former hobby room had become his combined study and bedroom. His impressive IT equipment had been confiscated and taken to police HQ in Malmö. One of their experts had managed to get into Mattias's computer and had found thousands of images of child pornography, mostly very young teenage girls. Several of the pictures showed serious abuse, stopping just short of outright sadism. Apart from that there was nothing in the basement to suggest Mattias's more morbid tendencies. No sadistic porn films, no magazines or books with similar content. Nothing.

"Something tells me that his mom went looking, but couldn't get into his computer. It would have been password protected," Jens said.

Fredrik gave a wry smile. "He keeps all his kinky stuff here in Göteborg."

THE EVENING PAPERS had the whole story of how Mattias Eriksson had found his victims on the Internet. Of course, the details weren't quite right; according to the articles a young teenage girl had felt something was wrong and had gotten in touch with the police. They had taken over all online contact with the man because they immediately suspected he was the perpetrator they were looking for in connection with the murders of Alexandra Hallwiin and Moa Olsson. When the police were sure he was the right man, they had set a trap at Göteborg's central station, and Mattias Eriksson had walked straight in. Unfortunately, he had grabbed hold of an innocent bystander when he realized that he was about to be arrested, and had taken the young teenage girl along with him as a hostage. When he was surrounded he had threatened her with a baseball bat, at which point a police officer had been forced to stop him with a well-aimed bullet to the leg. The police had decided that there was a definite risk to the girl's life, bearing in mind the abuse to which the homicide victims had been subjected. She was left traumatized by the terrible experience, and had received emergency counseling from a child psychologist. At her parents' request, her identity was being kept secret. The suspect had initially been treated in a hospital for a minor bullet wound; he had managed to smuggle out a strong bandage when he was transferred to the custody suite, and had hanged himself in his cell.

"Someone has very carefully leaked this story," Irene said; she couldn't help smiling.

"Madam Thylqvist," Jonny said.

No one had any other suggestions.

THE MORNING PAPER had also published Mattias Eriksson's picture. The article stated that he was definitely guilty; video film found in Eriksson's van showed the murders of Alexandra and Moa.

The story prompted Margot Asplund to contact the police.

"We've had a tip-off about what could be Eriksson's hideout," Tommy said as he walked into Irene and Åsa's office. He looked tired but pleased. He had gotten to bed late after Friday's operation, and had been on the go all weekend. Irene realized that he had put a lot of stock in the success of plan B. Even if he hadn't been totally convinced to start with, he had given one hundred percent when they decided to go for it. *The sign of a good boss,* Irene thought warmly.

"An elderly woman has been renting out a room and a garage to a guy she's sure is Mattias Eriksson, although he's been using a different first name—Östen. Östen Eriksson."

"Are you kidding me?" Åsa said.

"Östen is the last name in the phonetic alphabet," Irene pointed out with a shudder. "That's where he was intending to get to."

"Go and take a look at his little lair," Tommy said, dropping a piece of paper on Irene's desk before he left the room. Irene checked the address and looked it up on the map in the telephone directory.

"Halfway between Biskopsgården and Bräcke. Just as we suspected; he knew the area."

THE HOUSE WAS small and nondescript, with a separate double garage. The steps leading up to the front entrance had been replaced with a ramp, and when Irene rang the bell she heard a faint humming noise approaching the door.

"Who's there?" asked a woman's voice.

"DI Irene Huss and DI Åsa Nyström. We've come about your phone call."

There was a click and the door swung open. The owner of the house was in a wheelchair that she maneuvered using a small lever on the armrest. She was small and white-haired, and somewhere between seventy and eighty years old. Her back was bent, making it difficult for her to look up at their faces.

"Come in," she said, leading the way indoors.

Irene could see that all the doors had been widened. There were no rugs, and all the floors were tiled. The tiny kitchen had also been adapted for a wheelchair user.

"Please take a seat," Margot Asplund said.

With an elegant spin she parked herself next to a high coffee table, where a tray with cups, cookies, milk, sugar and a large red plastic thermos was already laid out. Irene and Åsa sat down in brown leather armchairs.

"The girls from the home-care service are so kind. They went and bought the cookies and made the coffee. I'd never have been able to stay here without them. Please help yourselves," Margot said.

"Do you live alone?" Irene asked.

"Yes. My husband died almost twenty years ago. We never had children; I developed rheumatism the year we got married."

"So you've been renting out your garage for some time?"

"That's right; my husband ran a cab firm, which was why he had such a big garage built. He used to have three cars, but toward the end he just had the one. Employing other drivers got too difficult. Then he retired, and the following year he had a heart attack. The garage stood empty for a year or so after his death, but it actually has a small bedroom with a shower and toilet. One of my husband's drivers was from Vänersborg, and sometimes when the weather was bad he stayed there. And since I became a widow I've been renting the room out too."

"And when did Mattias Eriksson become your tenant?"

"It's on those papers over there. I still think of him as Östen; it's a very unusual name for such a young man."

With a crooked finger Margot pointed to a large brown envelope on a small desk by the window. Åsa went to fetch it.

"He showed me his ID card from the railroad company. He said he needed to be able to stay overnight in Göteborg occasionally. The card looked genuine, although I didn't think the photograph was a very good likeness. When I mentioned it to Östen . . . Mattias . . . he just said that anyone who looked like the photo on their ID card needed to see a doctor. I didn't pursue the matter, because I wanted to rent out the room to bring in a little more money."

Åsa passed the envelope to Irene. She took out the papers and began to read. The lease was made out in the name of Östen Eriksson, date of birth July 2, 1975. He gave his home address as Annetorpsvägen in Malmö.

Mattias had added four years to his real age. The address was false. The ID card was obviously fake or stolen. Even if her body no longer obeyed her, Margot Asplund's mind was razor-sharp. And yet she had accepted the proof of identity, in spite of the fact that she suspected there was something wrong with it. The only explanation was that she really needed the money from the rental.

The lease dated from November 1 the previous year. Mattias Eriksson had rented the room and the garage for almost a year.

"Did he say why he wanted the garage?"

"Yes, he said he was fixing up some kind of camper van so that he could go traveling around Europe."

"Did you ever get a close look at the vehicle?"

"No, I only caught a glimpse of it when he drove in and out of the garage. I can't get down there in my wheelchair; there's only gravel outside, not tarmac. When my cats disappeared I went out to look for them, and my wheels almost got stuck."

Which must have been perfect for Mattias. No chance of his landlady snooping around when he wasn't there. Irene was keen to get out there and take a look at the room and the garage, but she realized it was important to find out as much as possible from the old lady.

"What was your impression of Mattias Eriksson?"

Margot Asplund straightened up as best she could, and gave Irene a long, appraising look before she replied. "He made it very clear that he preferred to keep himself to himself; he didn't want any kind of social interaction. That was fine by me, as long as he paid the rent every month, which he did."

"Do you know if he was away at any point over the summer?"

"He was—both he and the van were gone during the second half of July and part of August."

Nothing connected to Mr. Groomer had happened during that period; had he been operating elsewhere? Overseas?

Irene got up and thanked Margot Asplund for the coffee.

"The keys are in the cupboard in the hallway," Margot said.

THE GARAGE WAS poorly maintained. The paint was flaking, and there were patches of rust all over the metal roof.

Years of accumulated dirt made it virtually impossible to see through the windows. Irene unlocked one of the doors.

The smell was the same as in the van. It wasn't overwhelming; it was more of a faint perception that gradually made itself felt, until it was impossible to ignore.

"There's stuff here. Maybe trophies. Be careful," Irene said.

Åsa gave her a weary look. She was already putting on plastic gloves, shoe protectors and a paper cap. *I have to stop sounding like her mother,* Irene cursed herself.

She found the light switch by the door, and the old fluorescent tubes flickered reluctantly to life. They were festooned with cobwebs, but still provided a surprisingly good light.

Shelves and worktops lined one wall, with tall closets on the other side. They began to go through them, starting on opposite ends. Most were empty, but in some they found traces of Mattias: a piece of the red nylon carpet, along with a Stanley knife and some carpet glue. Everything had been dumped in paper bags, along with empty Coca-Cola bottles and chips wrappers. When Irene opened the door of the last closet, she inhaled sharply. She had found the source of the smell.

Clothes were neatly displayed on a series of hangers. Presumably they were the clothes Alexandra and Moa had been wearing when they went missing, although it was hard to tell because they were ripped to shreds and covered in blood. There was also blood on the inside of the closet. On the floor Irene saw a laptop and two pairs of shoes, with a cell phone pushed inside each pair. Everything was spattered with blood.

"There's a hell of a lot of blood. Strange. And I assume that's Moa's laptop and cell, and Alexandra's cell."

She closed the door to escape the smell, and called CSI. As she ended the call Åsa was already heading toward a rickety wooden staircase at the far end of the garage.

"The room is up here," Åsa said.

At the top of the stairs they found an attic with a sloping

roof, divided by a wall. One half was an open, empty space. Irene unlocked the door leading into the other half.

Once again they were met by an unpleasant smell, but this time it was because no one had done any cleaning in a long time. The room measured approximately twelve to fifteen square meters, and there was a small window. The bathroom was immediately on the left; if you didn't know where it was, all you had to do was follow the stench. On a desk beneath the window were a laptop and a palmtop. Dirty socks and underpants were draped over the chair, and the unmade bed was in urgent need of clean sheets. The closet was empty apart from a few used towels thrown on the floor. Irene noticed large rusty-red patches on them; it looked like dried blood. Could the towels have been lying there since the murders?

"I guess cleaning wasn't his thing," Åsa said.

Dirt and grit crunched beneath her feet as she walked over to open the window. They left the door wide open to create a cross draft; a breeze blew through the room, rustling all the papers pinned up on the wall.

"He's collected everything that's been written about the murders of Moa and Alexandra," Åsa said. "He's even printed stuff off the Internet. Look!"

She pointed to two color pictures of the girls; Mattias had obviously enlarged them. They were school photos, and Irene recognized them from the case. Perhaps the girls had actually sent them to Mattias, or maybe they had posted them online when they were trying to hook up with some guy on snuttis.se. Next to them were two other pictures of the girls that Mattias himself had taken after their deaths.

"I seem to remember Tommy saying that Mattias was one sick puppy; I guess he's right," Åsa said. She looked away from the terrible pictures and turned her attention to the computers on the desk.

"The laptop is an iBook; the palmtop is a Fujitsu Siemens

Pocket. Those are probably the stolen computers he used on the train when he was chatting with the girls."

She nodded in the direction of the window, where Mattias had neatly arranged pictures of girls between the ages of twelve and fifteen around the frame. Åsa began to count.

"Nineteen. And here's one of My."

Without further ado she removed the picture of My and slipped it into her pocket. Irene didn't comment; it was just as well if My disappeared from the case as discreetly as possible.

"Eighteen. There's Alexandra, and there's Moa. The other sixteen must be girls he was working on. Can you see Lina Lindskog?" Irene asked.

Åsa looked carefully at each picture, then shook her head.

"No. He must have dumped her after the failed attempt to pick her up."

"He probably thought it was too dangerous to try again—and he had plenty more."

They looked so young, so innocent. And yet several of them were completely or partially naked in the pictures. Didn't they realize what they were doing? If a living, breathing seventeen-year-old guy they didn't know had walked into their room and asked them to strip, they wouldn't have done it, but being daring in front of a webcam was more like a game; somehow it wasn't real. They couldn't have been more wrong. They could be seen not by just one person, but hundreds, thousands, perhaps millions. And the pictures would remain on the Internet forever.

"This is where he keeps the juicy stuff!"

Åsa started to empty the desk drawers, stacking DVDs and CDs on the desk. It looked as if he had burned most of them himself. The covers of the ones he'd bought clearly showed what kind of films were involved: the most extreme form of sadistic porn.

"We'll leave those to forensics," Irene said. Suddenly she

felt tired of the whole thing. The police were fighting an unfair battle against new technology, and they were always light-years behind.

After nineteen years in homicide, Irene knew a great deal about different types of killers. She knew what drove them, and whether they were likely to kill again. Mattias Eriksson's type needs to be able to feed their fantasies, and the Internet provides everything they could want. Like all addicts, they need a stronger and stronger fix in order to achieve the kick they desire. By the time they move on to acting out their fantasies, they know exactly what they want; they've already practiced in the virtual world. Judging by his collection of CDs and DVDs, Mattias had been very well prepared, and there was no doubt that he would have gone on killing until he was caught.

CSI ARRIVED, AND Irene and Åsa left the garage. As they were about to get in the car, Irene was suddenly overwhelmed with exhaustion.

"Åsa, would you mind driving?" she said.

Åsa glanced sharply at her. "Don't feel well?"

Irene told her about her mother's sudden death. She hadn't slept well over the past few nights, and now it was catching up with her. She also explained that she was going to see the funeral director straight after work.

"Oh, that's terrible! She can't have been very old," Åsa said sympathetically.

"Well . . . she turned seventy-nine a few weeks ago."

"So she can't have been all that young when she had you."

"I don't think she'd be regarded as old these days, when so many women have their first child at about thirty-five."

"My mom had four kids by the time she was thirty-five," Åsa said. "I was two years old at that point."

"Didn't you say you had three older brothers?"

"Why do you think I started boxing?" Åsa said with a smile.

"Are your parents still alive?"

"Yeah. My dad retired last year; Mom works in a store selling eco-friendly goods in Haga. She's got two years before she retires, but I can't see her wanting to stay at home and look after Dad. He's taken up painting. Pictures, I mean. To be honest, they're pretty bad, but he's happy."

"What did he do before he retired?"

"He was a journalist."

"What kind? Did he write about sports or politics? Or would I have seen him on the news?"

"He wrote about culture and the arts."

Åsa turned her head and looked out at the huge oil tanks looming at the foot of the Älvsborg Bridge on the Hisingen side. She nodded in their direction and said, "Just imagine if terrorists decided to blow up one of those! It would be a disaster!"

"Yes, but of course when they were built, they were a long way outside the city."

It was obvious that Åsa didn't want to talk about her parents anymore. A journalist . . . Irene's father had been a civil servant working for the customs office. And Åsa's mother worked in a store selling eco-friendly goods. Gerd had worked at the mail counter for thirty-five years. Irene was beginning to realize that Åsa had made some kind of journey from one class to another, which was unusual among police officers. And even if her background was different, it didn't change the fact that Åsa was a good cop.

IN A WEEK'S time the Cold Cases Unit would have its reinforcements: one man and one woman. However, right now the team consisted of only two active investigators, so they had to make the best use of their limited resources, as Leif Fryxender put it. He and Sven Andersson had discussed at length how best to proceed, and eventually they had decided to speak to Oscar Leutnerwall again. He was the only remaining link with the past, and if anyone knew what had gone on, it was likely to be the former diplomat. The only question was whether he would be prepared to tell them what he knew.

Fryxender called to arrange a meeting; he tried several times, but there was no reply. Just before he was about to go home for the day, he made one last attempt. This time Oscar Leutnerwall picked up; he seemed to be in a good mood.

"Good afternoon, Inspector! I could see from the display that someone whose number was withheld had called several times, but I've been out playing tennis. I play twice a week, all year round. I've missed very few training sessions since I started back in the summer of '32."

Fryxender asked if they could meet again. Oscar was available for the next few days, but not during the following two weeks.

"We're having a party to celebrate Astrid's ninetieth birthday on Saturday, then on Monday we're going to

Mauritius for two weeks. That's my birthday present to her," he explained.

They arranged to meet the next day. Oscar suggested they come over to his apartment, as he had a number of things to do before the party.

OSCAR LEUTNERWALL OPENED the door wearing nothing but a dressing gown. It was an elegant garment made of thick silk with a paisley pattern, but it still wasn't exactly what Fryxender and Andersson had expected. It stopped just below the knee, revealing white legs. He had black leather slippers on his feet.

"Please excuse my casual attire, gentlemen, but my tailor is here. He's made a few minor adjustments to my dinner suit, and I've just been trying it on. Do come in and sit in front of the fire."

Oscar led the way into the living room.

A large desk stood over by the tall window. It was an imposing piece, and was adorned with beautiful marquetry; the corners were gilded. *Probably not from IKEA,* Andersson thought.

Winston was asleep on the wine-red leather writing pad. He woke up as the men entered the room, extended his pink tongue in an elegant curve as he yawned and blinked those sapphire-blue eyes. He got up in one smooth movement, then stretched first his front legs, then his hind legs before starting to wander around.

Bursting with enthusiasm, Oscar started to talk about his preparations for Astrid's upcoming birthday party. Andersson wasn't really paying attention, and gazed around the room. Suddenly an object caught his eye. Or several objects, to be more accurate. A whole armory of weapons, in fact. Above the door hung two crossed sabers, with beautiful ornamentation and gold tassels. The rest of the collection consisted of guns; Andersson counted twenty around the door. Some looked very old.

"I see you collect weapons," he said.

Oscar glanced over at Andersson, looking distinctly irritated.

"Weapons? Those aren't really mine. I inherited them from my father; they've been there for many years. Some of them are extremely rare."

"He never had a Tokarev pistol in the collection?" Andersson asked.

"A Tokarev? No. My father was only interested in older weapons; the newest item is this one."

He went over and took down a gun that looked quite modern.

"A Colt-Browning 1911. He bought it when he was in the USA in the early twenties. It was regarded as one of the best handguns ever made. Needless to say the model has been refined since 1911; between the wars and during the Second World War, many countries produced Colt copies of various types."

"So your father never owned a Tokarev?"

"No. Such a thing wouldn't have interested him."

Oscar replaced the Colt.

"Was he keen on shooting?" Fryxender asked.

"Absolutely! But he used other guns for that, not these old things."

"Did you also learn to shoot?"

"Of course. It was part of a young man's education. Calle and I were dragged out to the range at Delsjön to learn. We both hated it. Neither of us turned into either a sharpshooter or a huntsman; my father was both."

Oscar pursed his lips slightly as he finished speaking. He stared at the Colt on the wall, and for a moment he seemed to be lost in memories.

The crash made all three men jump. It was totally unexpected, and Andersson felt his heart flip over in his chest.

"Winston!" Oscar said reproachfully.

The cat was sitting on the desk, meticulously licking a front paw; he seemed to have no idea how the orchid in the glass pot might have ended up on the floor. The flower had broken off, but the pot had survived.

"Thank goodness it landed on the rug," Oscar said, sounding extremely relieved.

"These thick Persian rugs are beautiful and practical at the same time," Fryxender commented.

"You're right. I collect those too." Oscar nodded.

"Did Carl-Johan collect Persian rugs too?" was Fryxender's instant follow-up.

Oscar frowned slightly as he looked sharply at Fryxender. No doubt he sensed that there was something behind the question.

"No. Calle didn't collect rugs. Or anything else," he said slowly.

"I'm just thinking about the rug Mats Persson was lying on. I mean, he'd been walled up in the chimney breast in your cousin's house, and he was lying on a genuine Persian rug."

Oscar didn't reply; he merely raised a quizzical eyebrow. But Sven Andersson thought there was a glimmer of something in his eyes. Fear? Surprise?

"So if cousin Calle wasn't interested in Persian rugs, I'm just wondering how Mats Persson came to be lying on such a fine example," Fryxender went on.

"You can't be sure the rug belonged to Calle." Oscar Leutnerwall's tone was distinctly chilly.

"No, exactly. In which case the question is, who did it belong to if not Calle?"

Oscar didn't move a muscle, and he made no attempt to answer. Fryxender smiled, but the smile didn't reach his eyes.

He turned to look at Winston, who was balancing on the edge of the desk, idly batting at the lamp cable with one paw.

"Have you always had cats?" he asked.

"Yes, except occasionally when I was working overseas. My mother always had cats; Astrid and I grew up with them. Astrid's Siamese died last summer; she's not sure whether to get another. If you'll excuse me I'll just go fetch the vacuum cleaner," Oscar said, disappearing into the hallway.

Fryxender bent down to pick up the flower and the pot. He stayed like that for a long time. *Jeez, his back's gone!* Andersson thought. He looked on in surprise as his colleague reached out and removed a number of books from the bottom shelf. Slowly he straightened up and handed them to Andersson.

H.-K. Rönblom's *The Spy Without a Country*, Stig Wennerström's *From Beginning to End*, and John Barron's *KGB: The Secret Work of Soviet Secret Agents*.

All three were covered in clear plastic and were unmistakably library books.

SEVERAL OFFICERS HAD interviewed every employee who had been working on the X2000 train on which Irene had traveled from Göteborg to Malmö. One of them had sent Viktor Jacobsson to police HQ, having decided that the young man had interesting information.

Jacobsson was noticeably nervous. According to Irene's notes he was twenty-four, but looked younger. His straw-colored hair was carefully combed, Beatles style, to hide one eye. The clothes hanging off his slender frame could have come straight out of a photo from the mid-sixties: black corduroy jacket, crumpled red-checked shirt, skinny blue jeans and pointed black shoes. He sat opposite Irene scratching at the pimples covering his chin and cheeks. She tried not to think about what he did for a living.

"So how long have you worked in the restaurant car?" she asked.

"Almost three years," he replied in a broad Skåne accent.

"As I understand it you've been sent to us because you have important information about Mattias Eriksson."

"Yes. It was me who got him a job in the restaurant car. We're related. Distantly related. Second cousins. But we've never hung out. He's . . . he was . . . five years older than me. It doesn't feel good, being related to a murderer," he said with a nervous smile.

"So you were working in the restaurant car and you got Mattias a job," Irene clarified.

"Yes. Two years ago. His mom asked if I could fix him up. She and my mom are cousins. There was a temporary vacancy, then when Nettan came back he filled in sometimes. Then he applied to be a conductor. He is . . . or was . . . super smart. But weird."

Viktor started picking at an angry red spot on his neck.

"Tell me what you mean; in what way was he weird?" Irene asked.

"Well . . . he kept to himself. Didn't have any friends. I mean he spoke to the passengers, but he was kind of . . . abrupt with them. And sometimes he said weird things."

"What kind of weird things?"

"Like 'only virgins are pure. Everyone else is impure and should die.' It almost sounded religious, like Muslim or something. Once he said that girls should be sub . . . sub . . . subjugated until they bleed, and that will cleanse them. He said that blood cleanses—stuff like that."

"Did he say these things within earshot of the passengers?"

"Oh no . . . just to me. I thought it was . . . disgusting."

"Did this happen often?"

"No. A few times. When we were, like, having our break."

Irene brightened as a thought struck her.

"Do you have some kind of staff room in the restaurant car where you can sit during your break?"

Viktor stopped picking at the spot and looked at her in surprise.

"Yes. If we're not too busy we can go and sit in there."

"And did Mattias come and see you when he was traveling between Malmö and Göteborg?"

He nodded.

"Always. He said he didn't want to sit with the riffraff, so I used to let him sit in the staff room. Although he wasn't really supposed to because he didn't work in the restaurant car anymore. Nettan used to let him sit there too when she was on duty."

Irene could feel her pulse rate increasing.

"What did he do when he was in there by himself? When you were busy with customers, I mean?"

"He used to sit there tapping away on his computer. He was brilliant at that kind of stuff. He got into Chalmers to study computer science, but he dropped out. He said he already knew everything."

Irene was growing more and more certain that she had the final piece of the puzzle in her hand.

"I believe you were working on Thursday evening almost two weeks ago. Do you remember if Mattias was in the staff room during that journey?"

Viktor thought for a little while.

"Yes, he was," he said eventually.

"And did he have a computer with him?"

"Yes, a little one, kind of like a big cell phone. He often used it; he said it was easy to carry around."

At last she knew why she hadn't found Mr. Groomer when she checked the train.

"So he was sitting in a staff room where no one could see him. Viktor Jacobsson had his hands full in the restaurant car, so Mattias could chat away to his chosen girls in peace. And if anyone came in, he could shut down in a second. It's very difficult to see what's on those small screens," Irene said.

The team was gathered in the meeting room. They all felt they were well on the way to closing the case; it was just a matter of tying up the last few loose ends.

"He's definitely guilty of the murders, one hundred percent. Moa's and Alexandra's blood is in his van. His semen is in the van and on the girls' clothing, and we found fibers from the red nylon carpet on both girls. We also have his video footage of the girls, and we have the knife. It's watertight. We're assuming he had the camera with him because he intended to film what he was planning to do to little Ann."

Tommy fell silent and looked down at the papers in front of him. He picked up one document and gazed at it for a while, then continued. "You thought there was a lot of blood on the victims' clothes when you found them in the closet, and you said the place stank. The amount of blood didn't match the injuries the girls had suffered. And now we know why; he poured cat blood over the clothes."

Tommy's expression said it all as he put down the sheet of paper.

"Cat blood? And is there cat blood on Moa Olsson's body too?" Fredrik asked.

"No, it was done after the event. Probably some kind of ritual, according to the profiler."

"Blood . . . His landlady's cats disappeared; I have my suspicions about where they went. And he allegedly told Viktor Jacobsson that women should be cleansed with blood," Irene said.

"The guy was seriously creepy, if you ask me, but there is one thing I've been wondering about," Åsa said. "He was so smart, stealing computers and chatting online on the train, doing everything he could to make sure we couldn't trace him. And Jens hasn't found much on his computers either; he covered his tracks very skillfully. There wasn't a thing on the laptop in Malmö to connect him to the murders, and yet he left all that evidence lying around in the garage. Why didn't he try to hide the things he'd kept?"

"It's actually not all that uncommon," Tommy replied. "Some psychiatrists believe that somewhere deep down, a serial killer wants to be caught. At the same time he feels invincible when those stupid cops can't find anything to prove he's guilty."

"So you think Mattias was a serial killer," Åsa said.

"Absolutely. He managed to kill two girls, but he was planning to take the lives of many more. If he had gotten to them, he would have killed them too. Thank God there aren't many killers like him, but they do exist. According to many of our experts, the Internet has made it much easier for serial killers to find their victims, and this case is a shining example of exactly that. Unfortunately, I think we'll find ourselves investigating plenty of similar homicides in the future."

"They picked up a guy not long ago who was suspected of having killed five gay men. I think they've found evidence tying him to two or three of the murders; all five victims had come into contact with him online," Fredrik told them.

"I don't think I'm going to run out of work anytime soon," Jens said.

THE WASHED-OUT MORNING light created a perfect working atmosphere for the two detectives in the Cold Cases Unit.

"He slipped out of the net," Andersson said gloomily.

"Very gracefully," Fryxender concurred.

They were both thinking back to the events of the previous day. When Oscar Leutnerwall returned to the library, dragging a huge vacuum cleaner that would have sent the experts on *Antiques Roadshow* into a trance, Fryxender had confronted him with the discovery of Mats Persson's missing library books. The former diplomat had listened expressionlessly. When Fryxender asked how the books had ended up on his shelves, he had answered calmly: "Calle gave me a lot of books for my birthday. He said he'd been to a sale at the library and picked up some interesting items. I'd already read the two books about Stig Wennerström, but I didn't have the heart to tell him. To be honest, I just put the whole lot on the bottom shelf and forgot about them." When asked when Calle had given him the books, he had answered with complete conviction: "Eight years ago. It was my eighty-fifth birthday."

So Calle Adelskiöld had allegedly had Mats Persson's library books in his possession for sixteen years before he gave them to his cousin as a birthday present.

"It's Friday today. Astrid's birthday party is tomorrow, and then they're off to Mauritius. By the time they get back, I'll have only three weeks to go until I retire. And I hope you'll forgive me, but I intend to ignore this goddamn case and spend my last few days of active service showing your new colleagues in the Cold Cases Unit the ropes. This is a tough job," Andersson said firmly.

Fryxender was staring out of their grubby window and didn't appear to be listening to his colleague's statement of intent. Instead he was slowly drumming his fingers on the desk; to his surprise, Andersson realized that he recognized the beat. Beethoven's Fifth. He was just about to ask if he was right when the phone on Fryxender's desk rang, breaking the silence. He picked it up and listened, then suddenly froze. His answers were monosyllabic, until he eventually said, "We'll be there at two. See you then."

Slowly he put down the phone. "That was Oscar Leutner-wall. He would like us to go over there for coffee this afternoon. He has something to tell us."

A PALE SUN was doing its best to filter some light through the remaining leaves on the treetops. It was a calm day, and the air felt cool. It had been a mild fall so far, and hopefully it would be a while before the last of the leaves came down. But Andersson was too old to be under any illusions; the winter would soon be here. The trip to Thailand with Elvy shimmered like a candle in the darkness. *As long as it's not too hot*, he thought pessimistically from time to time.

Oscar Leutnerwall opened the door. He was wearing dark blue chinos and a blue-and-white-striped shirt under a woolen sweater of exactly the same shade as the blue stripes. The well-worn slippers were on his feet, and even Andersson noticed that his socks perfectly matched his sweater.

"It's very kind of you to spare the time," Oscar said.

They hung up their coats in the closet, then Oscar led them

into the living room. As usual the fire was blazing away, spreading a pleasant dry heat.

Oscar had pulled another armchair up to the copper table in front of the fire. He invited the two officers to sit down in the comfortable wing-backs while he took the extra chair, where Winston lay fast asleep on his back with his paws in the air. Oscar picked up the cat and unceremoniously placed him on the floor. Winston was unimpressed and stalked off in the direction of the library, his tail in the air.

Oscar poured coffee from the silver pot made by Vivan, or whatever the silversmith's name was. Andersson noticed that there was a brandy glass next to each cup. Without asking if they would like a drink, the retired diplomat poured a generous amount of Cognac into each glass.

"Please help yourselves," he said. "Believe me, you're going to need this."

Andersson thought he looked tired and hollow-eyed. For the first time Oscar Leutnerwall actually looked his age.

"Your good health, gentlemen. Here's to the truth, which can now be told. The time has come," Oscar said solemnly.

They raised their glasses. Andersson inhaled the aroma before he took his first sip. He rarely drank Cognac, but the bouquet and the rounded taste told him that this wasn't a cheap bottle.

Oscar put down his glass. "Yesterday an old friend called; someone I hadn't heard from for twenty-five years. Staffan Molander. He told me you'd found a witness who saw us together outside Calle's house back in the summer of '83 . . ."

He paused and picked up his glass. With a wan smile he raised it once more and said, "Kudos to you, gentlemen. I'm impressed that you managed to dig up the information after all these years. We tend to believe that time obliterates our footsteps, but the truth is nothing disappears as long as there is someone left alive who can tell the story."

He nodded to the two officers and took a sip of Cognac, then cleared his throat. "I've had a sleepless night. You could say that I've been battling with my conscience. The truth has to come out sometime, and if feels as if that time is now. I've been wondering how to tell you what happened and have come to the conclusion that there is only one way: start at the beginning."

Cut the crap and get on with it, Andersson thought.

"Astrid told you that Calle and I grew up more like brothers than cousins. We went to the same schools, and our families spent a lot of time together. Our mothers were sisters, and the fact that they had no other siblings meant they were very close. We both studied law in Uppsala, though he started a couple of semesters after me. We had a great time. The two of us also met up often and rented rooms in the same building. I lived on the top floor, Calle on the ground floor. But we also had separate groups of friends. After a while I noticed that Calle seemed particularly friendly with one of his fellow students. His name was Sverker, and he was the son of a prominent financier. One day I went to pick up a book that Calle had borrowed from me, and when no one answered, I walked in and found Calle and Sverker lying naked in his bed.

"The general attitude in the 1930s wasn't exactly broad-minded," he continued, "so you might think that I reacted badly, but in fact I wasn't so innocent myself. I had realized as a teenager that I was bisexual, even though I couldn't put a name to it at the time. During my years at the university in Uppsala, I had many opportunities to explore my sexuality. My looks appealed to both men and women. I was always clear about who I was attracted to: individuals. I was drawn to young, good-looking individuals, not to one specific gender. That's the way it's always been, and it has definitely enriched my life."

"Why did you never marry?" Fryxender asked.

Andersson noticed that his colleague's glass of Cognac was still full. *Good. Let him drive us back*, he thought.

"Marriage . . . It's never appealed to me. I've never felt the slightest desire to tie myself down and to be faithful to just one person."

"But I assume Calle and Sverker were a couple?"

"Yes. They were together. Calle told me there was a group of young men who met up from time to time; they would have parties and just hang out. That kind of thing was a normal part of student life in Uppsala; the difference with this group was that they were all homosexuals, so their activities had to be kept secret. The members were invited to join after careful consideration and with great discretion. The existence of the group wasn't something to be publicized; after all, we're talking about a criminal association here."

"Criminal? Who said it was criminal?" Fryxender sounded surprised.

"The law. According to the law in Sweden back then, homosexuality was illegal and was punished with a jail sentence. It came under the rubric of sodomy. The law wasn't repealed until 1944."

"I didn't know it carried a jail sentence until the midforties. I just remember learning at the police academy that homosexuality was a symptom of psychosis and other serious mental illnesses," Fryxender said.

Oscar fell silent and gazed into the fire, which was beginning to die down. When he got up to put on more wood, Andersson noticed that his hips seemed stiff—something he hadn't picked up on previously.

"Yes, during the 1930s and up until 1944, convicted homosexuals were sent to jail. From 1944 to the end of the 1970s, they were admitted to a mental hospital. In other words, there weren't too many gay pride parades," Oscar said with a wry smile.

"What did they call themselves? These student groups usually have a name," Fryxender said.

"They called themselves the Ovidii network of friends, although often they just said the Network. Their motto was *Nitimur in vetitum semper cupimusque negata*, which is a quotation from the poet Ovid. We are drawn to forbidden things, and always desire that which is denied to us."

Both officers registered the fact that he had mentioned the Network, but neither of them reacted. Instead they allowed Oscar to continue his story.

"I was invited to some of the parties; they were very pleasant and well organized."

"Were you a member?" Fryxender asked.

"In a way . . . I suppose I was. But I didn't attend their gatherings on a regular basis. I spent time with my other friends, and I went out with girls. Which was why I wasn't at the ill-fated midsummer party in 1941. I was in Marstrand with close friends, while Calle had stayed in Uppsala. He was supposed to be studying, because he was due to resit some exams in August. However, the real reason he was there was that Sverker was there too. Sverker was going off to spend the whole of July and the early part of August with his family at their summer cottage in Skåne, but he and Calle spent Midsummer's Eve together, along with some of the other guys from the Network in a summer cottage out near Roslagen. For some reason Officer Elof Persson was on an assignment nearby."

Oscar broke off and topped off both coffee and Cognac for himself and his guests. His hands trembled as he poured the drinks.

Andersson enthusiastically accepted another glass of Cognac, but Fryxender declined; he still hadn't touched the first one.

"It was a beautiful evening. Calle said that for once some of the boys were really relaxed, and drank more than they usually did. The cottage was in an isolated spot, and they didn't think there was anyone around. They couldn't have known that the diligent General Security Service would be working on Midsummer's Eve . . . but Elof Persson was out there—presumably trying to track down spies. There was a lot of activity along the Swedish coast during the war years."

Oscar fell silent once more. His expression lost its sharpness, and he suddenly looked as if he were far away. The story was a bit too long-winded for Andersson's taste, but in spite of himself he had been drawn in. With a glass of excellent Cognac for company, he was happy to listen to the rest of the tale.

"The light summer night was perfect for a dip in the sea. The cottage had its own small beach and jetty; the boys ran down and jumped naked into the water. Afterward a few couples sneaked off, including Calle and Sverker. They found what they thought was a sheltered spot and had sex, but Elof Persson was lying on a hillock close by, taking razor-sharp pictures of them with a telephoto lens."

Oscar took a deep breath. "At the beginning of July, Elof Persson contacted Calle. He demanded five thousand kronor, otherwise he would take the photographs to the police. He had probably tried to get a hold of Sverker, but without success; he was in Skåne with his family. That's the only explanation I can think of. Calle had no money of his own. He lived on whatever my father and Aunt Vera sent him. He managed to convince Persson that he could only get his hands on three thousand kronor, and Persson went along with it. The money and the photographs changed hands late one night in Tantolunden. Calle told me how relieved he felt, in spite of the fact that Persson spent the whole time hurling insults at him. A month later, Persson got in touch again. He hadn't given Calle all the pictures and wanted more money. Poor Calle went into a complete panic. Somehow he managed to borrow three thousand kronor from his mother; he spun her a tale about having to travel to Moscow for an interview. He told her he might be eligible for a post at the embassy there after he graduated, so he needed the money for the journey. Luck was on his side when he was actually posted to Moscow later on; Aunt Vera never suspected a thing."

Oscar paused briefly; all this talking seemed to have left him with a dry mouth. Andersson and Fryxender waited patiently for him to continue.

"Once again the handoff took place at midnight in Tantolunden, but I don't think Elof Persson could ever have imagined what Calle would do afterward. Persson went straight home to Hornsgatan without looking over his shoulder once. Calle snuck along behind him, and found out where his blackmailer lived."

Oscar took another sip of coffee.

"When Persson got in touch the third time asking for the same amount of money again, Calle had worked out his plan. He was going to murder Elof Persson. He simply stole the Tokarev pistol from a friend of my father's at a firing range."

"Didn't this friend of your father's wonder what had happened to his gun?" Fryxender asked.

"Probably. But he couldn't exactly inquire openly into its whereabouts. There was never any suspicion that Calle had stolen the Tokarev; it simply disappeared, and nobody asked any questions."

Oscar gazed into the fire; only Winston's purring broke the silence in the room.

"Elof Persson informed Calle where the meeting was to take place. Calle didn't take any money with him for the simple reason that he didn't have any. Instead he took the loaded gun and waited for Persson, concealed in the doorway of the neighboring apartment block. When Elof Persson emerged, Calle stepped out and shot him three times, then hurried away. The weather was bad, and it was completely dark because of the blackout. The following day the Hårsfjärden disaster took place and became the focus for all the resources of the security service. The murder of Elof Persson slipped into the background, and was never solved. And that could have been the end of the story, if it hadn't been for Calle. And Aunt Vera."

He sighed, gazing into the distance once more. It was as if the old man could see people who were long dead standing here in the room. Andersson took a sip of his Cognac to chase away the ghosts.

"During the years in Moscow, I think Calle managed to suppress the memory of what had happened pretty well. However, when we came back after the war, it caught up with him. My dear cousin had already developed a distinct fondness for the bottle when we were students in Uppsala, and unfortunately the situation hadn't improved as time went by. On top of that, Aunt Vera was insisting that he get married; it was his duty to ensure that the family line continued. He was in despair when he came to talk to me, but unfortunately he didn't have the same inclinations as me; he was strictly homosexual. The solution was a very young, very shy girl called Greta Bergman. She was barely twenty when they got engaged just after the end of the war; Calle was ten years older. He liked her very much, but kept putting off any attempt at intimacy. Greta wasn't stupid, and I think she knew it wasn't going to work. She left him, blaming his drinking. Poor Calle had inherited his father's intermittent alcoholism."

"He never mentioned the murder to you while you were working in Moscow?" Fryxender asked.

"No. He never said a word. As I said, I think he managed to suppress the memory completely. But there was something he couldn't suppress: his love for Sverker. They started seeing each other again when Calle came home, and he was devastated when, after a year or so, Sverker said he was engaged.

Sverker married in '47 and had three children in quick succession. Calle married at the beginning of the 1950s; Lilly Hassel was an opera singer who was a few years older than him. It ended in divorce after eighteen months; the only thing they had in common was a fondness for booze."

"Divorce . . . was that why Calle stopped going out with women?" Andersson asked. It was the first time he had spoken since Oscar started his story, but he was genuinely curious; that particular detail had been bothering him.

"No. It was because Sverker killed himself. He couldn't cope with the deception any longer. Calle was devastated, and for a while I was afraid he might go the same way. Instead he decided to stop pretending to be heterosexual in the public eye; he became asexual, blaming his attitude on his failed marriage to Lilly. He threw himself into his work, and made a real effort to stop drinking. He succeeded most of the time, but occasionally he fell off the wagon. We were working in different countries, so sometimes we didn't see each other for quite a while. Poor Calle became a very lonely person beneath all that *bonhomie*. During his last few years in active service the relapses became more frequent, and in the end he was encouraged to take early retirement. He was given a very generous financial package, and was extremely relieved. He had already renovated Aunt Vera's apartment, and he moved back to the house he loved so much."

By now Winston was snoring loudly on his master's knee. Andersson was beginning to feel pleasantly drowsy, thanks to the Cognac and the warmth of the fire.

"What happened to Mats Persson?"

For a long time it seemed as if the former diplomat hadn't heard Fryxender's question.

"Mats Persson," he repeated eventually. "It was all so unfortunate. My telephone rang at about seven o'clock one evening, and it was Calle. It was almost impossible to work out what he was saying, but he kept on repeating: "The son is dead! The son is dead! And he's lying on your rug!" I was convinced he was in a bad way. I did my best to calm him down. Eventually I realized what he meant. I had given him several rugs when he moved into his newly renovated apartment. By now I was seriously worried; I told Calle not to touch anything, and said I would be right over. Never has a seventy-year-old man run through Näckros Park as fast as I did that evening. When I arrived, there was no denying that Calle was right. There was a dead man lying on the rug in the hallway. He had been shot in the head and chest, and Calle said he had done it."

Andersson's drowsiness disappeared in a second. So this was the explanation for Mats Persson's disappearance almost twenty-five years ago: He had been murdered by an ex–Foreign Office employee who happened to be an alcoholic. The same man who had murdered the dead man's own father. *Jeez, what a mess!*

"We went into Calle's room and I gave him another drink to calm him down. That was when he told me what had happened to Elof Persson in 1941. It had haunted him over the years, but as time went by he had begun to feel safer. Until the telephone rang on the morning of November ninth, 1983. A male caller introduced himself as Elof Persson's son, Mats. He wanted to meet to discuss the murder of his father. It came as a terrible shock to Calle. He managed to say that he wasn't available until after six o'clock in the evening, then he spent the whole day pacing around the apartment, getting more and more agitated. He came up with a nightmare scenario: Mats Persson had found his father's photographs from Midsummer's Eve 1941, and now he too was going to start threatening and blackmailing Calle. He might even accuse him of killing Elof. Being the man he was, my cousin attempted to fortify himself with a considerable amount of alcohol during the course of the day. Just before Mats was due to arrive, Calle went down to the cellar where he had hidden the Tokarev pistol and the ammunition after Elof's death. It had been lying there since 1941; he checked that it was still working, and loaded it. By the time Mats rang the doorbell, Calle was on the brink of hysteria. He shot the poor guy as soon as he stepped inside, then he wandered helplessly around the apartment. Eventually he started thinking a little more clearly, and called me."

"How do you think Mats Persson got a hold of your cousin's name?" Fryxender asked.

"I don't know. I suppose the most likely explanation is that Elof Persson had written it down somewhere, and Mats found it when he was going through his father's things. Bearing in mind that Elof was blackmailing Calle, it's not an unreasonable assumption."

Fryxender nodded, then said, "So you helped your cousin to wall up the body."

"Yes. What was I supposed to do? I realize now that it was wrong, of course, but in the heat of the moment . . . Calle was in such poor shape because of his drinking. I couldn't bear the thought of him ending up in jail. I found the bricks and mortar lying around in the cellar, then I went back upstairs. We each grabbed one end of the rug and carried the body down; it was easy to push the whole thing into the old wood store. We put the gun and the ammunition in first, then the rug and the body. Calle must have forgotten the bag Persson had been carrying with his library books in it. I didn't know anything about it until you told me. Presumably he whisked the bag away into his apartment and put it somewhere. He did give me books for my eighty-fifth birthday— that's true. But he didn't tell me those three came from Mats Persson. If I'd known, obviously they wouldn't have been sitting on the shelf where you found them."

He pulled a face and shook his head. "We spent the whole night walling up the opening in the chimney breast. It took a long time, because neither of us had any experience of that kind of work. But we managed it. In the morning I tidied up and cleared away all trace of what we had done. Then I hurried home through the park. It was so early that I didn't even meet anyone out walking their dog. I had a shower and went to bed; strangely enough, I slept for several hours. When I woke up I called Calle. He had calmed down, and we agreed never to mention what had happened the previous evening and night. And we never did."

"Did your sister know that cousin Calle had killed two men?" Fryxender asked calmly.

The old man gave a start and glanced at him sharply.

"No. Astrid has no idea about any of this. And I hope it will stay that way. Things will be difficult enough for her . . ."

He broke off and put the cat on the floor, in spite of Winston's noisy protests. Oscar got up and made his way somewhat unsteadily toward the library. There was the sound of a drawer opening, and he came back with a piece of paper in his hand.

"I got this report from my doctor at Carlanderska Hospital the day before yesterday. I lied when I told you I'd been playing tennis. The truth is that I was being given my death sentence."

He handed the paper to Fryxender, who didn't look at it; instead he said, "Tell us what it says."

Oscar sank back into his armchair. Suddenly he looked immensely old and weary. "It says I have a brain tumor. Inoperable. I have only a few months left. Personally I'm kind of okay with that; we all have to die some time. But I'm worried about Astrid; she'll be so lonely when I'm gone. I haven't told her yet; I'm going to wait until we get back from Mauritius. My doctor says I can travel, as long as I take my medication with me."

He sat in silence for a long time, gazing into the fire. The wood crackled as the flames began to die down.

"It's a relief to have told Calle's story," he said quietly.

It was as if Andersson had been waiting for the right moment, and now it had come. He straightened up in his chair, wide awake and firing on all cylinders.

"So it's not your story?" he said sharply. "Are you sure you didn't carry out the murders together?"

Oscar Leutnerwall stiffened. Slowly he turned his head and met Andersson's gaze. The sapphire-blue eyes were cloudy now, like half-frozen pools.

"CAN YOU GIVE me a ride home?"

"Of course. But three glasses of Cognac—what the hell were you thinking?"

"I've retired."

"You certainly have not—you've got just over a month to go."

"In my head I've retired."

Andersson folded his hands over his stomach and shut his eyes.

"Case closed," he murmured.

My THANKS TO:

Erik Lemchen, who recently retired from his role as detective inspector with the Police Authority in Västra Götaland. He has been a great help to me over the years, and has always come through when I have needed to consult him. He spent the last two years leading up to his retirement working on the Cold Cases Unit, which is an important aspect of this particular book.

Karin Alfredsson, my fantastic editor, who has been there ever since my debut novel.

Continue reading for a preview from the next
Irene Huss investigation

WHO WATCHETH

THIN VEILS OF mist lingered in the glow of the street lamps, but soon they would disperse completely. The gusts of wind were getting stronger all the time, carrying the first drops of rain. Dampness clung to her face as she leaned forward, fighting her way across the parking lot. Nobody was out and about without good reason; even the dog owners in the area seemed to have abandoned the idea of a last walk. The neighborhood was dark and silent; most people had already gone to bed. Only Bosse Gunnarsson's kitchen window showed a warm, inviting light. He was sitting at the table with a sudoku puzzle as usual, his reading glasses slipping down his nose.

Her own house lay in darkness, but she would soon change that. Switch on the lamps, make a cup of tea, fix herself an egg and caviar sandwich. Light some candles on the coffee table. Wrap herself in a thick, soft blanket and watch the late news. Then off to bed, she promised herself.

She reached into the mailbox: nothing but bills and flyers. She continued toward the door, searching in her purse for the key. As she was about to insert it in the lock, she noticed a rapid movement in the darkness by the shed. Suddenly someone was right behind her. An iron grip around her chest pressed her close to her attacker's torso, forcing the breath out of her body. She was paralyzed by the man's strength and by the acrid stench emanating from him. Only when she realized what he was doing did she manage to offer some resistance. The man was using his free hand to try to loop something around her neck but was having difficulty getting it over her head—not because he was so much shorter than her, but because she was struggling, twisting from side to side as she tried to free herself from his grip. He growled and hissed something unintelligible but managed to hang on to her. After a brief battle he had the noose where he wanted it. Instinctively she reached up and slid one hand under the twine. The attack itself had been so sudden that she hadn't had time to scream. She tried to call for help, but the only sound that came out was a faint whimper; the noose had already been drawn too tight. She felt him loosen his hold on her body so he could put more force into the act of strangulation. Even if she could manage to keep her hand between her throat and the twine, she was getting hardly any air. The darkness flickered before her eyes, and she realized that she would soon lose consciousness.

She managed to slip her other hand into her pocket and rummaged around feverishly. Paper tissues, a box of painkillers, her cigarette lighter . . . Wasn't it there? It must be there! She panicked even more, her movements growing clumsy. Was it in the wrong pocket? The pain in her throat was unbearable. She couldn't breathe.

All at once she felt the car key against her fingertips. She managed to find the little cylinder attached to the key ring and grasped it with trembling fingers. Her thumb slipped on her first attempt, but she could feel the button. Summoning up the last reserves of her strength, she pressed it again.

The screech of the attack alarm sliced through the silent neighborhood. She felt her attacker stiffen, and for a few vital seconds he lost concentration. She lifted one foot and kicked backward as hard as she could. The heel of her leather boot caught him just below the knee. He doubled over and groaned, loosening his grip for a fraction of a second. At the same time, she heard Bosse Gunnarsson open his door and yell:

"What the hell is going on out there? I'm calling the cops!"

Then the presence behind her was gone. She heard the crack of the gate as he flung it open and disappeared in the direction of the parking lot.

"Hey, stop right there! What are you doing?"

Bosse's voice again. Thank God for Bosse. She sank to the ground, trying to call for help, but all that emerged was a pathetic croak.

She had survived. She was alive!

Panic had locked her hand around the slim cylinder in a vise-like grip. She couldn't bring herself to let go of the object that had saved her life.

The screech of the alarm stopped abruptly as the darkness closed around her.

UNDER NORMAL CIRCUMSTANCES Irene Huss was not a morning person, but there were days when she seriously considered trying to become one. Mornings like this, for example. The air was crystal clear, with a hint of crispness left over from the chill of the night. Above the horizon an amazing sunrise filled the sky with intense shades of gold. Could there be a more perfect start to the day?

She drew her robe more tightly around her body as she paused on the top step and inhaled deeply. The moisture from last night's rain intensified the smells. The garden looked as if it had just woken up feeling refreshed. The luxuriant asters glowed deep red in the cast-iron urns on either side of the steps, a final defiant protest against the inexorable approach of the fall.

She padded down to the low gate in her slippers, leaned over and took the newspaper out of the mailbox on the fence. As she turned to go back indoors, she stopped dead. It took a few seconds before she realized that the small garden seat that normally stood between the two kitchen windows had been moved and was now in the middle of the flower bed beneath one window. The newly planted rose bushes were badly damaged: several branches were broken. Annoyed, Irene picked up the seat and put it back against the wall. Strange—it had been there yesterday evening, hadn't it?

• • •

"I THINK SO," Krister said when she asked him a little later.

He was standing at the stove cooking eggs, with crisply fried bacon and halved tomatoes piled on a plate beside him. As far as Irene was concerned, preparing such a hearty breakfast was a total waste of time. Three cups of black coffee and a couple of cheese sandwiches had been her standard start to the day for decades, but now her husband had decided that this was unacceptable. Perhaps it was, but it suited her. When she wondered how fried eggs and bacon could be regarded as healthy in view of the bad cholesterol involved, he had waved away the argument: "GI foods! A whole world of dieters can't be wrong!" To tell the truth, Krister was the one who needed to lose weight, not Irene.

He put a plate of GI breakfast in front of her. As usual she could only manage to push the food around. At times like these she was seriously tempted to turn vegan, like Jenny. Their daughter had stuck to her principles for almost ten years and was now in Amsterdam, training to be a chef specializing in vegan dishes. Jenny was following in her father's footsteps, but perhaps not exactly the way Krister had expected.

"But you have to admit it's weird, the seat being moved," Irene persisted.

"Oh, it's probably just Viktor and his pals fooling around."

"Why would Viktor . . . You could be right."

The boy next door was ten years old, and he and his friends were always running around the neighborhood. As far as Irene could tell, they all seemed to get along with everyone, and she hadn't heard of them getting into any serious trouble. She found it difficult to imagine why they would have picked up a seat and thrown it into the rose bed; it seemed completely pointless. The kitchen window was so low that Viktor could easily look through it if he wanted to; he wouldn't even need to stand on tiptoe.

She shook her head and poured her third cup of coffee.

THE FOLLOWING MORNING Irene woke at seven, despite the fact that it was Saturday, and she didn't have to go to work. Krister had worked late at the restaurant the previous night, and the soft, regular breathing from the bed beside her suggested that he would remain deeply asleep for quite some time. She crept out of the warmth of the covers. When she had finished in the bathroom she put on her running gear, automatically reaching for her knee brace. Her knee was too painful if she didn't use it these days. *I'm starting to fall apart,* she thought gloomily.

She opened the door and jogged down the steps, then stopped and stared straight ahead. Slowly she turned around.

The glorious asters had been torn out of their urns and lay strewn all over the lawn.

"VIKTOR WOULD NEVER do such a thing!"

Malin, who was Irene's neighbor and Viktor's mother, folded her arms and looked deeply insulted. Irene tried to adopt a conciliatory tone.

"To be honest I don't think he would either, but . . ." she began.

"So why have you come here accusing him, then?" Malin snapped.

This was not good for neighborly relations, Irene realized. Nor did it constitute a successful interrogation, her professional side noted.

"I'm not accusing him, I just wanted to eliminate the possibility and ask him if he knew anything," Irene tried to explain.

"Fucking police abuse!" Malin yelled as she slammed the door.

Police abuse? Presumably she meant abuse of power. To a certain extent Irene could understand why Malin was upset, but if she was so sure of her son's innocence, why was she reacting so strongly?

As if in response to Irene's train of thought, Viktor came ambling along the street. He opened the gate and grinned at her.

"Hi!"

"Hi, Viktor. Listen, I just came to ask your mom something, but she got real mad at me."

Viktor's grin disappeared and he looked anxiously at her. Irene gave him an encouraging smile. "The thing is, someone's being doing weird stuff in our garden. They've moved a seat and pulled up some flowers. I just wanted to ask if you know anything about it."

The boy shook his head; he looked genuinely surprised.

Irene looked him in the eye and smiled again. His expression was still a little uncertain, but he returned the smile. A guilty ten-year-old wouldn't look that way.

Viktor wasn't behind the vandalism.

So who was?

My beloved is having a party. I don't like that. Lead her not into temptation, but deliver her from evil. She must be removed from the destructive influence. Behold, I shall send an angel before you to guard you along the way and to bring you into the place that I have prepared. I will take care of you, my darling. We will be forever united in our love.

I am here for her. She knows that I am watching over her. We are united by our love. For ever and ever. Amen. Two men and two women. They are sitting at the table, eating. And drinking. So much alcohol.

Now the other couple has left, and he is still there. They have kissed each other and . . . more. Even though she has switched off most of the lights, I can see more than enough. She has let down her hair. He has started to undress her. Her large breasts are . . . disgusting. She is revealing her true self. The façade has fallen away. She looks like a witch. A troll.

Thou shall not suffer a sorceress to live.

DOGS WERE NOT allowed in the churchyard, but nature called; Egon had to go out. Just a quick walk. At this time of night it was unlikely there would be anyone to complain if she didn't pick up after him. He was small, so he wouldn't produce too much, and the asthma made it difficult for her to bend down.

She was lucky enough to find a parking spot right by the gates. Puffing and blowing, she clambered out of the Škoda. She put Egon on the leash before letting him out, then she entered the churchyard, dragging the dachshund along behind her. He wanted to stop and check out all the interesting smells.

"Come along, Egon! We haven't got time for all that!"

She carried on grumbling at the dog, who was becoming increasingly reluctant to cooperate. In the end he sat down, and with a little twist of his head he managed to slip out of the worn, stretched collar.

Free at last! Egon took off across the grass as fast as his short legs could carry him. Sniffing with pleasure, he buried his nose in the wet leaves, inhaling all the pheromones left behind by some unknown beauty. He could have spent hours there if it hadn't been for his mistress. He could hear her heavy tread lumbering across the grass, and even though he was trying to ignore her shrill voice, he couldn't misinterpret the tone: she wasn't happy. In fact, she sounded angry. As she approached with the leash at the ready, Egon realized it was best to stay out of reach for a while. Resolutely he plunged deeper in among the rhododendrons. His mistress's voice grew even more shrill, but she couldn't reach him.

Another smell began to penetrate through the strong scent. At first Egon stood still for a few seconds, unsure of what to do, but then curiosity took over. He had to find out what that strange smell was. He put his nose to the ground and started to follow the trail. Safely hidden behind the bushes, he moved along by the wall. At the point where the rhododendrons came to an end, he tracked down the source of those peculiar odors. He was slobbering with excitement. He started biting at the thick plastic enveloping the smelly object. He forgot to remain alert, and suddenly he felt the collar slip over his head. But instead of shouting at him and telling him off, his mistress was staring at the bundle wrapped in plastic. She started to make little screeching noises that hurt his ears. Egon crouched down. His sensitive nose had picked up another smell, overriding the interesting package. An acrid stench was emanating from every pore of his mistress's body: fear. She was terrified.

Other Titles in the Soho Crime Series

AGNETE FRIIS
(Denmark)
What My Body Remembers
The Summer of Ellen

TIMOTHY HALLINAN
(Thailand)
The Fear Artist
For the Dead
The Hot Countries
Fools' River
Street Music

(Los Angeles)
Crashed
Little Elvises
The Fame Thief
Herbie's Game
King Maybe
Fields Where They Lay
Nighttown

METTE IVIE HARRISON
(Mormon Utah)
The Bishop's Wife
His Right Hand
For Time and All Eternities
Not of This Fold

MICK HERRON
(England)
Slow Horses
Dead Lions
The List (A Novella)
Real Tigers
Spook Street
London Rules
The Marylebone Drop (A Novella)
Joe Country
The Catch (A Novella)
Slough House

Down Cemetery Road
The Last Voice You Hear
Why We Die
Smoke and Whispers

Reconstruction
Nobody Walks
This Is What Happened

STAN JONES
(Alaska)
White Sky, Black Ice
Shaman Pass
Frozen Sun
Village of the Ghost Bears
Tundra Kill
The Big Empty

STEVEN MACK JONES
(Detroit)
August Snow
Lives Laid Away
Dead of Winter

LENE KAABERBØL & AGNETE FRIIS
(Denmark)
The Boy in the Suitcase
Invisible Murder
Death of a Nightingale
The Considerate Killer

MARTIN LIMÓN
(South Korea)
Jade Lady Burning
Slicky Boys
Buddha's Money
The Door to Bitterness
The Wandering Ghost
G.I. Bones
Mr. Kill
The Joy Brigade
Nightmare Range
The Iron Sickle
The Ville Rat
Ping-Pong Heart
The Nine-Tailed Fox
The Line
GI Confidential

ED LIN
(Taiwan)
Ghost Month
Incensed
99 Ways to Die

PETER LOVESEY
(England)
The Circle
The Headhunters

PETER LOVESEY CONT.
False Inspector Dew
Rough Cider
On the Edge
The Reaper

(Bath, England)
The Last Detective
Diamond Solitaire
The Summons
Bloodhounds
Upon a Dark Night
The Vault
Diamond Dust
The House Sitter
The Secret Hangman
Skeleton Hill
Stagestruck
Cop to Corpse
The Tooth Tattoo
The Stone Wife
Down Among the Dead Men
Another One Goes Tonight
Beau Death
Killing with Confetti
The Finisher

(London, England)
Wobble to Death
The Detective Wore Silk Drawers
Abracadaver
Mad Hatter's Holiday
The Tick of Death
A Case of Spirits
Swing, Swing Together
Waxwork

Bertie and the Tinman
Bertie and the Seven Bodies
Bertie and the Crime of Passion

SUJATA MASSEY
(1920s Bombay)
The Widows of Malabar Hill
The Satapur Moonstone
The Bombay Prince

FRANCINE MATHEWS
(Nantucket)
Death in the Off-Season
Death in Rough Water
Death in a Mood Indigo
Death in a Cold Hard Light
Death on Nantucket
Death on Tuckernuck

SEICHŌ MATSUMOTO
(Japan)
Inspector Imanishi Investigates

MAGDALEN NABB
(Italy)
Death of an Englishman
Death of a Dutchman
Death in Springtime
Death in Autumn
The Marshal and the Murderer
The Marshal and the Madwoman
The Marshal's Own Case
The Marshal Makes His Report
The Marshal at the Villa Torrini
Property of Blood
Some Bitter Taste
The Innocent
Vita Nuova
The Monster of Florence

FUMINORI NAKAMURA
(Japan)
The Thief
Evil and the Mask
Last Winter, We Parted
The Kingdom
The Boy in the Earth
Cult X

STUART NEVILLE
(Northern Ireland)
The Ghosts of Belfast
Collusion
Stolen Souls
The Final Silence
Those We Left Behind
So Say the Fallen
The Traveller & Other Stories

(Dublin)
Ratlines

REBECCA PAWEL
(1930s Spain)
Death of a Nationalist
Law of Return
The Watcher in the Pine
The Summer Snow

KWEI QUARTEY
(Ghana)
Murder at Cape Three Points
Gold of Our Fathers
Death by His Grace
The Missing American
Sleep Well, My Lady

QIU XIAOLONG
(China)
Death of a Red Heroine
A Loyal Character Dancer
When Red Is Black

JAMES SALLIS
(New Orleans)
The Long-Legged Fly
Moth
Black Hornet
Eye of the Cricket
Bluebottle
Ghost of a Flea

Sarah Jane

JOHN STRALEY
(Sitka, Alaska)
The Woman Who Married a Bear
The Curious Eat Themselves
The Music of What Happens
*Death and the Language
  of Happiness*
The Angels Will Not Care
Cold Water Burning
Baby's First Felony

(Cold Storage, Alaska)
The Big Both Ways
Cold Storage, Alaska
What Is Time to a Pig?

AKIMITSU TAKAGI
(Japan)
The Tattoo Murder Case
Honeymoon to Nowhere

AKIMITSU TAKAGI CONT.
The Informer

HELENE TURSTEN
(Sweden)
Detective Inspector Huss
The Torso
The Glass Devil
Night Rounds
The Golden Calf
The Fire Dance
The Beige Man
The Treacherous Net
Who Watcheth
Protected by the Shadows

Hunting Game
Winter Grave
Snowdrift

*An Elderly Lady Is Up
  to No Good*

ILARIA TUTI
(Italy)
Flowers over the Inferno
The Sleeping Nymph

JANWILLEM VAN DE WETERING
(Holland)
Outsider in Amsterdam
Tumbleweed
The Corpse on the Dike
Death of a Hawker
The Japanese Corpse
The Blond Baboon
The Maine Massacre
The Mind-Murders
The Streetbird
The Rattle-Rat
Hard Rain
Just a Corpse at Twilight
Hollow-Eyed Angel
The Perfidious Parrot
*The Sergeant's Cat:
  Collected Stories*

JACQUELINE WINSPEAR
(1920s England)
Maisie Dobbs
Birds of a Feather